Killstraight

Johnny D. Boggs

LEISURE BOOKS NEW YORK CITY

A LEISURE BOOK®

January 2010

Published by special arrangement with Golden West Literary Agency.

Dorchester Publishing Co., Inc.
200 Madison Avenue
New York, NY 10016

ISBN 10: 0-8439-6307-7
ISBN 13: 978-0-8439-6307-6
E-ISBN: 978-1-4285-0801-9

The name "Leisure Books" and the stylized "L" with design are trademarks of Dorchester Publishing Co., Inc.

Printed in the United States of America.

10 9 8 7 6 5 4 3 2 1

Visit us online at www.dorchesterpub.com.

For the Burgess Boys: Nocona,
Quanah, and Chief Tachaco

Killstraight

Chapter One

They hanged Jimmy Comes Last forty minutes after Daniel Killstraight arrived in Fort Smith.

He came in from St. Louis on the old St. Louis & San Francisco line—The Frisco, folks called it—getting off at the depot on Garrison Avenue with nothing but a gaudy carpetbag, practically empty, and a stomach equally barren. Daniel couldn't believe how big the city had grown in . . . what had it been, seven years? Not that it compared to the cities he had seen back East, nor had he ever spent much time in Arkansas before leaving for Pennsylvania. Maybe he had thought Fort Smith would have reminded him of home, but smoke from the steamboats and factories along the big river stung his eyes, and the noise . . . his head split from all the shouts.

Adjusting his ill-fitting bowler, he suddenly staggered back in shock, confusion, even a touch of fear, when a stranger spit in his face.

"Take money from my chil'ren, you damned greaser!" a red-mustached man wearing a sweat-stained bandanna roared in an Irish brogue.

Daniel stepped back as the man lifted a baseball bat and started to swing.

Luckily the man never finished. Appearing out of nowhere, a city policeman struck Red Mustache from behind with a nightstick, and the bat *rattled* on the cobblestones as the man dropped to his hands and knees. Passersby hurried on. Few even stopped to glance at the ruction.

"Seamus O'Donnell, you bloody fool," the policeman said, his brogue equally thick. "Striking's bad enough . . . now you want to be hanged by Judge Parker, too!" The officer shoved the club in his belt and pulled groggy Red Mustache to his feet, then snapped at Daniel. "Away with you, lad. Frisco Depot's no place to be."

When Daniel hesitated, the policeman roared: "Scat! I have no damned use for a scab, either!"

Scab? Daniel wanted to tell them both he had been a passenger. Strike? No wonder he had the rocking, dirty Frisco car to himself. He said nothing though, merely pulled on his bowler and hurried down Garrison Avenue, away from the depot, weaving in and out of the throng, still hungry, but at least Red Mustache had scared away his headache.

He wandered the crowded streets, up and down the hills, over the cobblestone and boardwalks, until his feet hurt, walking aimlessly, hopelessly, still amazed at the number of people. Vendors hawked their wares. Men lounged outside grog shops and mercantiles, smoking cigars, cigarettes, pipes. Hansom cabs drawn by big draft horses *clopped* and *clanked* over stones and gravel. Ladies in fashionable dresses walked past him, never daring to make eye contact. What was it the conductor had told him? Well, not really told him, but Daniel had heard it in passing. Fort Smith had better than 17,000 souls now. Seemed like twice that many.

He had considered spending the night in town—he could never sleep well on trains, and he had been riding the rails since Pittsburgh. Not that he could afford a decent hotel. Or any hotel. Likely he would wind up spending the night in some wagon yard, if they'd have him. Buy a horse—although the idea of stealing one made him smile—and rig and head west, cross the Arkansas by ferry into Indian Territory. Go home.

If he could call it home.

If he had ever had a home.

The smell of fresh-baked bread and sizzling ham stopped him, and he looked into the window, stepped back, read the sign over the door: *Hotel Main.*

Well, he certainly couldn't afford a room here, and doubted if he could buy a meal as he'd need all the money he had just to get that horse and rig. The ferry wasn't free, either, and he couldn't swim. Besides, the look he got from one diner staring out the window told him they wouldn't serve him in a place like the Hotel Main.

He kept walking, managing only a few steps before a man in a sack suit staggered out of the hotel's saloon and clapped a huge hand on his shoulder.

"Howdy," he said in a Texas drawl. "Come for the hangin'?"

Daniel turned timidly. Timid? Had those seven years made him a coward? He frowned.

"Don't let folks in no more," the man said. He had brilliant blue eyes, beard stubble of two or three days, plaid trouser legs stuck inside tall brown boots with a green Cross of Lorraine inlaid in the tops, and large-rowel spurs. A battered hat, maybe gray, perhaps dust-caked white, topped his head, an outfit of contradictions. Part businessman with his suit, part drover with those boots and hat. His breath stank of whiskey.

"Folks here got citified," the man said, slurring his words. "Used to let anyone come see a body get his neck stretched, but not since. . . ." He jerked his thumb toward the saloon. "Well, the gents in yonder told me since 'Seventy-eight? Or was it 'Seventy-nine? No matter. It's your lucky day." He winked. "I got us a pass. Don't mind sharin'. I'd enjoy the comp'ny."

Daniel started to decline the invitation, but glanced across the street to find Red Mustache glaring at him. Daniel's drunken newfound friend had three inches over the Frisco striker, even without his boots, and a half foot over Daniel, so he let himself be steered down Garrison Avenue, leaving Red Mustache glowering, and rubbing the back of his head.

"Name's Henry," the stranger said a block later. "Cotton Henry. But if one of 'em marshals ask you at the gate, I'm Wooten with the Arkansas City *Republican,* and you's Palazzo with the *Globe-Democrat* up in Saint Lewey. Figgered you could pass for some Eye-talian." Cotton Henry snorted. "My maw would have a regular hissy fit if she knowed I was consortin' with a bean-eater, but you's all right . . . uh?"

"Daniel. Daniel Killstraight." He smiled, thinking: *My mother would have slit your throat and kicked me out of the lodge had she known you, and everyone else in this city, kept mistaking me for a Mexican.*

He couldn't blame Cotton Henry, though. His raven-black hair was close-cropped, and he wore Oxford ties—a going-away present, ordered from Bloomingdale's—that pinched his feet, and that scratchy suit of black broadcloth. Better than the uniform he had worn in Pennsylvania, or the muslin shirts and duck trousers on that hardscrabble farm in Franklin County and in those stinking, damp coal mines.

"Where is . . . where are Mister Wooten and Mister Palazzo?" Daniel asked as they turned down Third Street.

"In their cups at the Main," Henry said with a laugh. "Some ink-slinger with the *Times* said he'd fill 'em in on the particulars. I paid five dollars for these." He patted his coat pocket. "Come on, I ain't never seen no real hangin' before."

The deputy marshal at the gate scarcely glanced at either Henry and Daniel or the passes as they stepped inside the high-walled gallows area. Daniel had never planned on actually going to the execution. He thought he would slip away, but Cotton Henry never gave him the chance, and it finally registered with Daniel that Henry was just as scared, that he wanted, needed a companion to watch a man die.

No. Daniel stopped, staring at the huge gallows. *Not one man. Three.*

Another federal marshal pushed Daniel gently and pointed. "Reporters are over yonder," the lawman directed, and Daniel walked, or rather Cotton Henry practically dragged him, his spurs singing out some oddly merry tune, as he staggered toward the gathering of cigar-smoking men with pencils already scratching on their note pads.

Above the stench of tobacco, another smell, oddly familiar, triggered some old memories.

"Watch where you step!" a reporter called out, smiling. "Parker's deputies might be fine manhunters and peace officers, but they aren't worth a tinker's damn at mucking stalls."

"Huh?" Cotton Henry said, stepping into a mound of horse apples.

The reporter didn't bother explaining, and Cotton Henry, who didn't notice his misstep, forgot all about it, stopping and turning toward the gallows. Apparently Fort Smith wasn't quite as civilized as all those Eastern cities Daniel had seen, opting to use the compound as a stable when the gallows were not needed.

Daniel looked around. Men in suits circled the wooden scaffold, the backs of their heads somber. A doctor—well, he carried a black bag and hung a stethoscope around his neck—checked his stem-winder. Lawyers, or men he assumed were lawyers, chatted in whispers while a brute of a man waited on the top of the platform in front of three coiled nooses. Henry pointed at the man.

"That's ol' Maledon hisself," he said excitedly. "They say he ain't never botched no hangin'."

A priest began climbing the steps, reciting a passage from Psalms by memory, while a black marshal escorted the first manacled prisoner up the steps. To his surprise, Daniel found himself counting the steps. Twelve. Not thirteen. He remembered that half-dime novel the Lakota boy had smuggled into the barracks. Thirteen steps, but a man about to be hanged never stepped on the last one, fearing bad luck. The boys in the barracks had loved that line, the imagery. Every kid in school had thought the Beadle & Adams writer to have penned pure gospel in his macabre tale, but Daniel, with his own eyes, had just proven that story false.

"Charles Fenton!" a voice called out like some newspaper hawker as the condemned man stepped on the trap door beside the hangman. "Having been found guilty of the murder of Clark Edwards on the South Canadian River on the first of August, in the year of our Lord, Eighteen hundred and Eighty-five, and having been sentenced to death in the United States Court for the Western District of Arkansas, and having exhausted all appeals. . . ."

"Damn." Cotton Henry jabbed Daniel's arm. "That's a darky they's hangin'."

Daniel took a deep breath.

"Do you have any last words?"

The colored man shook his head, and his knees buckled slightly when the hangman slipped a mask over his face, then the noose.

"Lute Mosley!" the hawker called out.

Daniel didn't realize the second man had already made it up the twelve steps. He wet his dry lips. Pencils scratched on paper as the reporters tried to capture the final words Lute Mosley, convicted and condemned for murdering someone—Daniel hadn't caught the name—on a drunken spree near Fort Gibson in 1882, sang out for mercy and begged God again for forgiveness, blaming his impending death on the evils of demon rum and reminding Marshal Williams of his promise to inform his dear mother in Little Rock of his departure and that he'd meet her on the streets of gold. He finished his speech with: "And damn you, Judge Parker, I'll see you in hell for this, you pompous Yankee bas. . . ."

Maledon cut him off by jerking the black mask over his head, then roughly tightening the noose around his throat.

"The bloke's a mite confused," one reporter said. "First he's meeting his mother in heaven, and then he's seeing Parker in hell."

"Like God gives a damn what goes on in this hell-hole," another newspaperman commented.

Daniel decided to stare at his brown shoes. One

string was untied, he noticed, and he started to bend down to tie it, and stay down, so he couldn't watch, when the shrill voice made him jump.

"Jimmy Comes Last, having been found guilty of the murder of Thomas A. Benton and Karen Benton, committed in the home of the deceased, in the vicinity of Gibson Station. . . ."

He shot up, jaw slack, tried to swallow, but suddenly had no spit. Slimmer, much slimmer than Daniel remembered him. A federal lawman and a taller man, copper-skinned and wearing striped britches and a stovepipe hat, led Jimmy Comes Last to the final noose. The tall man kept whispering in Jimmy's ear. One lawman fastened straps above Jimmy's ankles, and, before Maledon covered the last condemned man's face, Daniel realized something else. Jimmy's braids had been cut off, his hair now as shorn as close as Daniel's.

The face vanished underneath a black sack, and the carnival hawker's voice ended, replaced by a new sound, a guttural chant, loud, powerful, from Jimmy Comes Last.

"What's he doin'?" Cotton Henry asked no one in particular.

Without realizing it, Daniel answered: "He's singing his death song." He had spoken louder than he had intended, and felt a handful of the newspapermen staring at him, saw from the corner of his eye Cotton Henry step away, studying him. Daniel didn't care. He wanted to look back at his feet, but couldn't move his eyes off the masked face of Jimmy Comes Last.

It ended quickly. Mercifully.

A mechanical *thud*, the sound of rushing wind, or

so it seemed, and a violent, sickening *snap*. Almost as one. As if George Maledon, master executioner, had planned it that way. The rope above Jimmy Comes Last's head quivered, somebody spit, and Daniel looked at the dead man he had once known, his head tilted at a ghastly angle, and found himself wondering: *How does one travel to The Land Beyond The Sun with a neck so crooked?*

The doctor stepped underneath the platform to pronounce the three men dead. Not that there was any need. Anyone could tell that with a quick glance at the three masked heads visible above the platform.

"Poor bastards," said one reporter, sliding pencil and an unlit, soggy cigar into his inside coat pocket.

"Well," another said, "it's over. Let's have a snort at The Choctaw Club."

Yet it wasn't over.

A voice of anguish pierced the sudden silence, and a crowd parted, revealing a woman in a mix of calico and buckskins, standing at the foot of the gallows, wailing louder than Jimmy Comes Last had sung. She dropped to her knees, her whole body trembling. The tall, coppery man in the big hat started down the steps, but stopped, looking at the woman as she pulled a knife from a hidden sheath.

"How'd she manage to get that in here?" a deputy shouted, and started for her, but the man on the steps yelled at him to stop, and the lawman obeyed.

She sawed off her own hair, rather short anyway in the fashion for Comanche women, singing, crying, tossing her silver-streaked locks to the ground. She looked older than Daniel remembered, as he struggled for her name. Naséca. It meant Persimmon

Tree. Seven years might have been seventy as much as she had aged. The blade bit into her left forearm. Again. And again. Rivulets of blood stained the cotton fabric, pooled on the dead grass beneath her.

"Stop her!" shrieked a bald man in a gray suit. "She's killing herself."

Surprisingly Cotton Henry stepped forward, his spurs providing some eerie harmony to Naséca's wails of heartbreaking pain. The cowboy, or whatever he was, no longer looked drunk, but sober, shamed, sick.

What shocked Daniel even more was when he reached out and took Henry's hand, pulled him back. He shook his head. "Leave her alone." He spoke in a dry whisper.

Naséca switched the knife to her other hand, cut three long gashes along her right arm, then, with a shriek, placed her hand on the ground and chopped off the tip of her little finger, then another.

"Jay-sus!" yelled a reporter, who spun, dropped, retched.

The grieving woman threw away the knife, buried her face in her bloody hands and, moments later, lifting her head, turning to stare at her son's body, choked out another cry. Removing his hat, the man on the steps completed his descent and walked toward the sobbing woman.

"She. . . ." Cotton Henry blinked. "She needs. . . ."

"She's in mourning." Daniel let go of Henry's hand, and headed toward Naséca.

One of the reporters spoke, his tone icy and rude. "For a Mex, Italian, Spaniard . . . whatever you claim to be . . . you seem to know a lot about those savages."

Stopping, Daniel turned and stared the journalist

down. He swallowed, and spoke, his voice powered by the rage he had felt, the shame of his cowardice, and he summoned up the words, the language they had been beating out of him, trying to make him forget for years in Carlisle, Pennsylvania.

"I am," he said in Comanche, "Nermernuh!"

Chapter Two

He had been given his father's name. Killstraight, only that wasn't the way The People said it, and his father had earned, not been handed, that name: His Arrows Fly Straight Into The Hearts Of His Enemies. A warrior with many honors, one of the cap wearers of the Kwahadi. Daniel could still picture his father in that hat of otter fur with buffalo horns, carrying a lance decorated with crow feathers. Big medicine. Even Quanah, the strong, young leader of the Kwahadi, often sought counsel with His Arrows Fly Straight Into The Hearts Of His Enemies. His *puha* came from the marsh hawk, and he had decorated his buffalo-hide shield with hawk feathers and vermillion drawings of talons. Even today, after all those years, every time Daniel heard a hawk's shrill cry, be it a marsh hawk, red-tailed or some raptor he couldn't see, he saw his father and felt that Comanche power.

Often Daniel remembered that day in the land of The People, what the pale eyes called El Llano Estacado, when he had earned his father's respect, and eventually his name, counting coup for the first—and only—time.

Back then Daniel's name had been Oá. Horn. How he got it, he had long forgotten. Yet he would never forget how he came to take his father's name.

They had ambushed four *Tejanos*, those who were killing all the buffalo, stripping them of the skin and leaving the meat to rot on that rugged plain during the spring of his eighth year. Too young, really, to count coup, but this had been a hunting expedition, not a raiding party. Led by Quanah, the band had come across the *Tejanos* by accident. His father killed one, Quanah had ridden down a second, three more young warriors chased a fleeing coward with no hair, and his father's friend—almost a brother, really, Isa Nanaka—had put an arrow into the last man's belly. Jimmy Comes Last, then known as Boy Who Comes Last To Eat, and Daniel had witnessed all of that. Seeing the man wounded by Isa Nanaka fueled the need for Boy Who Comes Last To Eat to prove his manhood, and he had swung onto his pony and raced ahead, yelling he would take first coup. Isa Nanaka merely laughed as Daniel, carrying a bow, had chased after his friend afoot.

Boy Who Comes Last To Eat would have won, easily, but his pony stepped into a prairie dog hole, and sent him tumbling into the dirt and mud, allowing Daniel to sprint past him. Slapping the wounded man's head with the end of his small bow, he had shrieked with joy: "I have first coup!" Cursing, holding a broken left arm, Boy Who Comes Last To Eat limped over and touched the man's stomach for second, final coup.

Not that there had been any danger for those two boys. The dying *Tejano*, moaning, blood bubbling between his lips, probably hadn't even felt those lame hits. He had never opened his eyes, hadn't even moved. Moments later, Isa Nanaka, still smiling at the escapades of Daniel and Boy Who Comes Last To Eat, had trotted over to cut the buffalo killer's throat and take his scalp.

"Boy Who Comes Last To Eat was very brave, and

very fast. He will be a great warrior for The People," Isa Nanaka had claimed at the celebration in the cañon where the Kwahadi had camped later that evening, a comment that drew Daniel's ire.

"Brave?" he had snapped. "Fast? Great warrior? How great can he be when I outran him on foot? He had a horse, and The People are supposed to be the best horsemen around!"

Boy Who Comes Last To Eat. Forgetting his friendship, Daniel had scoffed at that name. Comes Last? Sure, unless his mother was making that sweet candy of mescal beans and bone marrow. Comes Last? Yes, but always the last to get up, and never one to leave any morsel behind. It showed, too. The People were shorter, stockier than most Indians, but Boy Who Comes Last To Eat could put away more food, and put on more weight, than anyone in the Kwahadi camp. Even had he not broken his arm in the fall from his pony, Daniel felt certain he could have outrun his good friend. Probably the pony had collapsed under its rider's weight.

So Daniel had also reminded the men: "It was I who counted first coup!"

The warriors around the fire had exploded in laughter, and then his father had stepped up, face somber, putting his hand on Daniel's shoulder. "Hear this," he had said, "for from this night on, I give my name to my son, who has proved his manhood despite not yet reaching nine summers. No longer is he to be called Horn. He is His Arrows Fly Straight Into The Hearts Of His Enemies. I take a new name, Marsh Hawk, for it is my power."

"Good names," Quanah had said, "but your son did not kill the *Tejano* with his bow and arrow. His new name might be premature."

"He will." Daniel would never forget his father's smile. "He will kill more than I ever have. Scores of scalps, hundreds of coup. I had not counted coup at his age. He is brave."

"Considering his mother. . . ." someone had said in disgust, but Quanah had silenced that warrior with a sharp rebuke.

Ignoring the comment, his father, caught up in pride, had squeezed his son's shoulder. "You will be a great leader."

Not hardly, Daniel now thought in shame.

The Kwahadi would be the last band of The People to come to the reservation, but eventually they had no other choice. Bad Hand, the bluecoat, had seen to that. And all those *Tejano* killers of buffalo. The People surrendered at the soldier fort called Sill a little more than a year after Daniel had taken his father's name. Had limped in starving, ruined, those who had survived. Many hadn't.

Even Quanah had seen the hopelessness of resisting the pale eyes, telling the younger ones that they would have to learn to follow the White Man's Road. Eat the pale eyes' beef instead of buffalo. Go to the pale eyes' mission schools to learn the pale eyes' language. Become pale eyes.

At the mission school, these "Christians" had shortened Boy Who Comes Last To Eat's name to Jimmy Comes Last. His name shrank, but not his body. It was easy for a boy to get fat, and hard to kill the appetite of a hungry boy who had been starving for the past year on the plains, forced to eat grasshoppers, even ignoring taboo by consuming turkey and dog, and little of those, for the buffalo were all but gone.

Daniel had joined his fat friend at the school. His Arrows Fly Straight Into The Hearts Of His Enemies proved too tough for the pale eyes to translate, so his name became Killstraight. "Daniel" would come a few years later, after they put the thirteen-year-old Comanche in a wagon with several Arapahoes and sent him to Pennsylvania to learn to follow the White Man's Road. They didn't ask his mother for permission, just grabbed him as he walked from the mission school. Besides, Quanah had told the pale eyes it would be all right, and later Quanah would explain the kidnapping to Daniel's mother.

So he had gone to the Carlisle Industrial School, one Kwahadi among 136 frightened Lakotas, Cheyennes, Kiowas, and hated Pawnees.

There, the blue coat named Pratt and his pale eyes teachers had made him, and all the children, point to some "word"—strange white markings that covered rows upon rows on a black board, and, hesitantly, he had done so. He had stared at School Father Pratt, who had informed him: "Now your name is Daniel."

At least his father hadn't lived to see that shame. He had traveled to The Land Beyond The Sun shortly after Quanah had led the remnants of his Kwahadi band to become prisoners of the bluecoats. Many of those—and not just warriors of The People, but several Cheyennes and Kiowas, a couple of Arapahoes, even one old Caddo—had been taken away, much as Daniel and the others would be sent off four years later. The man named Pratt had Daniel's father and many others loaded into eight wagons, hauled them off, sent them East by wagon and train to some place called Fort Marion. They had stayed

there three years before coming back; only his father
had not come home.

Closing his eyes, Daniel could picture Isa Nanaka
telling Daniel and his mother that Marsh Hawk had
been shot by the bluecoats on the train tracks somewhere in Flo-ri-da, before ever reaching Fort Marion.
Many others would leave for The Land Beyond The
Sun as well, dying of rot in the hot, damp confines
of the fort, dying of heartbreak.

"The brave die young," Quanah, who had remained on the reservation, had commented, repeat-
ing a saying too often proved true by the best of The
People.

"Lucky," was all Isa Nanaka had said. Isa Nanaka
had been younger than his father, but now he looked
old, gaunt, almost dead. He had received his name,
Wolf's Howl, for the strength of his voice, but after
Fort Marion, when he opened his mouth, more often
he merely coughed, wiping flecks of blood from his
lips. He had left one of the strongest Kwahadi warriors, only to return with the lung sickness.

He's likely traveling to The Land Beyond The Sun, Daniel thought as he slowly walked to Naséca at the Fort
Smith gallows. She reminded him of old Wolf's Howl,
the death on her face, the pain in her eyes, how old
she had become.

"*Nevia*," he said, addressing her in the familiar.
My mother. She looked up, her song of mourning
softer now, and strained to see him through tear-
filled eyes. Words came hard for him, for it had been
so long since he had spoken in the language of The
People.

Another voice caused Daniel to turn. "Get her out
of here, Gunter. The fingers she cut off . . . and her

boy." The black lawman poked a calloused finger in
the chest of the tall man with the stovepipe hat, the
one who had helped escort Jimmy Comes Last to
his death. The tall man ignored the black lawman,
his dark, penetrating eyes locked on Daniel, and,
when he spoke, he addressed Daniel, not the deputy
marshal.

"You're Comanch'," he said.

Daniel nodded. At least he had been Comanche.

"Pronto, Gunter!" the lawman demanded before
storming away.

The tall man called Gunter looked Daniel up and
down, his face a copper mask, sizing up the lousy
suit, stupid bowler, those damned shoes and the
stocky kid who wore them, yet he made no comment, and, unlike everyone else in Fort Smith, at
least Gunter hadn't seen him as some short, chubby
Mexican, Italian, or Spaniard. Likewise, Daniel recognized something in the tall man.

"You're Indian, too."

Gunter's head bobbed slightly. "Cherokee." He
jutted his jaw at Naséca. "You take care of her. I'll
handle Jimmy. Got a wagon out back." He disappeared underneath the scaffolding with a handful
of black men in shabby clothes who had appeared
after the executions. Daniel looked around. The
place had cleared out—even Cotton Henry—except
for the doctor, and one or two of the myriad reporters chatting with a federal peace officer—replaced
by men from the undertaker waiting to load the
bodies of Charles Fenton and Lute Mosley into pine
boxes. Jimmy Comes Last, too.

Daniel looked back at Jimmy's mother. She had
stopped singing.

"My mother," he repeated in Comanche, and knelt

by her, opening the carpetbag he had absentmindedly been carrying through the whole ordeal. He pulled out a shirt, began tearing it into strips to wrap around her bleeding arms and mangled hand.

"I know you," she said quietly in Comanche.

He nodded. "I am. . . ." He swallowed, ashamed, trying to remember how to say his name, his real name, in the language of The People. Other words he could remember, but not that. Why? Had those teachers with their wooden rulers that had slammed his knuckles like hammers taken it away from his memories? Or was it his own shame?

"I am called Killstraight," he said in English. "Daniel." Then in Comanche: "I knew your son."

She choked out a short cry, and started to look behind her, but Daniel stopped her, shaking his head. "Don't," he cautioned her. Remember him alive. Not with a broken neck, his prison pants soiled, being roughly handled by strangers, thrown like a sack of flour into a cheap wooden box over the Cherokee's protest.

Another song began.

Fresh tears cascaded over the crevasses in her leathery face, like spring runoff flowing down the Wichitas. Daniel wrapped her hand, blood soaking the cotton. He found another strip. She let him work, too numb, too weak, to resist, and at last closed her eyes moments before the men of color carried Jimmy Comes Last toward the gate. They had packed his coffin with charcoal to preserve the body. After all, it was better than 250 miles to the agency, and summer in Indian Territory came quickly.

The Cherokee walked past, shooting a quick glance at Daniel and Naséca but saying nothing.

"Don't forget her fingers," a voice grunted, and

Daniel looked around, then up, finally found the hangman, Maledon, staring down from the platform, a wicked grin twisting his face into a scowl. He pointed, spit, and pivoted. *Thumps* of his feet sounded hollowly, and Daniel watched the man walk down the twelve steps, spit again, and walk nonchalantly out the gate.

They were alone now, Daniel and Naséca, and she began chanting again. Daniel found another bit of cotton. He should have made some attempt to clean her wounds, but wanted to get her out of here, away from the gallows. Besides, he wasn't some white doctor, and far from a *puhakut*.

He wrapped her arm, tied the ends tightly to stanch the blood. At least her wounds were beginning to clot. If she felt any pain from the cuts, she never showed it. When he had finished, his eyes scanned the brown grass behind her until he spotted the remnant of one of her fingers, then another. Swallowing down bile, he started to leave her and retrieve the bloody bits of bone and flesh, following the orders of the hangman and the deputy.

"Leave those!" The voice, strong, startled him, and he spun to see the Cherokee towering above him. Daniel hadn't heard Gunter return. He stared, swallowed, and started to look away when he noticed a badge pinned on the lapel of Gunter's vest. A Cherokee lawman. He was curious, but didn't ask. Instead, he looked back at the tips of Naséca's two fingers.

"Let Maledon pick them up," Gunter said bitterly, and Daniel found his respect for the Cherokee grow. "Or the others who brought this on." Gunter sighed heavily, stepped around Daniel and squatted beside the bloody digits, apparently changing his mind, and mood. "Hell," he said softly. "I brought this on, not George." Gently he lifted the two tips, wrapped them in a handkerchief he withdrew from his coat. "I'll put them in Jimmy's coffin." The handkerchief disappeared in the pocket, and he faced Daniel, removing his stovepipe hat and wiping his high forehead with the back of his left hand.

"Is she ready to travel?" Gunter asked.

Before Daniel could answer, Naséca stopped singing, and her eyes opened. She looked at Daniel, wetting her lips, studying him.

"I know you," she said again, and her head bobbed. "You were gone. We thought forever. Now you have returned to The People."

Have I? Daniel wondered.

Chapter Three

Jimmy Comes Last moaned.

Daniel heard his old friend's low groan, rising in pitch almost to a wail, heard him stumbling around the campsite, wandering, singing, lost. Daniel knew he should help, but he couldn't move. Wouldn't open his eyes. Instead, he pretended to be asleep, hoping someone else would wake up and go help that loco Comanche.

But . . . you're dead! The sudden thought caused Daniel to tighten his eyelids.

"Help me, brother!" Jimmy called out clearly, and Daniel could feel the young Comanche standing over his bedroll, feel those haunting eyes drilling through his body. Jimmy had found him, was waiting. "Help me. Tell her I am sorry. Help me!"

He didn't know what to expect, although he feared it would be gruesome. Maybe Jimmy held a war club over his head, ready to swing, crush Daniel's skull. Maybe. . . .

Summoning courage, Daniel forced his eyes open, tossed off the covers, looked up . . . and screamed.

At that point, seeing Jimmy, he knew he must be having a nightmare, shrieking in his sleep, likely waking Hugh Gunter and Naséca, probably sitting bolt upright in his bedroll. *Wake up!* he told himself. *Wake up! Shut up! Stop screaming. Move.* But he couldn't; Jimmy's dead eyes had pinned him to the ground.

Finally his eyes shot open, awake at last, freed

from the ghost of Jimmy Comes Last, and he heard . . .
silence. He hadn't been screaming in his sleep, just
in the dream. He wasn't even sweating, but he sure
couldn't go back to sleep, so he dragged himself out
of the bedroll, surprised to smell coffee.

"Bloody bone after you?" Hugh Gunter asked.

When his eyes grew accustomed to the darkness,
Daniel stared at the Cherokee. "Something like that,"
he said, barely audible.

"Almost dawn." Gunter gestured at the small fire
in front of him. "Got some chicory brewing. Couldn't
sleep much myself."

They had left Fort Smith immediately after the hangings. Daniel hadn't even considered riding along
with the Cherokee and Jimmy Comes Last's mother,
had figured he would just buy a horse at some old
livery in the city, but when Gunter asked if he
needed a ride, Daniel realized he would not get a
better offer.

"I'm taking her back to the agency," Gunter had
said, motioning toward Naséca. "I don't speak Comanche, she don't speak Cherokee, English, neither,
and, pained as she is, I don't think she'll understand much signing. Comanches ain't much good at
sign, nohow, from my experience." Gunter's mouth
and eyes hardened. "It ain't no paying job," he informed Daniel, then, face softening, he had almost
smiled. "But I won't charge you no fare."

"I'd appreciate the ride," Daniel had said. Horses
came cheaper on the reservation than in Fort Smith
anyway.

Using a bandanna as a mitt, Hugh Gunter lifted the
battered enamel coffeepot and filled a cup, passing

it to Daniel, who warmed himself by the fire. The cup burned his fingers, and he set it down to cool, then shot a glance over at Naséca.

"Still sleeping." Still bothered by the nightmare, he spoke just to hear his own voice.

"Snores like a sumbitch," Gunter said. "Not like you."

Daniel swallowed, made himself look at the wagon, although he couldn't make out the coffin in the back.

"Jimmy don't snore," Gunter said, and laughed at his own joke.

"Who did he kill?" Daniel finally asked, abruptly killing Gunter's laughter.

Before answering, the Cherokee stood, knee joints creaking and popping, walked to the wagon, rummaged through a canvas sack in the driver's boot, found another cup, and came back to the fire, pouring himself a hit of bitter brew.

"Thomas Benton," Gunter answered at last.

Daniel nodded, remembering the name mentioned at the execution, and picked up his cup.

"He was a squawman spitting distance of Gibson Station," Gunter said. "Had a cabin on the Verdigris. Ever seen what a Greener'll do at close range? I hadn't, and I've seen a lot of dead folks in my time. Blowed his face clean off. Gave him both barrels."

The coffee didn't sit well in Daniel's stomach. Maybe he had grown used to that weak Dutch coffee they brewed up in Pennsylvania. Maybe he remembered how The People liked coffee, heavy with sugar. Maybe he pictured Jimmy's face from that nightmare, the neck broken, the face a bloody mess, as if it had been blasted with a double-barrel shotgun at close range.

"There was . . . a . . . woman," Daniel remembered.

"Uhn-huh. Karen. Benton married her some years back. She was full-blood Creek. Not bad to look at, for a Creek." Gunter spit out the coffee. "Well. . . ." He swore under his breath. "Not bad to look at . . . poor choice of words."

"Shotgun?" Daniel asked.

Gunter's head shook. "Axe. Blood everywhere. It. . . ."

Silence. Eventually Gunter tossed a small limb on the flames, poking the coals with another stick. The eastern sky began turning gray.

"Why did he do it?" Daniel asked.

"Jimmy never said." Another long while passed without conversation, and Daniel heard Naséca's soft snores. "Not during the trial. Not no time. Noble, he's one of Judge Parker's deputies. Harvey P. Noble. Decent guy. His guess was that Jimmy was in his cups. Kid wasn't more than a walking whiskey keg anyhow. So Marshal Noble reckons Jimmy was hunting for some Creek whiskey. He come to the Benton cabin. Thinks he can find some rotgut there, and, when he don't, he just goes wild." He looked Daniel in the eye. "You knew him?"

"Knew him." Daniel nodded. "But a long time ago. Not the man you just described."

"White man's whiskey, Creek whiskey, any whiskey, it can change a man."

"And . . . the *taibo* that hanged?"

"*Taibo*?" Gunter asked.

"White man. Both of them, I mean. Did they . . . ?"

"I didn't have anything to do with them. Those two were charged with different crimes. Just because they stand on the same gallows, that don't mean a thing. You heard them read the charges. Didn't know them others, but I ain't sorry they're gone from this country."

"Did you know Jimmy?" Daniel asked.

"Some. Not much. Met him a few times when he was with your Indian police."

Daniel's eyebrows arched. "Jimmy? A Metal Shirt?" Vaguely he recalled the Indian agent recruiting Comanches as tribal policemen, although most of The People laughed at those so-called peace officers. They didn't even have guns—pale eyes certainly had qualms about arming any Comanche—and, whenever they were asked to go chase some felon, they had to ride over to Fort Sill to plead for rifles. Couldn't arrest pale eyes, of course, even if the white men— Texians mostly—had stolen horses or cattle. Only a white man could arrest another white man, so the Comanche lawmen settled disputes, chased their own, sending them off to Fort Smith for the serious offenses. Metal Shirts, The People called them, after those stupid badges they wore on hand-me-down uniforms. Jimmy Comes Last? A police officer? He couldn't picture that.

"Best way to get whiskey," Gunter offered, "is to be a Metal Shirt." He laughed. "Best way to know if the Creeks are running whiskey on the reservation is if you have a bunch of drunk Metal Shirts."

Daniel pointed at the badge on the Cherokee's vest. "You're one yourself."

Gunter nodded. "United States Indian Police. Got jurisdiction over all the Five Civilized Tribes." He sniggered. "Civilized. Like there's anything civilized west of Van Buren. Colonel Tufts . . . he'd been the Union agent in Muskogee . . . he recruited us five, six years back. District sheriffs used to pull me out of

bed whenever they needed a posse. 'Course, it's ille-
gal for any Cherokee citizen to refuse to serve on a
posse, and I had some experience. Rode with the
Cherokee Nation Lighthorse before it was disbanded
in 'Sixty-six. So when Tufts come calling, it struck
me that I might as well pin on a badge permanent-
like. Marshal Noble, he'll hire me on when he's in
the Nations. Some of Parker's other deputies'll do the
same. Pays all right . . . on top of the eight dollars
a month I get with the Indian Police . . . if you don't
get shot."

"You like it?" Daniel asked.

"Sometimes," Gunter said. He hooked a thumb
toward the wagon. "Not always."

The fire *hissed* as Gunter tossed the dregs on the
coals. "I am good at it," he said flatly.

Daniel stared at the cup, surprised to find it
empty. A mule snorted, and Naséca began singing
softly. He pictured Jimmy again, on the gallows,
and saw Hugh Gunter talking to the condemned
man. Talking? Saying what? Daniel had thought
the Cherokee had been translating, but Jimmy
Comes Last knew English, a smattering, at least,
and Hugh Gunter had just told him he didn't speak
Comanche.

Yet he said nothing, asked nothing, just reached
over and refilled the cup.

They moved slowly over the next several days, the
two mules, named Ross and Watie, seldom acting
like mules, following the military road from Fort
Smith to Fort Sill. *Not much different than Pennsylvania*, Daniel thought, *with the rolling hills and timber.*
He slapped his neck. *Or the mosquitoes.* He rode along-
side Hugh Gunter, while Naséca sat in the back, one

hand resting on the top of Jimmy's coffin, singing every once in a while, crying a little, mostly just sitting there, bouncing, rocking, never complaining. At a crossroads community two days out, Gunter bought grain for the mules from a squawman and a hogshead of cheese and crackers from a stout Choctaw woman. Daniel offered to help pay, but the Cherokee refused.

The following night, Naséca began talking.

"My son did not kill the pale eyes man and his woman," she said, touching Daniel's arm. "You remember him. You knew his heart. You know I speak the truth."

Gunter's lips tightened, and he stared coldly, but made no comment. Instead, he fished a piece of jerky from his pocket and tore off a hunk with his teeth. She spoke in Comanche, but Gunter must have understood part of the conversation, or, at the least, her tone.

"You. . . ." Naséca wet her lips, squeezed Daniel's arm. "You will help me."

"Help you . . . what?" Daniel felt himself trembling. It was too late for Jimmy Comes Last. Boy Who Comes Last To Eat would wander eternity with his twisted neck, doomed, unable to reach The Land Beyond The Sun.

"You make things right," she said. "Make things right with my son." Following the custom of The People, she remained careful not to mention the name of the dead. "Make things right with the pale eyes. And tell me, when you make things right. Find the truth. Tell me, so I can rest. So . . . he . . . he can . . . rest."

He drew a breath, held it.

"You are of The People," she reminded him.

He thought of his mother. Mescalero, not Comanche, until his father had taken her. And for seven years he had lived in the white man's world. His hair was close-cropped, and Comanche men loved, to the point of vanity, their hair, keeping it long, glistening. He spoke English, perhaps knew it better than his native tongue now. It had taken him practically two days after the hanging before he truly remembered how to say his name in his native tongue. Yet he also knew, in many ways, he would always be Nermernuh. At Carlisle, he had been one of the "wild ones," a savage bent on remembering his heritage, his language, his customs, who fought School Father Pratt and all the school mothers and school fathers. Fought . . . but lost. Eventually all students lost. Or died.

"Yes, mother, I will help you," he told her, and stared across the campfire at Hugh Gunter as she walked away.

"What did she want?" Gunter asked.

"Help her. . . ." He shook his head. "Prove that Jimmy was innocent, I guess."

The Cherokee spit. "Bit late for that."

The country hardened as they moved west, the trees thinning out, the water turning more brackish, the jack rabbits skinnier, the terrain more brown, the sun more blistering.

"I hate your country," Gunter said.

Daniel smiled.

Gunter reported in at the Comanche agency, while Daniel, staying close to Naséca, looked for familiar faces, but found few of The People. Hardly anyone could be seen at the agency, and, when Gunter returned and climbed back in the wagon, they rode south two more miles to a small clearing, where Na-séca leaped from the back of the wagon before Gunter could rein Watie and Ross to a stop.

Daniel looked around, finding a teepee made of white canvas, rather than buffalo hides, a rawhide-looking corral with two horses in it, nothing much else. The People had always preferred space, pitching their lodges far from others, spreading out to enjoy solitude, and make things harder for their enemies. Naséca turned at the entrance to the teepee, barked out instructions, then disappeared inside.

"What she say?" Gunter asked.

"Telling us where to bury Jimmy."

The People had never been formal when it came to what pale eyes would call religion. No men with paper collars to read scripture. Few, if any, songs. No organ. No crowds. Corpses petrified many other tribes, but not the Comanches. They didn't fear death, so why should they be afraid of a dead man? The Cheyennes and Lakotas would put their dead on a scaffold, but The People buried their dead underground, much the same as the pale eyes. So Daniel Killstraight and Hugh Gunter buried Jimmy Comes Last a few rods behind a lean-to near Cache Creek.

Sweating from the digging, Daniel and Gunter used the reins from the wagon team to lower Jimmy Comes Last into the grave. Daniel smelled the smoke as Naséca came walking down, leading one of the horses from the corral, carrying a flour sack, medicine pouch, and a beautiful Comanche war shield in the other hand. Behind her, flames engulfed the teepee, and the Cherokee wiped his eyes with his bandanna, staring at the inferno in disbelief.

"She'll burn most of his possessions," Daniel said as he gathered one of the reins from the pit. "The stuff's not important, anyway. It's our . . . it's the way of The People. His medicine . . . that she will either throw in that oak or into the creek." He watched. "Creek," he said.

They stepped back as Naséca led the horse, a rangy bay, to the grave. She emptied the sack, and Daniel saw a knife and pipe, some other trinkets he couldn't make out, fall into the hole for Jimmy to have on his journey, followed by the shield.

"And the horse?" Gunter whispered.

Daniel felt uneasy. She might present the horse to her son's best friend. The People sometimes did that, and Daniel needed, wanted a horse. He felt like a *taibo* then, greedy, coveting something he had no reason to expect. Or. . . .

Naséca swiftly drew a knife, the same one she had used in her mourning, from inside her blouse and sliced the bay's neck. Gunter grunted as the blood spurted, the horse cried out in terror, pain, shock, but the old woman was singing softly, helping ease the dying animal on the ground beside her son's grave.

"Damn' waste," Gunter said softly. "Not a bad horse."

"When my mother heard of my father's death," Daniel said, "she killed every horse in our herd. And she wasn't even . . . well . . . some of The People will just cut the manes and tails of the dead man's horses and mules, throw the hair in the grave." Naséca, still singing, dropped a Comanche saddle and bridle into the grave atop her son. "But those who do that are considered . . . misers."

She turned, wiping blood on her blouse, and walked into the smoke, away from the grave.

"Maybe we are civilized, after all," Gunter said.

"I thank you for the ride," Daniel told the Cherokee the next morning when he climbed into the wagon.

"You are welcome." Gunter held out his hand, and they shook. "What's next for you?"

Daniel shrugged. He'd need to report in at the agency. He could have done that when Gunter stopped, but he hadn't wanted to leave Naséca alone.

"Good luck helping the old woman."

Daniel's eyebrows arched, not understanding.

"You promised you would prove Jimmy was innocent."

"Oh." Daniel stared at his feet, finally looked up. "She should have asked you. You're the detective."

"I'm not Comanche," he said, and Daniel thought: *Am I?*

"Besides, I don't think the old crone likes me," Gunter said before releasing the brake and clucking at the two mules. "Certainly don't trust me. Hell, it was me who arrested Jimmy for those murders."

Chapter Four

He stayed with Naséca for another day, just to make sure she would be all right, then left for the agency. He had shunned those lousy city shoes for a pair of Jimmy's moccasins, which Naséca had presented him. The moccasins didn't fit well, but Daniel found them more comfortable than the brown Oxfords, especially considering he would be walking two miles back to the agency, and who knew how much farther after that. She came with him, explaining that it was ration day, and didn't seem to notice vultures circling the sky, reminding Daniel of the bay horse Naséca had killed, to carry Jimmy Comes Last on his journey. Daniel couldn't help but notice, and remember.

As a kid, Daniel had hated ration day. The People never cared for beef, and the cattle driven onto the reservation by Texans always seemed tough, barely digestible. Come winter, the longhorns grazing near the agency had become too weak, much like many of reservation Indians, and couldn't be driven off, so The People had slaughtered the animals near the corrals, to the horror of pale eyes agents and missionaries.

Yet now, and maybe even back then, ration day had become something for The People to celebrate, like a buffalo hunt, a reminder of the times when they had been free. Women sang songs as Indian men shot down the cattle in the corral, and then the women went to work with their knives, carving up the tough, leathery meat, leaving the hearts behind but eating the livers raw, as they had always done to honor the great *chutz*, although cow liver tasted nothing like buffalo liver. And, still, watching pale eyes looked on in either horror or disgust.

He stood in line with Naséca and others, patiently, and inspected the gangling, pockmarked man who issued Jimmy's weary mother a quarter pound of flour, the musky smell alone almost making Daniel sick, coarse sugar, coffee, corn unfit for even hogs to eat, and a bar of lye soap. Never making eye contact with the agency man, Naséca thanked him before hurrying toward the corrals to collect her beef ration.

The white man stared at Daniel.

"I need to report to the agent," he said, and the man's eyes widened in amazement at his English. "My name is Daniel Killstraight."

"Hell." The man sprayed tobacco juice over the barrels of corn. "They taught you good English up at Chilocco."

Chilocco was one of the newer industrial boarding schools for Indians. Prairie Light, The People called it, located somewhere north, near the Kansas border, a whole lot closer to Comanche country than Pennsylvania.

"Carlisle," Daniel said.

The man's face showed his disapproval of being corrected. He hooked a thumb toward a cabin a few rods beyond the corrals. "Get a move on," he said, swatting at a fly. "I ain't gonna stand here all day."

Daniel stepped out of line, wondering if he should have collected his rations, and started for the cabin. In front of the building, fanning himself with a *Harper's Weekly*, a blond-bearded man in a suit of dusty black broadcloth and a loosened gray cravat stood, talking absently to a taller man with a monstrous white mustache, a cowhand from the cut of his clothes. A *Tejano* from that small star cut into the crown of his big hat.

Suddenly a hand slapped Daniel's back, grabbed his shoulder, and spun him around, knocking his bowler into the dust. Daniel blinked, stepped back, staring into a smiling face, some teeth broken, a couple rotting, several others missing.

"I thought that was you," the face said in Comanche. "I knew it was you. Brother, it is good to see you."

Daniel swallowed, trying to remember. The man stood about his height, a little thinner, wearing denim trousers, Comanche moccasins, and a filthy gray coat, sleeves dripping in blood, buttons missing, over a muslin shirt. He carried a battered Spencer rifle in his left hand, with a knife secured in a bloodstained sheath belted around his waist. Daniel guessed the man had been helping butcher cattle. Women's work, he scoffed. The belt also held a holstered revolver, butt forward, and, when the man pushed back his coat, Daniel glimpsed a tarnished shield pinned on the dirty shirt.

"Have you forgotten your brother?" The man's eyes twinkled. "It has been five summers."

"Seven," Daniel corrected, and suddenly smiled. "But not too long for Ben Buffalo Bone to be lost among my memories."

"Killstraight," Ben Buffalo Bone said in English. "Speak good Comanch'." His eyes shone as if to say: *I thought you would have forgotten our language.*

He had met Ben Buffalo Bone, of the Kotsoteka band, at the missionary school on the reservation. Together, they had stolen chickens from pale eyes' coops, releasing the frightened, squawking, unruly birds in the pastures and laughing as coyotes tried to run them down for supper. It had never occurred to Daniel and Ben Buffalo Bone to eat the fowls, although that's what the pale eyes teachers had believed. Eat a creature with feathers? Among The People that was as awful as eating a fish or snake.

"Seven summers." Ben Buffalo Bone shook his head, switching back to Comanche. "But now you have returned. Come. . . ."

"I need. . . ." Daniel jutted his jaw toward the cabin.

"Ah. It is good. I will introduce you to our new white agent. Then I must get back to work."

The big-mustached drover shook the agent's hand, bit off the end of a cigar, and spit it out, then pivoted, his spurs chiming, and strode toward a horse hobbled near a lean-to behind the cabin. He scarcely glanced at either of the approaching Comanches.

The agent sighed heavily, wiped his brow with a handkerchief, and turned to go inside the building, stopping when Ben Buffalo Bone called out his name. The white man grimaced at the Comanche's bloody outfit.

"This is. . . ." Ben Buffalo Bone started to use Daniel's Comanche name, thought better of it, and said: "Killstraight. Of the Kwahadi. He come home."

The agent's eyes appeared bloodshot. Almost dead. He looked Daniel up and down, and eventually his head bobbed. "Yes. Daniel, isn't it?" Daniel nodded. The agent's voice, twangy but strong, surprised him. He had figured the agent to be like all those others he had known, meek, soft-spoken, with accents sounding more like Pennsylvania than

Texas. "Yes, Captain Pratt wrote that you would be returning."

"He *bávi*," Ben Buffalo Bone said. "Brother. Make good Metal Shirt."

"I didn't know you had a brother," the agent said.

"We were friends," Daniel explained. Pale eyes would never understand The People. "Not related by blood."

The agent wet his lips. "Your English is pretty good."

It should be, Daniel thought bitterly. *You people have been beating it into me for seven years. Punishing me whenever I spoke my own tongue.*

"See," Ben Buffalo Bone said. "Good English. Good Comanch'. Good policeman."

"Get back to the corrals," the agent ordered Ben, then motioned Daniel inside. The cabin felt stifling, and Daniel stood in front of the agent's desk, uncomfortable. The white man filled a tumbler with water, drank about half before sitting, shuffling papers that cluttered the desktop along with an ashtray, three books, a Bible, and an inkwell.

"Well, I can't find that letter." The agent looked up. "I am Ephraim Rueben. Came here last year. You really interested in being on the police?"

He hadn't considered it, even after Ben Buffalo Bone had made that announcement.

"I could use one," Agent Rueben added.

To replace Jimmy Comes Last? Daniel wondered.

"Pays eight dollars a month," Agent Rueben said.

The same as Hugh Gunter got with the United States Indian Police, Daniel thought, *but a whole lot less than the Army paid Indian scouts over at Fort Sill.*

A drawer *squeaked*, and the agent withdrew a plain tin badge, shaped like a shield, and tossed it atop the cluttered papers. "You get this, and a uniform, and a Remington revolver if it don't blow up in your face, if it'll pop a cap at all."

Armed police? That had changed.

"I need a good policeman, one who speaks English pretty fair, and you speak it better than fair. Some of these bucks I got I can't make heads or tails what they're telling me. Some interpreters aren't much better. And I'd like a policeman with some education, which that Yankee Pratt saw to. If I recollect right, you had been working on a farm a while, and then. . . ."

"Coal mine."

"Never liked being underneath the ground."

"I didn't, either."

The blond agent, a slight man, Daniel realized, but powerful, pointed at the badge.

"It's yours if you want it."

"I want it," Daniel said, although he wasn't sure he really did want the job, but that's another thing they had drilled into him in Pennsylvania. Work. Find a job. Earn a living. Forget your savage ways. He picked up the badge.

"I'll sign you in after we get rid of those rations," the agent said. "Right now, I got a chore for you. Report to Sergeant Sitting Still."

"Is he at the corrals?"

"No. We got rationing covered, I warrant. The sergeant and a few men . . . prisoners mostly, some other policeman . . . are working on the road to Camp Supply. If you quickstep it, you can be there by noon. The sergeant'll put you to work, then you come back here. I'll have the paperwork ready for you to make your. . . ." He looked up, his eyes questioning.

"I can write," Daniel said, pinning the badge on his shirt.

"We'll get your uniform and revolver issued to you then. Got a horse?"

"No, sir."

"You'll need one, eventually. Some of J. C. C. Mc-Bride's boys are bringing in some stock tomorrow. If you're not here, I'll pick one out for you. It'll come out of your wages."

"And my rations?" Daniel asked.

Rueben shook his head. "Indian Police don't get rations. Sorry, but that's what Congress decided when they upped your pay to eight bucks a month." He shook his head. "Besides, you don't want that hog and hominy we serve your people nohow." The agent took another sip of water. "Best get moving, Killstraight. Sergeant Sitting Still needs help."

He had just stepped through the doorway when the agent called his name.

"One thing you ought to know, Killstraight. I don't like whiskey-runners on the reservation, and I don't like drunken lawmen. You pull a cork, and I nail your hide to the barn. You savvy?"

"I don't drink," Daniel said.

"See that you don't start."

That first week he loathed his decision. Noihqueyú-cat, the Indian police sergeant known as Sitting Still, hated Daniel, hated any Comanche who had been sent off to one of those boarding schools, even though Daniel had never had any say in the matter. "You learn the pale eyes' way," Sitting Still had said with a sneer. "Well, I will always be one of The People."

Inwardly Daniel had laughed. Sergeant Sitting Still acted more like a white man than any Comanche he had ever known. He worked his men savagely, ruthlessly, only to bow down to Ephraim Rueben like a pale eyes dog, never quite understanding that white men were using him, much as he used, and abused, his policemen and prisoners.

At Ben Buffalo Bone's invitation, he left Naséca, where he had been sleeping underneath a blackjack. Ben's father, who started the journey to The Land Beyond The Sun five winters back, had been among the peace chiefs, if there could be called any such thing with the Kotsotekas, so when they came to the reservation, the pale eyes agent, then a balding, humble man from some place called Indiana, had built a fine cabin for the peace chief. Preferring a teepee, Ben's father had never lived in the cabin, but had used the cabin as a barn for his favorite horses. Ben Buffalo Bone didn't care much for the white man's houses, either, but he had fewer horses than his father had owned, so he let Daniel have the house. After all, Daniel was used to sleeping with a roof over his head and a square wall instead of the circular Comanche lodge of buffalo hide. That's how Ben Buffalo Bone saw it. Daniel didn't try to explain that he sure wasn't used to sleeping with horses.

When it rained, though, he appreciated the roof, and found the smell of horses as pleasant as the *patter* of raindrops and the wind whistling through the cabin's log walls, well in need of chinking.

After two days, Daniel and his squad had finished the road project, so Agent Rueben next put them to work digging an irrigation canal for the agency. So this is being a policeman? More like a slave. Daniel had a badge, though, which prompted snickers from old Comanche women and children, too young to attend either the mission school on the reservation or one of those boarding schools. He had a uniform, a gray coat about two sizes too small for his broad chest, the itchy wool tormenting him mercilessly. The uniforms, he learned, were leftovers from the Centennial Exposition. Moths, or rats, maybe both, had gotten into the pants he had been issued, so he wore the trousers from his broadcloth suit until they were torn and ruined, replacing them with a spare pair of duck trousers until Ben Buffalo Bone's oldest sister, Rain Shower, presented him with deerskin pants. She also altered Jimmy Comes Last's old moccasins so that they fit much better. He stuck a turkey feather in his bowler, decided to let his hair grow, and relished the frown Ephraim Rueben gave him while digging the canal.

Gone Injun, the agent had to be thinking. What a shame.

Daniel knew better. Gone back to his people? Not hardly.

He had a horse, a pretty good piebald gelding that was worth, maybe, $10, although the agent said he would deduct $22 from Daniel's wages, $6.25 a month over the next four months. Daniel didn't argue over the math, or interest the agent seemed to be charging. He liked the horse, and busied himself making a saddle and bridle when he wasn't sweating while performing his police "duties" or cursing Sergeant Sitting Still.

He also had an old Remington revolver, battered and scarred, but at least it fired, or had when he had tested it the day after Rueben had given it to him. Mostly he used it as a hammer, doing chores for the agent.

His palms were blistered, hands, arms, and legs cut and bruised, two fingernails blackened, and he smelled of sweat and horse dung. When he woke up one morning, washed his face, combed his hair, he decided that today he would quit his job with the tribal police.

"Come on!" Ben Buffalo Bone called out cheerily as he emerged from his lodge.

"Where?" Daniel asked bitterly. *What does Agent Rueben need done today? Patch his roof? Dig his privy? Pick his nose?*

"Let's go for a ride, see if that pony of yours is any good. I have an extra saddle."

He wiped water from his face. "What about Sergeant . . . ?"

Ben Buffalo Bone's laugh cut him off. "Didn't they teach you about the Sabbath in your school? We don't work on Sundays, unless we are pursuing some enemy. Let's ride, *bávi*. Feel the wind in our hair. Feel like Nermernuh again. Let's go see an old friend."

Chapter Five

He had named the piebald gelding Nabohcutz because the Texas pony reminded him of a skunk. Yet he hadn't ridden Skunk much. Agent Rueben kept him busy on his feet, digging ditches, mending roofs, fixing roads, things like that. That Sunday morning, Ben Buffalo Bone kicked his palomino into a gallop, and Daniel felt Skunk explode into a smooth gait, catching up with the palomino, lunging ahead, loving the race. Ben Buffalo Bone laughed; so did Daniel.

Wind whipped his face, blew off his bowler, but Daniel didn't care. It was a stupid hat, anyway. He had forgotten how good it felt to be on a horse, riding into the wind, feeling free. Had forgotten how good a horseman he was, but that was the way of The People. Even School Father Pratt, who had served with the bluecoats in Indian Territory before taking charge of his industrial school in Carlisle, had called Comanches the best horsemen he had ever seen. The way Daniel remembered things, he had been able to saddle his own mount by the time he was five years old.

Briefly they turned south, then west, maintaining a gallop for about a mile before slowing into a gentle lope, and only falling into a trot when they came across a cavalry patrol from Fort Sill. The soldiers eyed the two Comanches with distrust, saying nothing, and, as soon as they had disappeared around a bend, Ben Buffalo Bone kicked his horse into a lope. Neither the palomino nor piebald showed signs of tiring, and Daniel laughed. Maybe that paint horse was worth more than $22, certainly more than $10. Maybe Daniel had cheated Agent Rueben, not the other way around.

"Where are we going?" Daniel called out.

Ben Buffalo Bone answered with only a grin.

After a few more miles, they slowed their mounts to a walk, and Daniel followed his friend as they turned off the road and headed down a well-traveled path. He saw the teepee—made of buffalo hide when most lodges he had found on the reservation since his return had been pieced together using old Army canvas—in the center of a grass lawn, shaded by several trees. Behind the teepee stood a spacious, two-story house, wooden frames painted white, a porch wrapping around both floors for as far as he could see. The windows, and there were many, had been pulled open to catch the breeze, and a Comanche woman stared down from a rocking chair on the upper porch, working her awl on leather. In Pennsylvania, he had seen many fancy homes, and he remembered riding to town with a Lakota boy, spotting some mansion, or what they considered a mansion, for the first time, and the Lakota boy had marveled about what kind of pale eyes must have owned such a lodge.

A similar, boyish, thought struck Daniel now as they reined in their horses. *A king must live here.*

Painted on the red shingles were four enormous white stars, like those one would find on the uniforms of the Army soldiers, or on their flags.

The front door opened, and a tall figure emerged, carrying himself with dignity, like a king, stopping at the edge of the porch, calling out a welcome in the language of The People. His black locks were braided, falling in two tied plaits down his back, with deerskin pants and Comanche moccasins, yet an Army blue vest, its brass buttons gleaming, covered a silk shirt of lighter blue, and a black cravat, with a diamond stickpin, hung in place around his neck, as did a bear claw necklace. Part white man. Part Comanche.

But that had always been Quanah.

His mother had been a pale eyes, captured when The People raided into Texas long, long before Daniel had been born. The People had named her Nadua, and she had remained with them until the pale eyes attacked the village. Nadua, the way Daniel recalled the stories, had been returned to the pale eyes, where she had died of a broken heart. Quanah's heart had also broken, yet when his father, a great leader, a great fighter of The People, had fallen in battle, Quanah had risen in power. He had joined the Destanyuka band, becoming a great warrior, then came to lead the Kwahadis, the greatest of all The People. Yet he had also led his band to Fort Sill, and while others, including Daniel's father, had been sent to that prison in Florida, Quanah had remained behind. The pale eyes gave him the title of Comanche chief, leader of all The People, although The People had never, ever been governed by just one man.

Pale eyes loved Quanah. So did most of The People, although some loathed him because of his white blood. Remembering his own mother, Daniel knew The People could hate as much as pale eyes.

He had taken his mother's name. Quanah Parker. He had seen better than thirty winters, perhaps closer to forty now, fighting the pale eyes, surrendering to them, now trying to work together with them and The People.

"Pale eyes want to make him more white," Ben Buffalo Bone whispered as he dismounted. "But he remains true to his blood." He slapped Daniel's back. "He has seven wives. When the old agent told him he had to get rid of all but one, Quanah told him . . . 'You pick.' That silenced that agent."

"My sons!" Quanah called out. "It is good that you have returned home, His Arrows Fly Straight Into The Hearts Of His Enemies. Come into my Star House. We will smoke and talk."

"So you have joined the Metal Shirts," Quanah said after they had finished the pipe. "It is a good thing."

Daniel nodded, although he had found nothing to his liking working for Sergeant Sitting Still and Agent Rueben. "*Tejanos* and the Creeks, other pale eyes, too, they bring whiskey into the land of The People. Other *Tejanos,* those that raise the *pimoró* . . . not as good to eat as our *cuhtz* . . . they drive their beasts into the pastures of The People, to eat the good grass that should be used to fatten the ponies of The People. They do this without. . . ." He paused, thinking of a proper phrase. "To pay tribute to The People. They steal from The People. They steal our souls, our dignity, trying to make us like them."

Daniel found himself looking around the house as Quanah spoke. *It must have taken a lot of work to build a home like this,* Daniel thought. *The nearest railhead lay south of the Red River, and you couldn't find lumber like this in Indian Territory. It must have taken double teams of mules to pull wagons laden with such lumber. And the carpentry involved. Each of Quanah's wives had a bed-room for herself.*

Ben Buffalo Bone, Quanah, and Daniel sat in the Kwahadi leader's office, its walls decorated with photographs, paintings, mounted buffalo and deer heads, and furniture that smelled of rich mahogany and leather. When Quanah had given the two young Comanches a tour of the house—Quanah had insisted, taking pride in everything about it—Daniel had seen a photograph hanging on the wall in the chief's bedroom, a photo of Quanah's white mother and his sister, who had died after Nadua had been returned to her white relatives.

"The wind brings changes," Quanah said, and Daniel's head bobbed in agreement.

Many changes, he thought. Ben Buffalo Bone's father had used the house the Texans built for him as a livery, but not Quanah. Not now.

"Sad times for The People, and we must protect our brothers, our sisters, our fathers, and mothers. . . ."

Mothers. Daniel cleared his throat, waiting for Quanah to finish his speech, then asked: "And what of my mother?"

Quanah looked troubled. "It is impolite," he said softly, "to speak the names of those who have gone to The Land Beyond The Sun."

"I did not speak her name," Daniel said. "I just want to know. . . ."

Quanah tapped the pipe, set it aside, and tilted his head toward the door to the office. "Your mother came to us from the Mescalero."

Captured, you mean. Taken prisoner.

"When you left to follow Pratt, the woman of whom you speak felt her heart break. Her husband had gone to The Land Beyond The Sun, and she thought you would never return to her. She walked away. Just walked. A *puhakut* told us she left to rejoin her people, though she had become of The People. I tell you this out of the goodness of my heart. Water flowed high on the river, and she did not make it across. I don't think she wanted to."

Daniel felt the tear, quickly brushed it away.

"As I said, these times can be painful for The People. It was for that reason that you were chosen to go to the school far away with the man Pratt."

"You sent me!" He hadn't meant to shout, but the words exploded in anger. The white men had said no child could go to the school without permission of the parents, but Quanah hadn't asked his mother. Bluecoats had picked Daniel up roughly as he walked back to his lodge from the mission school on the reservation. Pale eyes had a word for that, Daniel would later learn. Kidnapping.

"I asked the woman of whom you speak to let you go to the school on the reservation, the same as I sent my own sons and daughters," Quanah said, "but I could not send you to the. . . ." He wet his lips, thinking again, and said the name in English: "Industrial School. That was not my place. It was Wolf's Howl who said you must go."

Blinking, Daniel sank, confused.

"Wolf's Howl?" he asked. Isa Nanaka? His father's best friend. He . . . ?

"It was his duty. . . ." Quanah frowned again. "With the passing of the man who wed the woman of whom you speak, Wolf's Howl. . . ."

"I understand," Daniel said. He remembered the school mother reading the letter that the Comanche agent had written, informing Daniel of his mother's death. At Carlisle, they wouldn't let him cut his already short hair, wouldn't let him mourn. For seven years, his anger had been aimed, mistakenly, at Quanah.

"Wolf's Howl thought it was best for you. To learn the ways of the pale eyes. Look at us, my son. We knew the pale eyes could not be trusted, that they cheat, they steal, they lie, but what did we know other than to fight, and fight them our way? What did we reap from our fights?" He swept his arm around. "I miss the buffalo. I miss the old ways, but they are gone, my son." His eyes fell down. "They are gone. Gone forever. So it was the bluecoat Pratt, and Pratt, your school father, was an honorable man. He told us the need to have our children educated as the pale eyes educate their children. Live with the pale eyes. Learn to read and write like the pale eyes." He switched to English. "I speak some. Make mark by name. But. . . ." He shook his head, and returned to Comanche. "That is it. I fight for The People, fight as best as I can, fight on the . . . terms . . . yes, terms, of the pale eyes, but I do not read the language other than my own name. Pratt, he said it would be good for pale eyes and all Indians to live together, to know each other. It was the only way to rid both of prejudice."

"I understand," Daniel said, and this time he meant it, although he wanted to add that while the intentions might have been good, it would never work. Pale eyes would always hate The People, and The People would be destroyed trying to live like pale eyes. They were practically destroyed already. And pale eyes weren't the only ones prejudiced. He thought of his mother, saw her, but forced the image away.

He rose, smiling, and thanked Quanah.

"We will speak again," Quanah said. "See each other often. After all, you are a Metal Shirt. And I am . . ."—he grinned—"a judge."

"Is Quanah really a judge?" Daniel asked as they rode away from the Star House.

"The pale eyes call it the Court of Indian Offenses," Ben Buffalo Bone said. "They just started it. Before, The People had to go across the Red River to Wichita Falls for trials before the United States Commissioner. Or on to Fort Smith if the offense was serious."

Like murder. Daniel frowned. He had meant to ask Quanah about Jimmy Comes Last, but that would have been awkward, speaking of a dead man, especially one killed for such a terrible crime.

"Where are we going now?" he asked, nudging Skunk to pick up the pace.

"To visit another friend."

They rode north to the Wichita Mountains. Not much in the way of mountains, Daniel thought, comparing them to the ranges he had seen in the East, or the stereoscope images of the Alps and Pyrenees one of his teachers had shown him at Carlisle. The tallest of the mountains didn't even reach 2,500 feet, but they dominated the horizon in Indian Territory, and The People had held them sacred.

Grama, blue stem, Indian grass covered the prairie that buttressed the ridges, wildflowers bloomed among the rocky outcroppings, and beyond that he saw patches of post oak, blackjack, and red cedar. Once The People had found elk in the mountains and prairies, but no longer, not in years. The elk had been killed off. Like the buffalo.

Daniel smelled wood smoke before he spotted the Comanche lodge. He wondered who lived here, alone, although he couldn't blame the man who had wanted to pitch his teepee here. A figure sat under a brush arbor, working on something, his hair silver. Daniel couldn't make out the face until the two riders reined in, and the old man looked up.

He set down the lance he had been working on, drew a dirty bandanna from a nearby stool, and coughed, grunting, then hid the rag. His face was gaunt, his body frail, but his eyes blazed with happiness when he recognized his visitors.

Daniel's mouth dropped. Long ago, he had believed this man had begun the journey to The Land Beyond The Sun, but now it made sense. Hadn't Quanah spoken Wolf's Howl's name? Quanah would never break such a strong taboo by speaking a dead man's name.

"I am not a ghost, my son," Isa Nanaka said weakly. "Come. Come closer." He motioned at his eyes. "I see not far. But I knew you would come, and my heart is filled with joy. Come."

Chapter Six

Isa Nanaka brought forth the rag again, coughing into it, then grimacing as he looked at the dirty piece of muslin. He hid it, but not before Daniel saw the specks of blood. Motioning for the visitors to sit, the old man gestured again toward a pipe, suppressing a cough brought on by the consumption. Ben Buffalo Bone began filling the red clay bowl with tobacco.

Isa Nanaka's body looked weathered and weak, wrinkled skin barely covering the bones, face gaunt, most of his teeth missing, his eyes rheumy, hair stringy, unkempt. How Isa Nanaka had managed to live this long with the lung sickness, Daniel could never guess, and never would have believed if he hadn't seen and heard the old warrior. He shook as if he had the palsy but smiled warmly, his long fingers, the tips scarred and calloused, pressing Daniel's forearm. Daniel tried to remember how Wolf's Howl had looked as a younger man, but couldn't.

"About all old men are good for," Isa Nanaka told Daniel, "is making lances, and other things." He hefted the one he had been working on before handing it to Daniel for inspection.

"It is magnificent." Daniel meant it. He had never seen a weapon that would equal the one created by Isa Nanaka.

"It brings me pleasure," the old Comanche said, "as does this place." Leaning back, he listened, smiled again, and his head bobbed as he thought of a story to tell.

Always, Isa Nanaka had been good at telling stories.

"In those days, there was nothing here but plains." His throat rattled like death, but as he talked, Wolf's Howl's spirit returned, and the coughing fits faded. "The People had camped here, just women, children, and old people. The men were out hunting, and a few scouts remained off, for protection. The scouts came riding in, riding hard, their ponies lathered with sweat. 'Pawnees!' they cried. 'Pawnees are coming!'

" 'How many?' an old woman asked.

" 'Too many,' a scout replied. 'We must run. There are too many for us to fight.'

"One scout rode off, to find the hunters. The other scout remained, telling the children and women and the old men that they must hurry. Run east. Away. Before the Pawnees came. It was an exciting time. Frightening. Everyone looked anxious, except for the old woman who had asked . . . 'How many?' She was a medicine woman, and she knelt on the earth, two small rocks in her hands, and she prayed. She prayed and prayed and prayed.

" 'We must go now, Grandmother,' the scout told her, but she just prayed.

"By now, the others were ready. And they ran off, and the scout begged the old medicine woman to come, but she shook her head and told him . . . 'You go. I will catch up. I will be all right.'

" 'The Pawnees will be here soon,' he told her.

"But she had closed her eyes again, praying over the two small rocks.

"They left her, and the old woman covered the

rocks with dirt. Finally she stood, and she went walking after The People. Soon, she caught up with them, and the scout and the others, they cried out to her . . . 'We must hurry. There are too many Pawnees.' But she said . . . 'No, there is no need to hurry. Look behind you.' And The People, they turned around, and there they were, these mountains. And the old woman said . . . 'The Pawnees will have to go around those mountains. Those mountains will hold off the Pawnees till our warriors come back.' That is how these mountains were born.

"That is why The People put such value on these sacred mountains, why young men come here to seek their medicine, their vision, why an old man lives here to make himself useful making lances, until he travels to The Land Beyond The Sun." He accepted the pipe from Ben Buffalo Bone, offered it to the six directions, and began to smoke. "But," he said when he was finished, passing the pipe to Daniel, "you did not come this far to listen to stories about old medicine women and an abandoned Kwahadi warrior."

Holding the pipe, Daniel suddenly felt like a white man, the fear, disgust, perhaps, stopping him. Smoke a pipe after a man wasted from consumption? Yet he fought back the revulsion. He would never insult a man at his home. He brought the pipe to his mouth, and let the thick, pungent smoke fill his mouth.

Isa Nanaka smiled, and Ben Buffalo Bone slapped his knee, laughing, and said something in Comanche Daniel didn't quite catch.

They smoked in silence, and, when they had finished, Isa Nanaka wiped his lips with the dirty muslin rag again, snorted, spat, and nodded. Another story began.

"Two moons ago, I had this vision. I was walking along the marsh, and came to a nest. In this nest, I saw three cracked eggs, and one that was not cracked. So I took the good egg to my lodge, put it under a buffalo robe, and waited till it hatched. It was a marsh hawk, and it spoke to me, telling me that it was lost, and confused. Then it flew away. I knew then that you . . ."—his head tilted at Daniel—"would come home."

Daniel nodded. "I have felt lost for a long time."

"Yes. The. . . ." The old man coughed, shook his head, and snorted, struggling for the word. "The school far from home, run by the Long Knife whose name I have lost."

"Pratt."

"Pratt." Isa Nanaka tested the name. "Pratt sent your father away with me." He tapped his lungs. "Where I got this." He shook his head. "I thought it was right to send you to the . . . In-dust-reel School," he said, saying the final two words in guttural English. "I looked into this man Pratt's heart and felt that it was good. He did help us at Fort Ma-ri-on. He sent us back home, those who did not travel to The Land Beyond The Sun. I thought the In-dust-reel School would be better, for you. That you would learn the ways of the pale eyes, then you would understand them. Much better than Quanah. Much better than me. Much better than Marsh Hawk."

"I think. . . ." Daniel hesitated.

"You can lead The People," Ben Buffalo Bone said softly.

"I'm not sure I belong to The People." Daniel looked

into the old man's eyes. *I should hate this man,* Daniel thought. *He sent me away, caused my mother, and me, such grief, but I . . . cannot. I can be nothing but honest with him.*

"I have spent seven years with the pale eyes. They gave me a new name. Daniel. They taught me their language, their trades. They cut my hair, made me take baths, made me pray to their God, learn their ways." He took a deep breath, afraid to look at his friend Ben Buffalo Bone, exhaled slowly, and went on. "Yet even before, I felt myself being pushed away by The People. Pushed away by all but a few friends like Ben Buffalo Bone."

"Pushed away?" Isa Nanaka wet his ancient lips. "I do not understand this."

"My mother, who has traveled to The Land Beyond The Sun, was not born of The People. She was Mescalero. Many times boys my age, and even older men, not you, but others, they always reminded me that my blood was not pure, that I was not wholly of The People."

"I never . . . ," Ben Buffalo Bone began, but Daniel cut him off.

"I never said you did, my brother. But others did. You must remember that."

Ben Buffalo Bone shook his head, until Isa Nanaka raised his right hand.

"Now I understand my vision," the silver-haired relic said. "You were lost." The weathered man reached for his pipe, tamping it absently. "That is why you returned. To find yourself. To find your place among The People. The woman of whom you speak, it is true, that she was not born of The People, but she became one of us. This is the way of many. The woman who raised Quanah was not born of

The People. Even her name said as much. But she became one of us, much as the woman of whom you speak did. Did she not kill every pony, mourning when Marsh Hawk left his body? Did her heart not break? She was Kwahadi. So are you. But I think you must learn this for yourself. That is why you returned."

In silence, Daniel considered this.

"Perhaps you need to seek your vision," Ben Buffalo Bone said at length.

"I have never had a vision," he said.

The old man laughed. "Pale eyes, they think visions come to The People like salt comes with their supper. You are not alone, my son. I have known men who have seen more summers than I who have never had a vision. It is nothing that should shame you. Marsh Hawk did not find his medicine until he was older than you."

Daniel thought of this. "My father," he said. "You were on the train . . . when . . . when he . . . died."

The old man's head shook. "If he had died, my son, I would not mention his name. No, Marsh Hawk did not die. He simply left his body." He motioned for Ben Buffalo Bone to light the pipe again, and, after he had smoked, he coughed twice, and told the story.

"We were on the train, in this place Flo-ri-da. Hot. Terrible. Marsh Hawk's heart was heavy, because he had left his family behind. I did not see him go, but he managed to step off the train when the. . . ." He tried to think of the word, but couldn't. He gestured with his hands. "The thing that breathes wretched black smoke."

"The engine," Daniel said.

"Perhaps. It needs water. All living creatures need water."

"It was taking water."

"I suppose that is so. It was during this time that Marsh Hawk disappeared. A Long Knife with three marks on his coat came to this Pratt, told him of the missing prisoner. We stared out the windows, as the Long Knives searched the woods and up and down the iron rails for Marsh Hawk, but he would not be found. I thought perhaps he had flown away. Much time passed, and the man who made the . . . engine . . . move, he told Pratt that they could not wait any longer. Pratt told the man with the yellow marks on his coat and another Long Knife to stay behind, that he would use the talking wire at the next place to send more Long Knives to search. The train started to move, when all of the others had climbed upon the cars, and that is when Marsh Hawk rose from beneath the pine straw in the woods near the iron rails. He did not know two Long Knives remained behind.

"I heard the gunshot. Pratt leaped from his seat and yanked on the string that told the . . . engine . . . to stop. I looked out, and saw Marsh Hawk stagger into the woods. Two Long Knives chased after him. Pratt and others leaped from the train and ran into the woods."

He paused to smoke the pipe again.

"They told us Marsh Hawk was dead. Lung shot. They told us he would be buried here, where he fell. They told us we must not try to escape or we would also die. But I knew my brother, Marsh Hawk, who had given you your name, His Arrows Fly Straight Into The Hearts Of His Enemies, I knew he had fooled the Long Knives."

Another cough.

He passed the pipe to Ben Buffalo Bone. "After he staggered into the woods, after the Long Knives chased after him, I saw the hawk fly from a tree in those woods. I saw it circle, heard its cry, and it kept circling, laughing at the Long Knives below. Marsh Hawk had fooled them. He had turned himself into a hawk, for the hawk was his *puha*. His medicine. The hawk in the sky seemed to speak to me, and I knew Marsh Hawk would always protect you. This knowledge helped me make the decision to send you with Pratt to the In-dust-reel School."

Daniel took the pipe, smoked, and handed it back to the old man.

"The hawk has always protected you, and it will keep you safe. Always."

"I . . ."

Daniel thought back to that time at Carlisle. His second year there, maybe. He had been walking along the grounds, policing the area, as the school fathers told him, picking up trash, collecting kindling for the fireplaces. A hawk had startled him, its size enormous, not more than twenty feet in front of him, flying off toward the woods, carrying a snake in its talons. Later, a Lakota boy had told him that it had been a rattlesnake, and, if the hawk had not been there, that snake surely would have bitten Daniel.

Coincidence, the pale eyes would say. Imagination. For all Daniel knew, the snake hadn't been poisonous, and the Lakota boy had been mistaken.

"I thank you for your stories," Daniel told Isa Nanaka as he rose. "But it is time for us to return."

Isa Nanaka's head bobbed. "I am here to help you," he said. "Do not forget your promise."

He barely heard the old man's last sentence.

They rode off in silence, keeping their horses at a trot, while Daniel wondered about the day's events.

His hatred had vanished. Quanah and Isa Nanaka had quashed it. Besides, he couldn't hate a dying man like Isa Nanaka. He had learned about his mother and father. His mother drowning herself in the Red River. His father shot dead trying to escape the train carrying prisoners of war to Fort Marion. Maybe Isa Nanaka thought Marsh Hawk had changed himself into a hawk and flown away, but Daniel had spent too many years in Pennsylvania to believe in such miracles.

When they reached Ben Buffalo Bone's place, Daniel volunteered to rub down and feed both horses. He thanked his friend for taking him on the visits, and Ben Buffalo Bone told him to get some rest. "Agent Rueben and Sergeant Sitting Still will have much work for us to do in the morning," he said with a laugh.

Daniel smiled without humor, and led the horses away.

He brushed his teeth, a habit he had picked up in Pennsylvania, brushed with more vigor than usual, trying to cleanse his mouth of the taste of the old warrior's tobacco. Not that it helped much.

He didn't eat that night, and sleep evaded him. He lay on his blankets, listening to the horses snort and paw the sod floor, and stared at the ceiling. The wind picked up, bringing with it a hint of rain, and at some point Daniel finally closed his eyes.

If he slept at all, it hadn't been for long before the voice, carried by the wind, woke him. He sat bolt upright, caught his breath, tried to listen.

Nothing but the wind. Even the horses had quieted.

He fought to remember the dream. Was it a dream? Just a voice?

Have you forgotten your promise?

That's all the voice had said, and then Daniel remembered Isa Nanaka, telling him: "Do not forget your promise." *What did the old man mean? No, how did he know about that promise he had made to Naséca?*

Then Daniel shuddered, recalling the voice in his nightmare, imagination, whatever. Or maybe from a ghost. Isa Nanaka had not spoken those words that startled him out of his sleep.

It had been the voice of Jimmy Comes Last.

Chapter Seven

"Got a chore for you, Killstraight."

Daniel finished dragging the rake across the ground before straightening his back and looking at Ephraim Rueben, who stood in the doorway smoking a rubber-stemmed apple-wood pipe. The agent motioned for Daniel to follow him inside, then disappeared, and, with a grunt, Daniel dragged the rake behind him, leaning it against the hitching post, and stepped inside the cabin.

Rueben crumpled a sack of Old Raleigh tobacco and pitched it into an almost overflowing trash can.

"Take that out back," the agent said, "and empty it on the fire you got going."

Without comment, Daniel picked up the container and headed for the door.

"It ain't always like this, Killstraight!" Rueben called after him.

He didn't bother acknowledging the comment. He dumped the trash onto the burning heap, and stepped back, ignoring the smoke and heat from the flames, wondering why he had not quit. Indecision, maybe. Not wanting to let Ben Buffalo Bone down, perhaps. The teachings of the Carlisle Industrial School tightening their hold. Just plain laziness.

Well, $8 a month wasn't much money, but raking leaves, burning trash, fixing roads, digging ditches, and repairing shingles were not well-paying jobs. He watched the flames engulf the papers, losing himself in his thoughts, his doldrums, and didn't even hear the hoof beats.

Fighting the urge to toss the can into the fire, to go slap the agent's face and tell him to find a new boy to do his meaningless chores, Daniel thought of his father, and his mother, and Isa Nanaka out by the Wichitas making lances while waiting to die of consumption. He thought until his thoughts turned into ash, like Rueben's papers, and then he just stared at the smoke.

"Killstraight! Boy, are you deaf? The hell are you doing? Come here!"

Blinking, he turned as the shouts finally registered, stepped from the fire as Rueben put his hands on his hips and glared, and set the trash can onto the dirt, took another step, realized what he had done, and picked up the can, and walked to the cabin.

"I been calling you for five minutes, boy," the agent said. "Like you were sleeping standing up. Come here."

He saw the horses as they rounded the front of the building, and found Sergeant Sitting Still, another Metal Shirt named Twice Bent Nose, and Ben Buffalo Bone inside the office.

"These are all I could round up, Sergeant," the agent said as he sat behind his desk. "You want to get some soldier boys from Fort Sill?"

"No," the sergeant grunted.

Daniel put the trash can down.

"Your hair smells like smoke." Ben Buffalo Bone grinned.

"Fool was just staring at the fire," the agent groused. "You get paid for working, Killstraight. Remember that."

"What's going on?" Daniel asked.

From a desk drawer, the agent pulled out a box of cartridges and slapped it on the cluttered top, rose, fishing his pipe from his vest pocket as he stood, and walked to a map pinned on the far wall. Using the pipe stem, he pointed at the map. "The sergeant found some longhorns in the pasture along Middle Creek. Free grazers." He tapped the spot. "Eating Comanche grass." Turning, he asked the sergeant: "You read the brand?"

"No."

"Figures." He returned the pipe. "The sergeant saw one rider. Might be more. You sure that boy didn't see you?"

The sergeant's head bobbed once.

"And you don't want no help from the fort?"

The head moved slightly again.

"Suit yourself. I'm issuing five extra cartridges per man, but I expect an accounting for each cartridge when you return. Control your boys, Sergeant. Don't let them go shooting rabbits and tree trunks for the sport of it. Get those cattle off Comanche land, Sergeant. Run those free grazers back across the Red. Try not to get killed."

"And . . . the white men?" Twice Bent Nose asked timidly.

"You can't arrest them. Not white men. Most likely they'll show yellow and light a shuck, but if they shoot at you, shoot back, damn their hides. I'm sick and tired of those free grazers. That ought to get my name in the newspapers. Our names, I mean."

For once, the sergeant looked happy.

It took better than two hours to reach the pasture. The last two miles, they covered slowly, riding along the banks of Middle Creek, hearing only the gurgling water and the wind rustling through the blackjacks that dotted the water's edge.

A bawling calf told the policeman they had reached their prey, and Sergeant Sitting Still reined up, drawing his Remington revolver, and motioning Daniel to dismount.

"I can smell them," Twice Bent Nose said in Comanche.

So could Daniel, at least their cook fire. He handed the hackamore to Ben Buffalo Bone, rubbed Skunk's neck, and, unholstering his own Remington, carefully crept through the brush, climbing up the slippery bank, and kneeling behind an oak.

The cattle, tough, leathery longhorns, paid him no attention. Across the field, 400 yards to the west, maybe 500, he spotted a tendril of white smoke. He saw no white man.

Grumbling, he backed away, then slid down the embankment, holstering his revolver.

"How many?" Sergeant Sitting Still asked.

"Can't tell," he replied. "Let me have your spyglass."

Reluctantly the sergeant reached inside his canvas war bag, and withdrew an old telescope, the brass tarnished, the wood battered. Daniel took it without comment, and climbed back to his position, pulling open—the slide action felt way too loose—the telescope, about a foot-and-a-half in length, and bringing it to his right eye.

First, he found a brindle cow, and read the brand. *Lazy B.*

He sought out another animal, then a third, whose brands he could make out. All Lazy B.

After that, he found the smoke, but the longhorns

blocked a ground-level view. He slid the telescope shut, and scanned the pasture, trying to tally the number of cattle as he looked around.

"How many *taibo?*" Sergeant Sitting Still sounded more irritable than normal.

Daniel shook his head, and the sergeant grunted in disgust, and barked another insult. Ignoring him, Daniel found a better vantage point. Crouching, he headed south about twenty yards, and squatted next to another blackjack.

His hands felt clammy, and he wiped them on his trousers, then opened the telescope. Leaning against the tree, he scanned the far woods, stopping, moving back, focusing.

"There," he said, and looked at a picketed horse, an ugly liver chestnut with a white blaze. Slickfork saddle. Dirty slicker and bedroll tied behind the cantle. One horse. For about 100 head. Would that be right? Hell, he wasn't some Texas drover.

Moving from the horse, he found the fire, and saw the man squatting by a battered coffeepot, filling an enamel cup. The man had a thick handlebar mustache, battered, high-crowned hat, dark chaps. That's about all he could tell. A horse whinnied. Close. Daniel swung the telescope around.

A second later, he lay flat on his back, sliding down the bank, briars tearing at his forearms, the sound of the gunshot reverberating in his ears, his eyes stinging with bark that had exploded into his face when the bullet hammered the tree inches from his head.

Horses snorted. Hoofs pounded. Water splashed. Twice Bent Nose let out a yip, and the telescope rolled past Daniel's ear.

Another gunshot *boomed*, and Daniel rolled over,

trying to climb, slipping in the mud. His ears rang. He found his feet, desperately trying to jerk the Remington, saw Sergeant Sitting Still gallop past him, mouthing something. Daniel couldn't understand what.

The palomino carrying Twice Bent Nose climbed up the bank, slipping once, finding its feet, lunging ahead as the policeman pulled an ancient musket from the scabbard, and charged across the pasture. Like a Comanche of old.

"Let's go!"

Ben Buffalo Bone had dropped from his saddle, leaving his horse and Skunk in the protection of the creekbed, hoping they wouldn't run from the shooting, the noise. His friend charged past him and up the bank, and Daniel, shaking his head, trying to clear his vision, staggered after him.

Another shot.

Both dropped to their bellies.

Daniel blinked rapidly, his eyes tearing, caught a glimpse of Ben Buffalo Bone loping after Twice Bent Nose, heard the sergeant's pistol *popping*, then drowned out as the cattle stampeded south, toward the Red River.

A shout came from one of the free grazers. The ringing had left Daniel's ears. He fired, without really aiming, at the same time Ben Buffalo Bone's pistol *boomed.*

Two riders—no, three—chased after the cattle. Ben Buffalo Bone fired again, and the Remington kicked in Daniel's hand. The drovers yipped, slapping their horses' rumps with their big hats. One turned slightly in the saddle, lifting his hand. A puff of white smoke. Another. Then the cowboy holstered his gun, or tried to. At a gallop, it looked like he dropped the weapon in the grass. If that's what had happened, the Texian didn't stop to get his pistol.

The two mounted tribal policeman reined up, and the Texans were gone. So were most of the cattle, except for three or four killed during the mêlée. Trampled, most likely. Hell, for all Daniel knew, one of his bullets had killed a longhorn.

Ben Buffalo Bone rose, pulled Daniel to his feet, and slapped his friend's shoulder.

"Pretty exciting," he said, his eyes beaming. His open palm whacked Daniel's back once more. "That's almost better than stealing chickens, right, brother?"

The Remington felt hot, and he shoved it in the holster.

His heart *thumped* against his ribs, and his throat felt parched. His vision had cleared, though, and now that he realized he hadn't been killed, or even hit, he wet his lips, and nodded. A moment later, his grin matched his friend's.

Exciting? Absolutely. He had never felt anything like it. He felt alive.

"This is better than burning trash." Leaning back, Ben Buffalo Bone roared with laughter. "You're too good a policeman to be burning that agent's garbage. That wasn't even fit for Jimmy. . . ." The laughter died in Ben Buffalo Bone's throat, and he looked away. "I'll fetch our sergeant's spyglass."

Daniel scanned the pasture as Ben Buffalo Bone raced back toward the creek, retrieving the telescope and catching up with the two horses.

"Come on!" Twice Bent Nose yelled, laughing, waving. "What kind of warriors of The People are you two? No horses! Come, you cowards, and let us give chase."

* * *

The herd they found, milling about five miles south, but the drovers had vanished. They gathered the longhorns and drove them the final few miles to the Red River, Twice Bent Nose joking that no one had ever seen cowboys who rode so well, smelled so sweet, looked so handsome.

By chance, they came across three deputy marshals who agreed to push the cattle across the river. When that task had been completed, one of the lawmen rode up to the Indian policemen, and pulled a notepad and well-chewed pencil from his saddlebags. The two other white men remained a few rods back, hooking legs over the saddle horns while rolling cigarettes.

"You say these boys shot at you?"

Sergeant Sitting Still grunted.

"Who shot first?"

"They did," Daniel answered.

The lawman stared, impressed by the directness and the English.

"Get a good look at 'em?"

"No, sir. It happened too fast. But the cattle were all Lazy B."

"Hell, boy, I can read a brand." The lawman snorted, shifted his weight in the stirrups, then looked at Daniel again, his face registering surprise that Daniel had accurately read the brand.

"What's your name?" the lawman asked.

"I am called Killstraight. Daniel Killstraight."

"Speaks damn' good English for a buck," one of the other marshals said.

"How the hell would you know, Dave?" the third man joked.

"I think one of the drovers dropped his pistol," Daniel said.

The lawman considered that. "Might help. Might have his name scratched on the butt or somethin'."

"One of them had a mustache," Daniel said.

The two other lawmen laughed in their saddles. All of the marshals sported facial hair.

"Well, iffen you find that pistol and it's got a name or letters or somethin' that might be useful, you let me know. Not that much'll come of this. You sure ain't nobody hurt?"

Four Comanche heads bobbed.

"Do you know this ranch that uses the Lazy B?" Daniel asked.

The marshal shook his head, and returned the pencil and notepad. "Not hard to find out, though, but it won't do no good. Foreman, rancher, or any waddie ridin' for the brand'll just say 'em beeves was rustled. They'll thank you boys and me for returnin' 'em home."

"You return?" Sergeant Sitting Still asked.

"Hell, no. We're leavin' 'em just 'cross the Red. I'll do some investigatin' next time I'm in Wichita Falls, but that's 'bout all I can do. But iffen you learn somethin' from that pistol, iffen you can find it, or iffen you remembers somethin' useful . . . like some identifyin' mark on one of 'em drovers, a scar or some such . . . you have Agent Rueben get a note off to me, Harvey P. Noble. Work out of Judge Parker's court in Fort Smith."

Daniel remembered the name. "You know a Cherokee policeman named Gunter?" he asked.

More surprise showed on Deputy Marshal Noble's leathery face.

"I know 'im. Friend of your'n?"

"We've met."

"Well, Killstraight, I'm sorry we can't be of more

assistance, but Judge Parker ain't payin' me to nurse cows or protect Comanche grass. There's a bunch of murderin' b'hoys in these parts, so the boys and me'll be takin' our leave. Much obliged." He tugged on his gray hat.

The white lawmen rode east, and the Comanche policemen turned back north. Ben Buffalo Bone and Twice Bent Nose exaggerated the shooting, bragged about their daring, and joked about Daniel's first taste as a real policeman.

"The soldiers at Sill would say you have seen the elephant," Ben Buffalo Bone said.

Mood souring, Sergeant Sitting Still demanded the return of his spyglass, then told Daniel that he was the sergeant and he should have talked to the lawmen. When they reached the pasture, Twice Bent Nose asked if they should stop and look for that pistol the *taibo* had dropped.

"No," the sergeant grunted angrily, and they kept riding.

Chapter Eight

Agent Rueben scratched his chin during Sergeant Sitting Still's report, took a few notes, and shrugged. "I'm not sure this will get us in the newspapers," he said, "but I'll send a report to this correspondent I know up in Wichita. Comanche policemen drive off free grazers. Make those boys know we mean business. Would have helped if you had killed one of them, though, or one of y'all had caught a bullet." He looked up sheepishly. "Not mortal, of course." His head bobbed, and his face turned serious. "All right. Good work, boys. How many bullets did y'all fire?"

The following day, Rueben ordered Daniel and Ben Buffalo Bone out again, southwest, to scout for any other free grazers. They didn't find anything, and the sun baked them, but Daniel had to admit this kind of work beat burning trash and working on roads. On their way back to the agency, Daniel suggested they ride over to the Middle Creek pasture and see if they could find that pistol the Texas drover had dropped.

They rode down into Middle Creek, then up the bank, ducking the low blackjack branches, and reining in their mounts.

"Something's wrong," Ben Buffalo Bone said uneasily.

The sight disgusted him. Daniel drew his Remington, pointed the barrel skyward, and pulled the trigger. Startled, Skunk bucked twice, but Daniel kept his seat, as turkey vultures noisily beat their wings and took flight from the remains of the dead cattle. After holstering his pistol, Daniel patted Skunk's neck, and nudged the horse into a walk, slowly approaching the remains of the nearest Lazy B carcass.

The stench of blood and guts turned Skunk even more skittish, so Daniel dismounted, handing the hackamore to Ben Buffalo Bone. No need in pressing his luck, getting bucked off, providing his friend with scores of jokes. He was lucky Skunk hadn't dusted him when he had fired his pistol. *Mighty green thing to do,* he thought. After covering the last few yards afoot, Daniel frowned. This wasn't the work of just turkey vultures and other carrion.

"Butchered," he said, and Ben Buffalo Bone nodded, then circled around, leading Daniel's horse, to the other dead longhorns.

To get his bearings, Daniel glanced behind him, trying to recall the previous afternoon's events. Studying the pasture, he could picture the Texas cowhand firing, stumbling, losing his pistol. He walked to the area. The bluestem had been trampled, by cattle, the fleeing cowboys, yet he still tried to read sign as he worked his way in a checkerboard fashion across the area. No pistol. He could have been mistaken. Maybe the Texian hadn't dropped a pistol. After all, Daniel's eyes had been filled with tree bark and the acrid smoke from his own revolver.

No, he thought. *No, I wasn't mistaken. That man dropped a pistol.* He knelt, finding a bare spot of ground, and fingered the track, faint, but there, left by a moccasin.

Someone had come earlier, and had found that pistol.

Hearing hoofbeats, he looked up, as Ben Buffalo Bone reined up. "Find anything?" his friend asked.

"The pistol's gone," he said.

Ben Buffalo Bone nodded. *"Pimoró."* He gestured at the remains of the other longhorns. "All butchered," he said in Comanche. "Maybe the same ones who came for the cattle found the pale eyes' pistol."

"Maybe so," Daniel said.

"Could have been anyone," Ben Buffalo Bone said. "They had a wagon." He pointed. "Tracks lead north."

"Maybe so." Anyone could have seen the vultures, or perhaps just come across the pasture, and found the beef. No sense in letting it go to waste, not with the rations The People received from the government. But the missing revolver bothered him. It had fallen nowhere near the dead cattle. Someone had to know about it, and that someone had been wearing moccasins. Who knew about that pistol? Sergeant Sitting Still, Twice Bent Nose, Ben Buffalo Bone, those three deputy marshals, and himself. And the drovers, of course. Agent Rueben, too.

The marshals? Only the one named Noble had shown much interest in the drovers, and he sure hadn't sounded like he would go hunting a dropped revolver that wouldn't likely prove useful in finding free grazers that really didn't weigh much on his scale of justice.

The cowboys? Yeah, but they wore boots. So did Rueben.

Daniel and Ben Buffalo Bone had been together all day. That left Sergeant Sitting Still and Twice Bent Nose. As far as he knew, neither owned a wagon, but the man who had found the revolver had not necessarily come with those who had butchered the beef.

Add it all up, and Daniel had nothing. *Quit trying to act like some pale eyes detective,* he told himself, and frowned again, thinking of Naséca, of Jimmy Comes Last, of his forgotten promise.

"What do you want to do?" Ben Buffalo Bone asked.

Shrugging, Daniel took the hackamore and mounted Skunk. "Go home," he said.

He spent the rest of the week covering much of the southern reservation with Ben Buffalo Bone or Twice Bent Nose, accomplishing little except toughening the insides of his thighs and his buttocks. He had told Agent Rueben about the missing pistol and butchered cattle, but kept his suspicions about Sergeant Sitting Still and Twice Bent Nose to himself. Rueben had merely commented—"I told you it wasn't always burning trash, Killstraight."—but had shown little interest otherwise, and Daniel couldn't really blame him.

Recovering a pistol? What did that mean? That the sergeant, Twice Bent Nose, or some other Comanche had been trying to protect the identity of the free grazer? Unlikely. A better theory would have the policeman keeping the weapon for his own, or selling it. If the pistol had been a newer single-action Army Colt, it might fetch $10 to $15, although, from what little Daniel had seen, the revolvers most cowboys could afford were as old and loose as his own Remington.

By Sunday, he had pretty much dismissed the missing revolver and the butchered cattle until he visited Naséca. He apologized for not coming to visit her earlier, but she smiled, patting his shoulder, and insisting that he take supper with her. She had plenty. Too much, she said, for an old woman with few teeth to chew.

Awkwardly he tried to summon the words, as she fetched a brass kettle from the inside of her lodge. "I have not forgotten what you asked me to do," he said. He wet his lips, cleared his throat. Jimmy Comes Last hadn't let him forget, haunting his sleep. "But I have been away from our country for so long . . . I need. . . ." She stepped out of the teepee, smiling.

"There is information I must have about . . . Jim . . . your . . . son."

"I think it will rain in the next few days," she said. She drew a knife, stepped toward the brush arbor. "The smell of the land after a good rain is always pleasing. I hope you have much appetite."

He rose, uncertain of his feelings. Naséca had not forgotten the ways of The People. She had brushed aside Daniel's words, refusing to hear him, knowing she could never bring herself to talk about her dead son, be so disrespectful. He didn't want to talk about Jimmy himself, didn't want to hurt Naséca, cause her to prolong her mourning, bring back that pain. Yet he also wanted Jimmy Comes Last to stop haunting him. What did that ghost want of him? Prove he was innocent? What good would that do?

Brushing dirt off his pants, Daniel rose, and followed her, stopping, watching, staring at the quarter of beef hanging inside the brush arbor. Too much for one woman to have received for rations. The daily allotment was one-and-a-half pounds, and ration day had been three weeks ago. That quarter of beef had scarcely been touched, by blade or sun.

"Hunting has been good to you," he said.

Naséca laughed. "I am no hunter," she said. "That is for our warriors." She brought the beef to the fire.

While she cooked, Daniel walked around, glancing once toward Jimmy's grave, then eyeing the corral, finally looking at the ground, finding tracks from a wagon. He returned to the fire, and knelt. Humming, Naséca looked up at him and smiled warmly.

"Who brought you the beef?" he asked.

"The *pimoró* of the *taibo* does not fill one's belly as much as *cuhtz*."

"Who brought you the beef?"

"The spirits," she answered at last, and went back to humming as she cooked.

Spirits indeed. Daniel sighed. Spirits. *Puha.* Medicine. Like his father changing himself into a hawk. A friendly apparition bringing a quarter of Texas longhorn to an old Comanche woman in the dead of night. He had been with the pale eyes too long to believe in such fantasies. At Carlisle, he had been taught to pray to the one God, the God of the pale eyes, and he wasn't even sure he believed in that any more, wasn't sure what he believed.

"I need to know about. . . ."

Naséca shoved a bowl into his hands. "It is time to eat," she said. "You must eat, and I must feed what few ponies I have left some grain. Eat. There is plenty. I will be back in a few moments."

He'd learn no answers from her. Daniel fingered the rare beef and watched her head to the corral. He fought down the urge to grab her shoulders, shake her, yell at her, slap her if he had to, demand that she listen, make her tell him who had brought her the meat. Sergeant Sitting Still? If he had a wagon. Had he charged her for it, or had he merely bought her silence? And why? *Make her tell me all about her dead son!* He felt himself trembling, and, when he looked down, staring at his fists, he saw his knuckles whitening. Why was she so certain he hadn't killed that couple in the Creek Nation? What had Jimmy's role been with the Metal Shirts? Why did his ghost keep tormenting him so?

She had not returned when he had finished eating, and he did not wait for her. He couldn't. He wiped his greasy fingers on his pants, and rose, mounted Skunk, and rode back to sleep in a pale eyes house that served as, and smelled like, a livery.

The longhorn did not set well in his stomach. Well, how long had it been baking in Middle Creek pasture before the butchers had found it? Or maybe it wasn't his supper, but the way he had felt toward Naséca. Rage.

He hadn't felt like one of The People, but like a white man.

Monday morning, he found himself repairing the agency roof, raking, emptying Agent Rueben's trash can on the fire again, but the following day he was back in the saddle, riding with Ben Buffalo Bone, southeast, scouring the countryside for Creek whiskey-runners rumored to be in the area. Sergeant Sitting Still had led another patrol southwest, and Twice Bent Nose and two other Metal Shirts rode north up Cache Creek. Whiskey-runners concerned the agent a lot more than free grazers, Daniel thought, or maybe The People took the matter more seriously.

They forded the Big Beaver, then moved south toward Hill's Ferry, and Daniel reined in Skunk at the sound of bawling cattle.

"Free grazers," he said, gripping the butt of his revolver.

"No." Ben Buffalo Bone laughed. "These cattle are. . . ." He searched for the word. "Legal. Come on."

The cattle scattered as the two Comanches rode, and Daniel read a brand. Bar TA Slash. Maybe he had hoped he would have found a Lazy B.

"Whose cattle?" he asked.

"Big *taibo*. But they pay a . . . tribute. At least, that is what Agent Rueben and Noihqueyúcat say. I see the man around the agency, but his name I do not know."

"He leases the pasture then?"

"I believe that is what they call it. Pays The People for the grass his *primoró* eat."

"I see," Daniel said, but he wondered how many of The People actually ever saw that money.

"You like this *taibo*?" Daniel asked.

Riding ahead, Ben Buffalo Bone looked back curiously. "I know not even his name. The new agent likes him. They are old friends, I have heard Noihqueyúcat say."

He wondered about the sergeant, and asked if Sitting Still liked the *taibo*.

"Noihqueyúcat likes no one." Ben Buffalo Bone pulled on the reins, and let Daniel stop beside him. "What is the meaning of these questions, my brother? I do not know this *taibo*, other than what he looks like. He pays a tribute to let his cattle eat our grass. Others do not. He does not bring whiskey to our lands to steal the souls of The People. He is *taibo*, worse than that he is *Tejano*, so he would be our enemy. We would have stolen his horses, perhaps taken his scalp, but those days are gone forever. We are supposed to be after the Creeks selling whiskey to The People." He nudged his horse forward, then turned back toward Daniel, a grin stretching across his face.

"You should like this man, though. It is his horse that you ride."

They gave up on pursuit, cutting no trail, finding no signs of whiskey, seeing nothing but 100 or so leathery Bar TA Slash longhorns, and rode back toward the agency.

Ben Buffalo Bone turned off the trail, and they headed toward a white frame building. "Where are we going?" Daniel asked.

"There is someone you might like to see," he answered. "She is *taibo*, too, but not unpleasant to the eye. Do you not remember this place?"

"No," Daniel said, but then the memories returned, and his stomach tightened. The missionary school. He had been on his way to his lodge all those years ago when they had taken him away from his mother, sent him to Pennsylvania. He remembered the pale eyes teachers, the man in black with the beard of iron, the gray-haired woman with bony hands, a growth on the tip of her nose, and what he always considered a mustache, although he had been told that although the pale eyes men often let their faces turn hairy, their women. . . .

He eyed the steeple, the cross, looked for children, but saw none. Instead, he found three horses tethered in front of the mission school, and saw three men in boots and a woman in a red calico dress, working on a frame structure being built beside the old school and church. The wooden beams looked naked. The three men looked stupid, hatted, in high-heeled boots, two of them holding a ladder, the third standing with a saw in his right hand and cigar in his left.

At the top of the ladder, the woman looked lovely. Ben Buffalo Bone had been right. She tossed a piece of wood onto the ground and, shaking her head, gracefully descended the ladder.

"It doesn't fit," she said. "We're going to run out of wood trying to put that piece in the corner."

"We got visitors," the man with the saw and cigar said, and everyone turned to face the two Comanche riders.

They stopped their horses a few rods from the construction crew.

"Why it's Ben Buffalo Bone," the woman said.

Her hair was blonde, like corn silk, her eyes blue, face freckled. She didn't sound like a *Tejano*, but more like one of those ladies from the city of Carlisle. Guessing, Daniel figured her to be about his age, no older.

He didn't look away from her until one of the cowboys who had been holding the ladder blurted out in an easy drawl: "Hey, I know that feller."

Chapter Nine

Underneath that battered old hat, the cowboy's face looked familiar to Daniel, as well. Bright blue eyes. Seemed to be trying to grow a mustache. Since arriving on the reservation, Daniel hadn't seen that many pale eyes, but, still, he could not place him, even when the cowhand spoke again in a pleasant drawl— "I know I seen you before."—causing Daniel to shudder, knowing he had heard the voice. But where? One of those Lazy B free grazers? He couldn't be certain.

"Likely he was scalpin' your ma," the tallest of the cowboys said, and Daniel studied that man. Dark-headed, with a mustache and under-lip beard, both starting to gray, unfriendly green eyes, sunburned face with a crooked scar over his left eyebrow, the string from a sack of tobacco hanging out of a vest pocket.

Desperately Daniel wanted to look at the brands on the horses these men rode.

"Shad Carter," the girl scolded, "that's a terrible thing to say."

"Yes'm," Carter said. "Not very Christian of me. I apologize to you, Cotton."

"No need, Shad." The cowboy named Cotton smiled at the girl. "He was just joshin', ma'am. My ma, she's in good health, last I heard, down 'round Indianola."

Cotton. The cowboy's name. Daniel knew it. But from where?

"You should apologize, Shad, to Ben Buffalo Bone's friend," the girl said.

Shad Carter's eyes blazed, and Daniel figured he should play peacekeeper. "No need, ma'am," he said. "Joke is all it was. Didn't bother me, hurt my feelings."

"You speak good English," said the third cowhand, a wiry man, older than the others, maybe forty, but shorter, pockmarked, wearing a bowler and pince-nez glasses.

Three cowboys. There had been three free grazers, including one who had damned near blown Daniel's head off. *No*, he told himself. *Coincidence.*

"This friend Kill . . . uh, Daniel," Ben Buffalo Bone said to make the introductions. "Back from. . . ." He pointed eastward.

"The Carlisle Industrial School," Daniel said.

The girl smiled. "Well, welcome home, Daniel. I am Randall Jordan, but my friends just call me Randi. And we are having a terrible time trying to get a piece of wood to fit in that corner." She walked over to him and held out her hand. Shad Carter didn't care much for that, either, but Daniel shook her hand briefly, a little embarrassed.

"New church?" Ben Buffalo Bone asked.

"Schoolhouse," she replied. "People have been coming over to help me build it. Soldiers from Fort Sill. Some nice folks from Riverland. He's a carpenter, and his son helps him. And today Shad rode over to offer some much needed assistance."

"But we ain't much good at hammers and nails," the first cowboy said. "Less'n shoein' a horse."

Randi laughed at that, and looked back at the schoolhouse under construction. "Well," she said, "I guess we'll have to try again."

Without thinking, Daniel swung off his horse, and led Skunk to a grassy patch to graze. Ben Buffalo Bone stared at him curiously, as did the three cowboys, when Daniel walked to the ladder and pointed.

"Is that the problem?" he asked.

"Why, yes, it is," Randi said.

"I'll need a ruler." Looking at the cowboys, he said: "And if one of you gentlemen could fetch me that protractor."

"A what?" the third cowboy said.

Daniel pointed. "See in that lean-to, atop the toolbox, that little half-circle thing?"

"Oh, yes," Randi said. "Mister Eriksson left some tools when he was here last. He's the carpenter from Riverland."

"Comanches ain't known for buildin' schoolhouses, Miss Randi," Shad Carter said. "Burnin' 'em down, maybe but . . ."

Daniel was already climbing up the ladder. He placed the ruler against the base, noted its size to an eighth of an inch, wished he had a pencil and paper to write it down, then measured the height. Quickly he descended, and pulled a piece of wood from the pile.

"It's called the Pythagorean Theory," he said. "At least, I think that's the name. I haven't used geometry in a long time. I'll square the length, multiply that by the base, and then I get the hypotenuse of the triangle."

"Hippo-what?" the first cowhand said.

Daniel grinned. "I need a pencil, ma'am, to do some ciphering."

"Paper, too?"

"No, ma'am. I'll just scratch it all out on the inside piece of wood."

Seeing the amused look on Ben Buffalo Bone's face almost made Daniel break out laughing.

When he had the measurements, he found the angle, marked the wood, and quickly but carefully sawed. Afterward, sticking a handful of nails in his mouth, and grabbing a hammer, he took his triangle-shaped piece of wood up the ladder, and hoped it fit. Tight, but he pushed it in, then hammered it in place.

"Why it's perfect," Randi said.

Not quite, Daniel thought, *but it will do.* He returned the hammer to her.

"Maybe this buck built your ma's house in Indianola," the third cowboy said. "Maybe that's where you know him."

"No. But I seen him before."

The voice triggered some memory he couldn't quite piece together . . . until Daniel looked at the cowhand's boots for the first time. Brown, although covered with dust, with a green Cross of Lorraine inlaid in the tops. Large-rowel spurs ornamented with circled brass stars and jinglebobs. His stomach tightened, and he remembered where he had first seen Cotton Henry.

Fort Smith, Arkansas, only then he had been wearing a plaid sack suit with those boots, spurs, and hat, with a whiskey-scented breath. Cotton Henry . . . the drunken cowhand who had bought two passes from a couple of lazy newspaper reporters at the Hotel Main's saloon. Together, they had watched Jimmy Comes Last, and two other convicted murderers, hang on Judge Parker's gallows.

Cotton Henry took off his hat to scratch his hair, and Daniel mounted Skunk.

"Thank you so much, Mister . . . ?" Randi said.

"I am called Killstraight," Daniel answered. "Daniel Killstraight."

"They learnt you good at that school, Killstraight," Shad Carter said.

"Glad I could help," Daniel told Randi Jordan, and kicked Skunk into a lope. He didn't bother learning the brands on their horses. He just wanted to get away from there, away from Cotton Henry, away from those memories of Jimmy Comes Last's death.

The glory of chasing those whiskey-runners back to the Creek Nation belonged to Sergeant Sitting Still, who said he had found them near the Chickasaw border, and within a week Daniel found his police duties as a peacekeeper reduced to solving disputes between a couple of Comanches and stopping an argument before it got out of control during ration day. By the following week, Daniel was back burning trash, raking leaves, mending fence. The whiskey-runners were gone, for now—Sergeant Sitting Still had seen to that. The Lazy B herd was gone, and no more free grazers had been spotted in the pastures south of Fort Sill and the agency. Ration day had come and gone in relative peace.

Boredom . . . again.

He and Twice Bent Nose spent much of that morning repairing the agency corral where the posts had been kicked down and splintered by one temperamental old Army mule. Two other Metal Shirts had raked up the ground in front of Agent Rueben's cabin, and had a trash pile ablaze, complete with wood from the fence too ruined to salvage. A pair of *taibo* riders loped up, but Daniel paid no attention to them, too busy worrying that Twice Bent Nose would miss his mark and nail Daniel's thumb with the hammer.

After surviving that chore, Daniel and Twice Bent Nose slaked their thirst with water. A moment later, Agent Rueben walked out of the cabin and called out: "Come here, Killstraight!"

He had a pretty good idea what that meant. Trash heap burning. Agent's office. Empty my trash can, Killstraight, be a good Comanch'.

Inside the cabin he recognized Shad Carter, the sour-faced cowhand he had met at the mission school, leaning against the far wall, biting off a mouthful of chewing tobacco. The other man was older, smoothing the ends of a huge white mustache while sitting in the chair in front of the agent's desk. Cigars rested in an ashtray. He wore a big brown hat, a small star cut into the crown. Daniel had seen this man at the agency once, back when he had first joined the police.

"Sawin' any triangles lately, Injun?" Shad Carter asked without humor.

"Only a rhomboid or two," Daniel said without looking at the cowboy. "You need me, sir?" he asked the agent.

The mustached man spoke. "You know this buck, Shad?"

"Met him," Carter told his boss, "down at the mission school a while back. He's a educated Injun."

Agent Rueben ran a palm across his blond beard. "Killstraight," he said, "this is J. C. C. McBride. He leases grasslands from the Comanches and Kiowas. It's his beef you people eat, and, in fact, it's his horse that you ride."

Daniel nodded at the rancher. "It's a good horse," he said.

"Glad you like him." McBride picked up his cigar, telling Daniel the conversation had ended.

"Take the trash out, Killstraight," Rueben said.

As he started to pick up the bulging can, McBride spoke again. "How much of an education did you get?"

Daniel stared, not knowing how to answer.

"You just some Comanch' carpenter?" McBride went on. "I mean . . . you boys live in teepees, not houses. How come you learned about ciphering, measuring, and such?"

Letting the trash can fall back to the floor, Daniel answered. "When we first arrived at Carlisle, we had to make repairs, put up buildings, things like that. Boys were turned into carpenters out of necessity. I wasn't sure I'd ever use any geometry again until that time at Miss Jordan's school."

"I see." McBride flicked ash from his long-nine into the trash can, and smiled. "What else did them damnyankees teach you up in Ohio?"

"Pennsylvania," Agent Rueben corrected.

The rancher returned the cigar to his mouth.

"I worked on farms, and later in coal mines."

"You speak pretty good."

"I learned English," Daniel said.

"You can write then? Read?"

"Yes, sir."

Using his cigar as a pointer, McBride motioned at Carter. "My *segundo* here, he never even learned his letters. Ain't that right, Shad?"

Carter spit out tobacco juice, and McBride laughed and stopped needling his foreman, giving him a compliment. "But he's a top hand. Best man I got riding for my brands. You like being a peace officer?"

A shrug.

"Ephraim and me, we was Rangers down in Texas for a spell. Wore out many a horse chasing after bucks like you, I reckon. Had us a few good rows with you Comanch'. And some I'd like to just forget. Tell you, boy, I've fought greasers, Yankees, and niggers . . . black and red . . . but you Comanch' was some of the toughest *hombres* I ever come across."

Daniel nodded at the compliment. At least, he thought it was a compliment, or as close to one as J. C. C. McBride could deliver to an Indian, or, for that matter, Shad Carter. "If you rode with the Texas Rangers, you earned the respect of The People," Daniel told him. "We called you Those Who Always Follow Our Trails."

The old rancher roared with laughter, jabbing the cigar in the air as he stood. "By grab, I like that name. Those Who Always Follow Our Trails. Yes sir, damnation, that's what we done, when we was chasing Injuns or thieving bean-eaters. Those Who Always Follow Our Trails. How do you say that in Comanch'?"

Daniel told him, and McBride tested the translation on his lips, butchering it, as would most white men. He took off his hat, ran his fingers through his hair, and returned the battered old Stetson, before stubbing out the cigar and tossing the butt into the trash pail.

"You're a good boy," the rancher said. "Too good, Ephraim," he added, turning toward the agent, "to be soiling his hands with your trash. That ain't no chore for an educated man like him. Get some other buck to do it."

Agent Rueben's head bobbed, and he walked back outside, calling Twice Bent Nose.

"That'll be all, Daniel," he said, and Daniel passed Twice Bent Nose on his way outside. He saw the horses tethered there, a buckskin and a towering blood bay. Daniel ducked underneath the hitching rail, and walked to the nearest horse, the bay. He found the brand. Bar TA Slash. Just like the cattle he and Ben Buffalo Bone had found down south. He slid around the bay, and checked the buckskin, too. Same brand. What had he hoped to find, the Lazy B?

Clopping hoofbeats turned his attention toward the road, and he frowned at the sight of Cotton Henry as the cowhand reined up in front of the agency. He had to see Daniel, but didn't look at him, didn't acknowledge him. Two minutes later, J. C. C. McBride stepped out of the cabin.

"Get the herd bedded down?" the rancher asked.

"Yes, sir, Mister McBride."

Shad Carter emerged next, spraying the nearest post with tobacco juice, stopping and staring angrily at Daniel. Then Agent Rueben walked out, and, spotting Daniel, called out in jest: "Better watch it, John, or Killstraight yonder might steal another horse of yours!"

"Get away from my horse, Injun!" Shad Carter wasn't joking. He sounded mad, the cowhand's attitude reminding Daniel of Sergeant Sitting Still's.

"Easy . . . ," Rueben began.

Daniel stepped back from the horses. "What next, sir?" he asked the agent.

"Cotton," McBride called out before Agent Rueben could give Daniel another order, "this here is Killstraight! He's. . . ."

"I know him," Cotton Henry said without looking toward Daniel.

"That's right." McBride nodded. "Reckon you was with Shad when he showed you his carpentry skills."

"I met him before," Henry said stiffly. "At Fort Smith. At the . . . hangin'."

"Hanging?" The pleasant features vanished from the old rancher's face. "You mean he was in town?"

"He was with me."

"With you? What the hell do you mean he was with you?"

For some reason, Daniel decided to speak up. Maybe he remembered how sick Cotton Henry had looked after the hanging. Sicker even than Daniel had felt. Maybe he just didn't want to see the young cowhand get into trouble, scolded, perhaps even get fired, for bringing a Comanche to a hanging.

"The son of Naséca was my friend," Daniel said.

"She was Jimmy Comes Last's ma," Rueben explained.

Silence. It lasted a long time, until Twice Bent Nose dropped the empty trash can inside the cabin, and stepped outside with a grunt.

"Friend of your'n?" Shad Carter asked, wanting an explanation.

Daniel didn't respond.

"That's right." Rueben suddenly snapped his fingers. "Daniel came in with Jimmy's mother. I had given her a pass. Figured it proper, let her go see her boy on his way to the happy hunting ground. Daniel came back with her. That Cherokee . . . can't recollect his name at the moment . . . he mentioned something about a Comanche coming back with him. I never made the connection till just now." He looked up at Daniel, his face masked in bewilderment. "But how did you know Jimmy was . . . ?"

Chapter Ten

Looking at those faces of the four pale eyes, without really knowing why, Daniel said: "Naséca doesn't believe her son killed that man and woman. She asked me to prove he was innocent."

"Bit late for that, boy." Carter's instant chuckle came out as more of a snort, and he started for his horse.

Then Daniel knew why he had asked. He wanted to see the reaction. Carter had laughed it off. Agent Rueben looked at him with suspicion, or wonder, maybe a bit of both. The old rancher just smoothed his mustache, but Daniel couldn't make himself look at Cotton Henry, fearing he wouldn't see the cowhand mounted on that dun, but the ghost of Jimmy Comes Last. Twice Bent Nose grunted, not understanding anything about the conversation.

After the longest while, J. C. C. McBride slapped his thigh and guffawed. Bowlegged, he walked toward the big blood bay, gathered the reins, and, for an old man, mounted effortlessly. "Yes, sir, Ephraim," he told the agent, "you got yourself one mighty good peace officer here. Too good, I warrant, to be taking out your trash. Hell, he's whiter than Shad." Turning his horse, he shot a glance at Daniel. "How do you say that again, boy? Those Who Always Follow Our Trails?"

Daniel repeated the Comanche phrase, and McBride laughed again before spurring his horse into a lope. Shad Carter and Cotton Henry quickly followed their boss.

"Killstraight," Rueben called out four days later, "got a chore for you!"

Swearing slightly underneath his breath (a habit he had picked up living with the pale eyes), Daniel set down the tack he had been mending in the shed, and stepped into the light to find Ephraim Rueben rubbing his dirty beard, waiting just outside his cabin.

Rueben had followed J. C. C. McBride's advice, or instructions. Daniel hadn't been burning the agent's trash, or even gone inside the agency office, since the rancher had ridden off. Not that Daniel had spent his time doing anything exciting. No, he had been working on the road to Fort Cobb and the Caddo village, and, this day, perfecting his saddle stitching. He brushed the dust off his clothes as he walked to the cabin.

"Yes, sir?"

The agent's hand disappeared inside his coat, and came out with several sheets of paper stuck inside an envelope.

"I told you it wouldn't always be like picayune chores," Rueben said, passing the envelope to Daniel. "You read the *Police Gazette* or something, folks think it's all exciting, pistol fighting and saving damsels. Trust me, I spent more hours than I can recall with the Rangers doing absolutely nothing more than what you're doing. But then, something exciting happens, and you realize that's why you do this for a living. That, and protecting people." Rueben stopped, apparently waiting for Daniel to offer some kind of acknowledgment.

"Yes, sir," was all Daniel could think of to say. He looked at the envelope. Nothing written on it. Should he look at the papers inside?

"Not that this will be exciting," Rueben went on. "Likely, there won't be anything to it, but it'll get you on your horse for a good spell, let you see something other than this godforsaken country." Rueben pointed with his pipe stem at the envelope. "Those are receipts. Sergeant Sitting Still and Ben Buffalo Bone are fetching prisoners from the Fort Sill guardhouse. You and Policeman Tach will escort these prisoners and turn them over to the federal marshal in Fort Smith. Once you have delivered them, have the marshal sign those receipts. They are duplicates. He keeps one copy. You take the other." Rueben jabbed the pipe stem at Daniel's face. "These must be signed, Killstraight. You must bring them back to me. Do not lose them. There is one for each of the prisoners."

"Yes, sir."

"You will travel by wagon. Tach will drive the wagon. You can ride horseback. The prisoners . . . there are five of them . . . must be chained at all times. You are to follow the Fort Sill-Fort Smith Military Road. Also in that envelope is a letter of introduction, requesting permission to house the prisoners at the guardhouse at Camp Arbuckle and at the jail in McAlester. That should not be a problem. We've done it often. Other times, you'll have to camp, keeping a sharp eye on the prisoners."

Rueben kept talking. He was a particular man, and he had everything planned out. Traveling twenty miles a day. One day to rest the horses in Fort Smith after delivering the prisoners to Fort Smith. If the cells weren't full, the jailer might put them up for the night and feed them breakfast the next morning. He was allocating them $15 in script for expenses. Daniel would file a report upon his return, and pay back any leftover sums. No extra ammunition would be issued. Rueben didn't feel it necessary. They could take pemmican and beef jerky, airtights of sardines, salt pork, coffee, and a sack of corn dodgers. Certainly they could kill any game they came across for fresh meat. He was sending along enough food for both the policemen and the prisoners. Rueben would expect him back no later than the first of next month.

"Can you savvy all that, Killstraight?"

Traces from a weather-worn Studebaker Brothers Manufacturing Company wagon sounded as Ben Buffalo Bone and Sergeant Sitting Still rode up with the prisoners.

"Yes, sir."

Rueben smiled. "I figured as much. You can read. You can write. Sometimes it's a pain in my arse to deliver prisoners to Fort Smith. Tach doesn't speak much English. Ain't a one of my policemen can read and write, except you. Anyway, I've drawn a map for you. Tach's done this a couple of times with Sergeant Sitting Still, so he knows the road, the routine. Map's in the carpetbag under a tarp in the wagon." He pointed at Sergeant Sitting Still. "Ask the sergeant for the keys. Make sure the prisoners are chained to the wagon while in the wagon. Make sure the manacles on their wrists and ankles remain on at all times. They may stretch their legs . . . with the irons on, mind you . . . and follow nature's call in the morning and when you make camp each evening. Do not trust them, Killstraight, even though they are Comanch'. These are desperate men."

* * *

Desperate? Maybe, but they didn't seem dangerous, not on that first day's ride. How dangerous could they be? Two men guarding five prisoners. Or was that standard policy? Shackled prisoners did not pose much of a threat, he guessed. Hell, Daniel thought, what did he know about being a peace officer?

The Comanches had been arraigned at the court in Wichita Falls, Texas, and ordered to stand trial at Fort Smith. Those charged with lesser crimes appeared before Judge Quanah Parker and his Court of Indian Offenses. Others faced sentence in Wichita Falls. Many other disputes were simply handled by the policemen themselves.

Beats His Horse, a silver-haired Penateka, had beaten more than his horse after buying forty-rod whiskey from the Creeks. Near the Fort Sill sutler's, he had busted one trooper's jaw, and carved up two others with the busted whiskey bottle, before the soldier with the ruined jaw drew his revolver and put a .45 slug in the old warrior's left thigh. Finder of Honey Trees, equally drunk, had then ridden up, on his skewbald mare, trying to run over the soldiers, but forgetting to duck. An elm branch left him with a concussion, not to mention the broken right wrist he received when the tree knocked him from the saddle. The heavy iron bracelets must have really hurt, tight as they were against that broken bone, but the old Kotsoteka, once a great *puhakut*, never showed any discomfort.

The Yamparika named Four Coyotes had stolen rations from two old women, putting up a pretty big fight when Twice Bent Nose had arrested him.

Those three were older men, warriors who might

have known Daniel's father, might have ridden on raids and counted coup with Isa Nanaka. Daniel could blame Creek whiskey for the trouble Beats His Horse and Finder of Honey Trees had gotten into, but Four Coyotes? That was just meanness, unlike most of the Yamparika he had met.

As far as the other two prisoners were concerned, Daniel didn't know what to think. He vaguely remembered Aaron Iron Skillet, another Yamparika, from the time when he had first arrived with Quanah and the other Kwahadis years ago. Aaron Iron Skillet was but ten years Daniel's senior; however time had ravaged his face until he looked more like Beats His Horse's age. He had slaughtered some Bar TA Slash cattle grazing, legally, in one of the Comanche pastures. Too much for one man, or even ten, and the Yamparika had not killed the beef for meat, but for some unknown reason. Vengeance? Boredom? Aaron Iron Skillet wouldn't say.

William Barking Dog he remembered pretty well. He was Kwahadi, born four summers after Daniel on the Llano Estacado. Taciturn, Daniel remembered, quieter even than Daniel, and the boy didn't say much now. Sixteen years old, and he had committed a crime, in Daniel's eyes, far worse than anything the other four prisoners had done. He had been arrested for working with the Creeks, selling whiskey to The People, bringing poison that would leave his relatives blind, disgraced, or dead.

Didn't say much—until they made camp.

"You call yourself The People," the boy lashed out in Comanche. "You have become *taibo!* You are dogs. No, you are worse than dogs. You are dung. I speak to you, Killstraight. I speak to you, Tach! You have betrayed The People."

He spat, kicked at the two policemen as they brought him a plate of salt pork, corn dodgers, and a cup of coffee. He managed to kick the plate out of Daniel's hand, leaving the food for red ants. "Dung I call you."

Tach poured the coffee on the boy's moccasins, turned, picked up the plate, and walked back to the wagon. Daniel just stared, keeping his distance from William Barking Dog's legs.

"Dung of the snake. Dung of the coyote. Ha! Look at these brave Metal Shirts, my friends."

Within minutes, the other four prisoners joined in, singing out insults, laughing, spitting at the Comanche policemen. They kept at it for an hour. William Barking Dog went on for fifteen more minutes.

"Is this the way all prisoners talk?" Daniel asked Tach when he returned to the wagon to eat his supper.

Tach, a thirty-year-old Kotsoteka, shrugged and fingered a mouthful of pemmican. "I do not listen to what they say," he said.

A lie, for ten minutes later, when the Kwahadi prisoner resumed his tirade, Tach leaped up, strode over to the singing William Barking Dog, and clubbed the boy's head with the barrel of his pistol, stunning the kid, sending rivulets of blood down his forehead and over his nose.

"I am not the one who betrayed The People!" Tach yelled. "It is you, William Barking Dog. You who helped the Creeks bring whiskey to our country. You did this not to get staggering drunk like that old fool Penateka there. You did it for pale eyes money. Now, William Barking Dog, you will shut up?" Tach pointed the revolver, uncocked, at the boy's bleeding face. "You will shut up or you will not live to see the dungeon where the pale eyes judge will send you to rot."

The threat didn't work, though, for Four Coyotes and Finder Of Honey Trees resumed their torments, daring Tach to kill them, defending William Barking Dog, calling the policeman a coward, striking a young boy whose hands and feet were bound by iron cuffs. Defeated, Tach holstered his revolver and returned to his plate beside the wagon.

"It is a long way to Fort Smith," he said in resignation.

So the journey went. Exciting? Not hardly. Dangerous? No, just noisy. The prisoners would sing out their insults in the morning, chained to the Studebaker, until heat and dust forced them into silence, then they would resume their curses at camp that evening, scaring the birds, coyotes, and crickets into stopping their songs.

On the ninth day, near the Katy railroad in the Choctaw Nation, Tach and Daniel had unlocked the metal chains, allowing the prisoners to step off the wagon, one at a time, the policemen keeping their revolvers cocked, standing back from the five men. The last to drop off the tailgate, William Barking Dog, glared at Daniel, unbuttoned his fly, and began urinating right there, trying to spray Daniel's trousers while the others found a bush or tree behind which to do their business.

Daniel stared back, out of range from the Kwahadi's piss.

"Watch the others," Daniel told Tach.

The policeman grunted, and had managed just two steps before the first bullet struck.

Chapter Eleven

Whirling, Daniel dropped to a knee, stared at the woods, heard a gun speak, saw a puff of white smoke. He heard the shouts, in the bushes, in the woods. Skunk and the team still hitched to the wagon—Tach hadn't gotten around to picketing the livestock yet—snorted, whinnied, stamped their hoofs. A hawk sang out, flew from its nest. Another bullet *thudded* in the wagon behind Daniel. Absently he raised the Remington. Something *buzzed* past his ear.

In the corner of his eye, he spotted Tach, on the ground, crawling toward the wagon wheel, his left arm drenched in blood, his revolver left behind in the grass.

Dirt kicked up near Daniel's feet, and the reality of the situation struck him: *They're trying to kill us!* He stood there in the open, a perfect target, and quickly started backing up, started to take cover behind the wagon. Started to call out to the prisoners, warn them to keep their heads down—or were they trying to escape? Started to pull the trigger, started to breathe again. Then . . . William Barking Dog leaped on him.

The Remington flew from his grasp as the Kwahadi boy's handcuff chain bit into Daniel's throat. Choking him. Dragging him backward, lifting him upward, off his feet. Daniel reached with both hands, tried to break the stranglehold. Tried to breathe.

"I kill you," William Barking Dog said. "Dung!"

A man charged out of the woods, gripping a double-barrel shotgun. Daniel's vision blurred. William Barking Dog grunted, lowered Daniel, then jerked him again, pulling him backward, cutting off all air, almost crushing his windpipe. He couldn't believe the sixteen-year-old's strength. The iron bit the tender flesh. Blood trickled down Daniel's throat. In front of him, the man, still running, raised the shotgun. Tach shouted something. William Barking Dog had to lower Daniel to catch his breath, then leaned back, lifting him again, pulling Daniel tighter. Choking him. Hanging him. Killing him. Like Jimmy Comes Last died.

Laughing, the man with the shotgun brought the Greener to his shoulder, maybe ten yards away. No farther than that. Daniel remembered Hugh Gunter telling him: "Ever seen what a Greener'll do at close range?"

William Barking Dog didn't care that the shotgun blast would likely kill him, too. Probably he didn't even see the assassin.

Trying to fight back, Daniel heard a warrior's yell. The man with the shotgun turned, surprised. Manacles *jingling*, Beats His Horse, the ancient Penateka, stumbled forward, raising a tree limb over his head, savagely bringing it down. A gunman from the woods fired, but missed. Cursing, the man with the shotgun tried to deflect the blow with the Greener. Too late. A *thud*. The branch broke over the white man's head. More curses from the woods as the man toppled, dropping the double-barrel. Then . . . another round of musketry, knocking Beats His Horse to his knees. Swaying, the old Comanche began singing his death song. Two more bullets caused his body to jerk, and the warrior fell atop the Greener.

All the while, William Barking Dog never faltered from his task, pulling Daniel, choking him, trying to keep Daniel's feet off the ground. *I'm about to black out*, Daniel thought. *About to die.* Suddenly the young Kwahadi tripped over something. Tach's revolver, Daniel saw. William Barking Dog cried out in surprise, releasing his grip on Daniel's throat just a bit as another man stepped from the woods with a rifle, and fired.

Blood sprayed the side of Daniel's face. William Barking Dog's arms went limp, and he fell, pulling Daniel down with him. They landed on their sides, still facing the bushwhackers in the woods.

The man with the rifle swore, charged, jacking another round into the weapon as he ran.

Daniel tried to breathe. William Barking Dog's arms were still over his head, over his throat. Daniel pulled the handcuffs away, felt no resistance from the Kwahadi boy. He filled his lungs with one breath, then another. The rifle barked, a bullet singeing Daniel's arm. The man worked the lever, and kept running. Daniel saw Tach's revolver again, reached out, but the gun vanished a second before his hands fell on empty earth.

He only managed a glimpse of the moccasins, chains, and ankle bracelets, and slowly understood what had happened. Another prisoner had dashed from the bushes, reaching the Remington first.

Now it's over, Daniel thought. *Finished.* The prisoner would turn, kill Daniel and Tach with the pistol, join the men trying to break them free. No. No, Beats His Horse had fought back. Saved Daniel's life. This wasn't an attempt to free the Comanche prisoners. Something else.

Tach's Remington *boomed* twice, and the man with

the Winchester turned, unhit, ran back to the woods, like a pale eyes coward. Another shot came from the trees. And another. The Remington roared once more before *clicking* twice with misfires, faulty cartridges.

Daniel, still trying to breathe and regain his strength, heard the Comanche cuss, toss the weapon away, then lean down, pulling William Barking Dog's arms over Daniel's head. Another bullet slammed into the wagon. A horse screamed, died. Daniel recognized Aaron Iron Skillet above him, felt himself being dragged under the wagon beside a badly bleeding Tach.

A bullet kicked dirt and grass into Iron Skillet's eyes, and he roared, more from annoyance than pain, and shouted a question: "Where is your long gun?"

Daniel shook his head. "No rifle," he said hoarsely. Agent Rueben had not issued them any rifles, not even extra ammunition for their Remingtons.

Iron Skillet swore in English, then hugged the earth as lead whined off the nearest wheel's iron rim.

More bullets rang out. The man lying beside Beats His Horse stirred, rose weakly. From the woods, someone shouted something, and the man rolled over Beats His Horse's body, found the shotgun, brought it up. . . .

His muslin shirt exploded in a spray of crimson, and the Greener boomed, blasting the earth in front of Beats His Horse's legs. Dropping the shotgun, the man fell over the Penateka's body.

"The hell . . . ," came from the woods.

From the other side, toward the Katy line, a cannonade clipped branches and tore bark off the trees above the bushwhackers' heads.

"We're federal officers!" followed the rifle fire. "And we're gonna kill all you sons of bitches!" The deafening roar of gunfire resumed. Too many rounds for Daniel to count.

"Let's get out of here, Murt!"

A minute passed. Then another. Silence returned, but the smell of blood, of gunsmoke, of death, urine, and excrement lay heavily in the air. Daniel thought he heard hoofbeats, yet couldn't be sure. Slowly, cautiously he crawled from underneath the wagon, crawled past William Barking Dog's body, reached for his Remington, waiting for the bullets to begin raining again.

Nothing.

He glanced behind him. One horse lay dead in the harness. Spying Skunk standing near the other horse, both apparently unhurt, Daniel breathed a sigh of relief.

A lone man on a big mule left the cover of trees.

"*O-si-yo!*" the man called out. "You fellows all right?"

Slowly Daniel stood. His legs felt like water, rubbery, but, somehow, he didn't fall. He started to holster the Remington, but as the rider, the man who claimed to be a federal officer, drew closer, Daniel felt uneasy. Daniel looked, waited, but no lawmen followed. On came the rider, Winchester cradled in his arms, clucking at his mule, calling it Ross. A tall man, Daniel noticed, wearing a stovepipe hat.

It was the Cherokee, Hugh Gunter.

"Killstraight," Gunter said when he reached camp. "I'll be damned."

Unsure, Daniel stepped back. The Cherokee swung off his mule, still holding the repeater. Finder Of Honey Trees and Four Coyotes slowly came from behind the bushes, the latter's britches still down to his ankles. Aaron Iron Skillet turned his attention toward Tach's bleeding arm.

Daniel's eyes fell on William Barking Dog, then looked away, his stomach almost capsizing. He found himself staggering toward old Beats His Horse, then stopped, pivoting, not wanting to turn his back on Hugh Gunter. But why? Gunter had saved their lives, hadn't he? Or was this some Cherokee trick?

He backed away, covering the last few rods, while Gunter talked to Tach and Iron Skillet. Backed until he found himself standing over the bodies of Beats His Horse and the man with the shotgun. Slowly he kicked the pale eyes off the Penateka's body, and knelt, feeling for a pulse, praying he'd find one while knowing Beats His Horse, black eyes vacant, blood pooling from several wounds in his chest, was dead.

"They will mourn your loss in the lodges." Daniel spoke softly in Comanche, laying down his Remington to fold the dead warrior's arms over his bloodstained chest. "There will be much sadness, but all of The People will know of your bravery, that you died a warrior's death, that you. . . ." He choked out the last few words, surprised to feel a tear roll down his cheek, couldn't finish.

Swallowing, he glanced back at the wagon, picked up the Remington, and studied the face of the man Hugh Gunter had killed. Beard stubble covered his face, a bit of blood from the corners of his mouth, one eye closed, the other half open. Brown. Maybe black. A *taibo*. Perhaps half-breed. The corpse bore some features of the Choctaw, and this was the Choctaw Nation. Plaid woolen trousers, the seat and thighs reinforced with black wool. Cavalry boots and small spurs. Army issue, Daniel thought. A soldier then, or deserter. Muslin shirt, dark blood sticky. No vest. No bandanna, but a filthy handkerchief sticking out of one of his pants pockets.

"Know him?"

Daniel's heart leaped, and his hands tightened on the Remington. Hugh Gunter towered over him, still holding that cannon of a rifle, a Winchester Centennial .45-70. Daniel scrambled to his feet, almost tripping over the body of the Penateka warrior.

When Daniel didn't answer, the Cherokee's black eyes darkened. "I asked you if you know this *dila?*"

"*Dila?*" His question was barely audible.

"Skunk," Gunter translated, and Daniel looked at his horse. When he looked back, Gunter had raised his rifle slightly.

"You want to put that thing away?" Gunter motioned at the Remington. "You make me nervous. Way you're acting. Them that done this are long gone."

Rather than holster the .44, Daniel started to bring it up, but Gunter raised the Winchester, slipping his finger inside the trigger guard. "It's over," Gunter said. "You ain't used to this, I know, but it's over. We got some burying to do, and need to get your friend to a doctor. That arm's busted, and he's bleeding pretty bad."

"What are you doing here?" Daniel found his voice.

"Saving your life," Gunter snapped.

"You said you were a federal lawman . . . a posse. . . ."

"I lied, you idiot. Make them squat assassins think I had me a regular brigade of Judge Parker's deputies with me. Hell's bells, I had no idea how many boys they was shooting at you. Now, stop this fool interrogation. I ain't got to answer to the likes of you."

Yet Daniel thought differently. *Easy*, he thought, figuring out the plan. It made sense to Daniel. Gunter sees the ambuscade isn't going well, so he kills one of his own men. Make Daniel think he has rescued them, then murder them when they lower their guard. But why? And what had Hugh Gunter told Jimmy Comes Last when they went up the gallows? What was Hugh Gunter doing here now? This wasn't Cherokee country.

"You had quite a shock here, Killstraight." Gunter's words didn't come out soothingly, but angrily. "Had quite a shock since you got back from your white-man schooling, what with Jimmy Comes Last. Now this. But if you want your friend to live, we need to start footing it. I don't care about this man, or that kid that was trying to kill you, but this *e-qua a-ya-s-ti-gi* needs burying."

Daniel didn't move.

"You suspicion me?" Gunter roared out. "I risk my neck to save you fool Comanches, and you suspicion me?"

"What did you tell Jimmy Comes Last?" Daniel said. He felt light-headed, thought he might faint. Couldn't faint. Then Gunter would kill him surely.

"What?" Gunter squinted. "What are you talking about?"

"Who were these men? What are you doing here? Why do you want to kill me? Who killed that Creek girl and her husband, Gunter? The one they hanged Jimmy Comes Last for. You?"

Gunter stepped back, the barrel of the Winchester inches from Daniel's gut. "You're a damned fool. If I wanted you dead, I'd have let these skunks do their business. Why would I want you dead? No, don't raise that pistol, boy. I don't want to kill you."

"You. . . ."

"Boy . . . ," Gunter warned, his finger tightening on the trigger.

"You're a *taibo*," Daniel challenged.

"Me? Damn if you'll call me a white man! I am Hugh Gunter of the Long Hair Clan. I am full-blood. We Gunters go back all the way to Georgia. My mother carried me on the Trail of Tears. My father, he escaped the roundup, I am told, staying, having to call himself Black Dutch, denying he was Cherokee, living in the hills so he wouldn't be shot, killed, or rounded up and sent out here. Pretending he was not Indian. But it was pretend. But you. . . ." Gunter spat. "This man. . . ." His head tilted toward Beats His Horse. "He was Comanche. But you . . . you are nothing! You are, as you say, *taibo*."

"You lie," Daniel blurted out in anger, fear. "You told me you didn't understand Comanche!" He thumbed back the Remington's hammer, hoped he could kill Hugh Gunter before the Cherokee madman murdered them all.

Returning to its nest, the hawk *screeched*, startling Daniel, causing him to look up. A mistake. Not even a second passed. But enough. Daniel cried out, heard his Remington roar, saw the Cherokee step to his side, turning, swinging that heavy Winchester barrel like a coup stick.

Chapter Twelve

He felt himself rolling, surrounded by darkness, the far-off smell of cinders, a *clacking* noise, succumbing to a terrible torment, rolling, moving, being carried off to The Land Beyond The Sun.

A hatchet kept pounding his head. From the outside or inside, Daniel couldn't tell. All he knew is he had never felt agony like this since that time his pony had stumbled, pitching him into the rocky earth, on a buffalo hunt when he had been seven or eight. Pain and blackness, a deep void, except for that awful, splitting head. He had always thought that the road to The Land Beyond The Sun would not hurt, but he hurt. Hurt bad.

His eyes opened, but only briefly, blinded by the terrible light that caused his head to throb even more. "I'd rest easy, bub." The voice echoed in his brain, but Daniel forced his eyes open again, slowly, adjusting to the light, saw the fuzzy creature in front of him.

His vision focused, briefly, detecting a man with a beard of red and gray whiskers, a blood-soaked shirt. Almost immediately, the blackness swallowed him again.

"Ahhhh." He woke to darkness, head still throbbing, rolled over, and vomited. Caught his breath. The stench made him sick again. Where was he? Naked,

he thought, feeling coarse cotton sheets against his skin. Closing his eyes, he collapsed into his own disgorge.

On the fourth day, Daniel woke to only a mild throbbing in his head. A far-off voice called to him, and, slowly, the blurs lessened, and he looked up into the face of the man with the gray and red whiskers.

"Who . . . ?" He started in Comanche, closed his eyes, tried again in English. "Who are you? Where am I?"

"Name's Campbell." The accent was heavily Scottish. "Some call me a doctor, some a bloody bastard. I can vouch for the veracity of the latter. As to the former. . . ." He shrugged. "But I'm all you'll find at Gibson Station." The hands moved toward Daniel's head, and he cringed, expecting a flood of pain, but Campbell's fingers had a gentle touch. "As a doctor, I mean. There are plenty of other bastards here."

"What . . . how . . . ?"

Gibson Station? That couldn't be. If he wasn't dead, he should be . . . where? McAlester maybe. Or somewhere else in the Choctaw Nation. Gibson Station lay way north, in Creek Country. Maybe Cherokee. He couldn't quite remember which.

Doc Campbell removed his hands. "Can you eat?"

He shook his head. A mistake. Bit his lip against the pain.

"You took a bad crack to the head, bub. Wasn't sure you'd be with us for long, but your skull is harder than mine, I warrant."

"How . . . ?" Daniel let out a heavy sigh, sank deeper into the bed.

"You have questions. I have another patient, your

Comanche colleague. I'll send in someone who has some answers, and more questions. Then I'm bringing you some venison stew. You say you can't eat, but I want you to drink the broth. You need something."

He didn't hear the doctor leave, thought he might just drift off to sleep again, but the song of spurs forced his eyes open, and Daniel watched a tall man with a sunburned face and handle-bar mustache approach him, a six-pointed star pinned on his vest.

"You remember me?" Deputy Marshal Harvey P. Noble asked.

"Yes, sir."

"Good. How you feel?" The lawman didn't wait for a reply, pulled a pencil and notepad from his pocket, and crossed his legs after sitting in the camp chair by Daniel's cot. "I'm gonna ask you a few questions 'bout that fracas you had down in the Choctaw Nation. I talked to your pal, Tach . . ."—Noble couldn't quite pull off the guttural pronunciation—"but I'd like to get your version, since your pal didn't see much, and he ain't. . . ."

"How is he?"

Noble frowned. "Doin' fine." A lie. Daniel could see that in the old man's eyes. Noble uncrossed his legs, searching, found a spittoon, and spit out a mouthful of tobacco juice. "Doc Campbell had to saw off the boy's arm," he said bluntly, and Daniel closed his eyes tightly. "Nothin' else he could do. Your pal ain't out of the woods, but he's alive. Lucky. You're lucky, too."

Noble paused, to give Daniel time to respond, but there was nothing to say.

"Want to tell me 'bout it?"

Slowly Daniel related the ambush, from the first shots fired from the woods, being attacked by William Barking Dog, the heroism of Beats His Horse, and their deaths—the bullet that struck William Barking Dog in the forehead likely had been meant for Daniel—to his suspicion of Hugh Gunter. "Things went black after that," he said.

"Yeah." Noble spit again, wiping his mouth with his shirtsleeve. "You're lucky Gunter didn't kill you. Could have. You made a mistake, boy. I been ridin' for Judge Parker for nigh seven years, and Gunter ain't no bushwhacker. He's what we'd call a top hand."

"But. . . ."

Noble held up his hand. "The dead man, the one Gunter shot, was Jasper Cross. Least, that's the handle he used in the Nations. We got paper on him. Name mean anything to you?"

He shook his head, then remembered something else. "But I heard another name. When Gunter started shooting, after he had killed that Cross fellow. Murt. Someone in the woods yelled . . . 'Let's go, Murt.' Or 'Let's get out of here.' Something like that anyway. But the name was Murt."

The pencil scribbled. "Figures," Noble said. "Cross was knowed to run with Murt Jones and some Creeks, Choctaws, Texians. Kill a man, they will, for ten dollars or ten cents."

He returned the pencil and notepad into his pocket, and pushed himself off the chair. "You rest your skull, boy. We'll catch up with Murt Jones and his crew. They'll swing. One of these days."

"Can I see Tach?" he asked.

"That'd be Doc Campbell's department, so you

need to ask him. And, first, there's somebody else you need to talk to, I reckon." He nodded a farewell, and walked out the door.

A moment later, Hugh Gunter walked in.

"Guess I buffaloed you harder than I should have," Gunter said.

About two minutes, perhaps three, had passed in silence after the Cherokee entered the room. Daniel's head throbbed, and his throat felt like someone had filled it with sand. He coughed, tried to push himself up a little, which only made his head pound harder. Finally he looked the Cherokee in the eye, and held his stare.

"You understood *taibo*," he said again. "I. . . ."

"You told me what it meant," Gunter snapped. "When we were on the trail, bringing Jimmy's ma back to the reservation. Think back. We was sitting at the wagon, talking, just before daybreak after that first, maybe second, day out from Fort Smith. Think back, boy. Think!"

He sagged when the truth hit him, almost crying. Damn if he hadn't botched everything, almost killed an innocent man, had almost gotten killed. He started to apologize, but Gunter was already talking.

"Look, I was riled myself, and I'm sorry I almost broke your skull. Figured those bandits might change their minds and ride back to the fight, call my bluff. Killing a man with a gun I can handle, especially a piece-of-dirt quarter-breed Choctaw, but hangings eat at you. All I told Jimmy right before he was hanged was to keep his head up, his ma was out there, so were a bunch of . . . like you call them . . . *taibos.* Told him to show them he was a man, a Comanche. Hell, I was talking more for myself than Jimmy."

Silently Daniel let it all sink in.

"You're bound and determined to help Jimmy's ma, I guess," Gunter said, removing his hat and sitting in the chair, stretching out his long legs. "Fulfill your promise."

"I. . . ." He shook his head.

"If you want to be a detective, a real policeman, you can't go off jumping to no conclusions. That'll get you in trouble. You got to think. Think hard. And take notes. That's what Harvey Noble is always doing. You look at him, you hear him talk, you think he's just one of Judge Parker's hard-rock deputies with a gun, but he ain't all that. He's a thinker. Taking notes all the time. I'll be with him on the trail, and each evening he'll drink his coffee and thumb through his papers, reading all he had wrote about the vermin he's chasing, the murders and robberies he's investigating. I've seen him do that I don't know how many times."

Gunter reached inside his coat pocket and withdrew an Old Glory writing tablet, a Columbus lead sharpener, and a pack of Faber's No. 2 pencils, all of which he laid at Daniel's side. "Don't say I never give you nothing." He held out his hand.

Daniel shook it. Relief swept through him.

"Noble's sent word to the Comanche agency, told him what all happened, told them you'd be laid up a spell. He's taking your prisoners, them's that ain't dead, to Fort Smith."

"Tell him to get a receipt," Daniel said. "Agent Rueben, he's. . . ."

Gunter grinned. "And Noble, he'll tell Parker about what all Aaron Iron Skillet done for you, dragging you under that wagon. Might persuade the judge to go a bit easier on the boy's sentence."

"I'd appreciate that."

"Uhn-huh." The Cherokee hesitated, then pulled on his stovepipe hat. "One thing you best consider, though," he said as he walked toward the door.

"What's that?"

"That Jimmy Comes Last killed those folks. That his ma is just acting like any other ma would, not believing her child could do such ghastly business. I expect Murt Jones's mother believes he's almost a saint."

The thought stuck with Daniel as he sharpened the pencil. Think things through, he told himself as he opened the tablet. Jimmy might be guilty. But he wrote:

Why did Murt Jones ambush us?

He drew a line underneath the sentence, chewed on his pencil, then wrote down Jimmy Comes Last's name.

What did he know about the dead Comanche?

Metal Shirt, he wrote.

Another memory came to him, riding with Ben Buffalo Bone. "This is better than burning trash," Ben had said. "You're too good a policeman to be burning that agent's garbage. That wasn't even fit for Jimmy. . . ." So he wrote:

Burning trash?????

"Victims," he said out loud, and tried to remember the names. Benton. The man was Tim, no Tom. Thomas A. Benton . . . married to Karen Benton. "A squawman," Gunter had said. Lived in a cabin on the Verdigris. The pencil point broke when Daniel realized he was near the river now, in a bed at Gibson Station. He grabbed the sharpener, repaired his pencil, and took more notes, recalling that Gibson had been killed with a shotgun, his wife murdered with an axe.

Axe. Shotgun. Why? Two killers? he wrote. Then: *Talk to Noble about this.*

He turned the page, and kept writing.

He walked to the privy the following morning. Later that day, he visited Tach, but the Comanche slept, a bloody piece of plaster above where his elbow should have been. In a way, he was glad Tach slept. He didn't know what to say to a Comanche who had lost part of his arm.

Two days later, Tach was dead.

Infection, Doc Campbell said. Nothing he could have done, and Daniel's heart sank. He picked up the tablet, but couldn't write anything, couldn't think. He wanted to sing a song of mourning, wondered if Tach had any family back near Cache Creek.

They buried Tach that afternoon, and Daniel made himself go to the funeral. *A pale eyes funeral,* Daniel thought, *maybe Creek or Cherokee. But not Comanche.* The song the church lady sang on the piano seemed joyous, while no one cut their hair, carved their flesh, and they buried Tach in a wooden box. *How is Tach going to get out of that, with its cover nailed shut, to begin the journey that his ancestors had taken?*

Silently he returned to Doc Campbell's cabin, collapsed on the cot, and found the tablet, turning to the first page and reading and wondering: *Why did Murt Jones ambush us?*

He found the pencil, and wrote in the margin near this: *Why Tach?*

Ten days later, Marshal Harvey P. Noble and Hugh Gunter returned, the latter driving the Comanche agency wagon, pulled by Gunter's Cherokee mules, the surviving Comanche mule, and Skunk trailing the wagon with a long lead rope.

"Gunter, here, says he'll take you back to your people," the marshal said. "Sorry to hear about that friend of yours. I'll see that we add his killing to the pile Murt Jones is already suspicioned for. You up to the ride?"

"I'd like to see the cabin before we go," Daniel said. "The one where the Bentons were murdered."

The lawman looked surprised, then maybe mad. "What on earth for?"

Daniel shrugged.

"You can't, bub," the doctor said from the corner of the room. "It burned down."

"What?" Noble glared at the doctor. "When? How?"

"Lightning, we suspect," Campbell said. "I don't know. Three, four months back. I, for one, was glad to see it go. Nothing but bad memories there."

Hugh Gunter nodded. "Bad medicine."

"I never wanted to set foot in that place again," the doctor said.

Daniel considered this, sinking onto the cot. Well, what had he expected to find? Then he reached over and grabbed his pencil and paper.

"Marshal," he said, "Hugh Gunter told me you suspected that Jimmy had gone in search for Creek whiskey. That he hoped to find some whiskey there, didn't, and went crazy. Is that right?"

"Good a theory as any," he replied. "The boy never said one thing, never confessed, never denied doin' it. Acted like he wanted to die."

"Did you ever think of why two weapons were used?" Daniel started writing on a blank page. "Shotgun on the man, axe on the woman. Could there have been two people involved? Maybe even more?"

"I can answer that, Harv," the doctor said. "The Comanche used both barrels of the scatter-gun on Thomas. Threw it aside, grabbed the axe, and. . . ." He shook his head.

"That's the way we figured it," Gunter said.

Daniel felt like a fool. Obvious. The shotgun was empty. Of course, that's why he used the axe. He flipped back some pages and scratched through the words:

~~Axe. Shotgun. Why? Two killers? Talk to Noble about this.~~

"Doc," he suddenly asked. "You were there? In the cabin?"

"Doc testified at the trial," Noble said. "He examined the victims."

"I need to know about this," Daniel said, pleading. Pleading for himself, not only Naséca and the ghost of Jimmy Comes Last. "Tell me everything."

The doctor rubbed his whiskers and stared blankly.

"Tell him," Noble said.

Campbell filled a tumbler with amber fluid, killed it in three gulps, and shook his head. "Medicinal whiskey," he said with a wink, but his face showed no humor.

"Go on, Doc," Noble said.

Still, Campbell hesitated. "The Bentons are dead. So is their killer. The cabin burned. I don't see any reason to bring up all that. . . ."

"Come on, Doc." The marshal withdrew his own pencil and paper. "Let's just say I'm a mite curious myself. You sure lightning was the cause of that fire?"

"We just assumed," the doctor said.

"You recollect the exact date?"

"I'd have to check my calendar. Mary Sixkiller might remember. She told me about it. You might ask her."

"I will." Noble turned a page in his pad. "But right now I'd like to hear from you."

"Who's Mary Sixkiller?" Daniel asked.

"Lives on the river," Gunter answered. "Nearest thing the Bentons had for a neighbor."

"Did she see . . . know about . . . the Bentons?"

"No." Noble missed the spittoon. "I questioned her, but she didn't see nothin'."

Doc Campbell set down the empty glass. "I really think this case is closed, gentlemen. . . ."

"Tell me about the Bentons, please," Daniel begged. "How they were killed. Please, sir. I really need to know anything you can tell me. I think their deaths might be connected to Tach's."

Marshal Noble coughed. "Boy, that's a stretch."

"But . . . ," Daniel paused, nodding. Think things through, Gunter had told him. Think! He had nothing to support that claim, not a shred of evidence, not even a theory. "You're right," he said meekly. "My gut's just telling me. Maybe it's a forlorn hope. But I'd really like to know about the Benton deaths. Please, sir." He was staring at Doc Campbell again. "I grew up with Jimmy Comes Last. His mother. . . ." He swallowed down the rising bile. "Please, sir. You might be right. You probably are right. But I need to know, for my own sake, for Jimmy's mother's."

Sighing, the doctor refilled the tumbler. "Thomas took a blast of buckshot from two barrels of a Greener. I estimated the distance as six feet. He was killed instantly. Then the boy grabbed an axe and. . . ."

He looked for mercy from Noble, but getting none, he sipped the whiskey.

"The shotgun?" Daniel asked, still working his pencil.

"It belonged to Benton. I remember when he got it."

Daniel wrote: *How could Jimmy have gotten it?*

"Just grabbed it. Benton kept it by his door."

He heard the *ping* of Marshal Noble's tobacco juice striking the spittoon. "Just when did he get that Greener, Doc?"

Campbell shrugged, and Daniel stopped writing, his eyes landing on the marshal, then the doctor. He wouldn't have thought to have asked that question.

"I don't know exactly. A month, maybe two, before . . . before it all happened."

"Benton much of a hunter?" Noble asked, and wrote.

Another question that never would have struck Daniel.

"Not really. Good fisherman, though."

Daniel cringed. Eating fish disgusted him, and almost all of The People, unless they found themselves starving.

"But he'd shoot a quail or dove every now and then," Campbell quickly amended.

"Shotgun was loaded with buckshot," Gunter said. "Both barrels, if I remember right."

"You do," Campbell said. "It was."

"I got an old muzzle-loading shotgun in my cabin," Gunter said. "But I keep one barrel of buck, the other of birdshot. So I'm ready for either pheasant or white-tail."

"Benton had been traveling a lot recently," Campbell said. "Maybe he bought it for protection. Trails are dangerous all throughout the territory."

"Ain't that the truth," Noble said, chuckling, and the others joined the laughter, all except Daniel, too busy making notes, hoping he'd be able to read his writing later.

"There was a rumor, Doc . . . didn't come out at the trial, mind you, but I heard it," Noble said. "Rumor that the Creek woman was in the family way and that Benton wasn't the daddy. To get even with her husband who, the story goes, had him a strumpet somewhere down the pike."

"A bloody falsehood," Campbell said. The whiskey had soothed him, for he didn't say this angrily, and never lost his smile. "I told you I wasn't the only bastard in these parts, Mister Killstraight. And, Marshal, you should know better. Folks have been spreading that gossip since Benton started his work."

"What work?" Daniel asked at the same time Noble asked: "What makes you certain sure, Doc?"

The doctor answered the lawman's question. "I examined the bodies, remember, Harv?" The good humor had vanished. "Leave it go."

"What do you mean?" Daniel asked.

"You don't need to know." Campbell refilled his glass. Nervous. Not like Doc Campbell, from what Daniel had seen. He had always seemed pleasant, constantly joking, sometimes at his own expense, but talk about the Bentons left him on edge. Daniel wrote: *Why?*

"But I do," Noble said.

"Damn you, Harv!" Campbell sprayed whiskey on the wall. "Karen couldn't have been with child. I examined her body. She's dead. Thomas is dead. And their killer is dead."

"You checked her?" Noble said. "You mean . . . ?"

The doctor's voice dropped to a hoarse whisper. "She was menstruating, Harv."

Daniel felt sick. "Menstruating?" he said softly.

"This is your fault, Harv," Campbell said, trying to ignore Daniel, glaring at the federal lawman. "You brought this up. It's over. . . ."

"Menstruating . . . ," Daniel repeated.

"It's a female thing." Gunter whispered his answer, sounding embarrassed.

"I know," Daniel said. "But this means . . . Jimmy couldn't have killed her."

Chapter Thirteen

"How's that?" Noble asked.

Daniel took a deep breath, held it, then slowly exhaled. Explaining the ways of The People never came easy. Pale eyes couldn't, or wouldn't, understand these kinds of things. On the other hand, even after living with them for seven years, Daniel could never say that he knew much about them. He certainly didn't understand some of the things they did.

"It's taboo," he answered. "A woman like that, during that time, a Comanche man . . . he must avoid her. Touching the blood, that would destroy his medicine." He could picture his mother, being sent away to her own lodge away from his father during those times, could see the anxiety in his father's face. Marsh Hawk was fearless, bravest of all the warriors of The People, or so Daniel had believed as a child, but he would never risk losing his *puha*, would avoid a woman in that way be it his wife, mother, or some *taibo* on a raid.

"Maybe he didn't know," Gunter offered.

"He knew." Paling, the doctor sighed. "He had to know."

Questions raced through Daniel's mind, but he decided it best to keep quiet, not ask Doc Campbell anything. Daniel didn't have to. He knew what the doctor meant, and so did Marshal Noble.

"We thought it best not to mention it durin' the trial," Doc Campbell explained, both voice and face grim. "Let the woman rest in peace, not give 'em blue-birds something else to gossip 'bout. Bad enough she got chopped to death with an axe. . . ."

The lawman slid his notepad into his pocket, stuck the pencil above his ear, and shook his head. "You sure 'bout this, Killstraight? A Comanche buck wouldn't. . . ." He frowned.

"It is not the way of The People. Any warrior, any man believes in cleanliness. Maybe not the way you view clean, but important to us. We believe in harmony. That is why we offer the pipe to the six directions before smoking. That is why we avoid taboos such as eating fish, snake. Medicine is important, the most important thing to a warrior. I remember the stories of the fight against the buffalo hunters at that place in Texas." He strained at the memory. "I can't think of how it was called."

"Adobe Walls?" Noble said.

"Yes. That is it. The leader blamed the failure of that attack on some braves who had killed a skunk. The skunk had been his medicine."

"Karen Benton wasn't no skunk," Gunter said.

"No. But a Comanche man would not touch a woman who is. . . ." He felt as embarrassed as the other men.

He waited for the silence to pass, but when it was broken, it was only Harvey P. Noble hawking out his tobacco and saying in that Texas drawl— "Well. . . ."—before heading outside. The others followed. The interview, interrogation, whatever it had been, was over.

Noble mounted his horse, and Gunter and Daniel climbed aboard the wagon. Doc Campbell bid his good-bye before quickly entering the cabin, closing the door behind him.

"I hope you're wrong, Killstraight," the marshal said as he kicked his horse forward, moving closer to the wagon, and leaned in his saddle to shake Gunter's and Daniel's hands. "I'd hate to think I put an innocent man on the gallows. But if you learn somethin', somethin' more'n Comanche notion or a hunch, you get word to me. I can't promise you much help. My plate's mighty full." He tapped his badge. "But I'm duly sworn to uphold the law, and, if you find out someone else should have swung from that rope, I'll do my best to give ol' George Maledon another customer."

He returned to work the day after Hugh Gunter left him at the reservation, reporting to Agent Ephraim Rueben about the ambush and Tach's death. He decided not to mention his bit of detective work that might prove Jimmy Comes Last's innocence. Not that Rueben or Sergeant Sitting Still would have cared one way or the other.

The rest of the week he spent repairing the agency corral and digging a new privy before Sergeant Sitting Still sent him down toward the Deep Red to solve a dispute between two Kwahadis over a dog. Two days later, he rode south, scouting for any free grazers. He was riding alone now. Tach's death, Rueben said, left the police shorthanded, and Ben Buffalo Bone was needed at a Penateka lodge over by West Cache Creek, and Sergeant Sitting Still needed to check the pastures south of the Caddo village. Being alone didn't worry Daniel. Fact is, he enjoyed the solitude, and it gave him time to check the notes he had taken, and add any thoughts, questions, memories that came to him.

That's what he was doing when Randi Jordan surprised him.

"Well, hello there!" she called out as he sat in the saddle, letting Skunk drink his fill in the middle of a creek, absently rereading his Old Glory tablet, which he almost dunked in the water.

"Ma'am," he said, his Carlisle manners taking hold, reaching up to tip a hat that wasn't there, just a bandage he really should replace with something cleaner. He closed the tablet, slipped it into his war bag, and grabbed the braided hackamore.

"I didn't mean to startle you. . . ." She waited.

"Killstraight," he said. "Daniel Killstraight."

"Right," she said. "I'm dreadful at names. You're Ben Buffalo Bone's friend. The great carpenter."

Her smile warmed him.

"Don't think I'd call myself great."

"Well, Mister Eriksson, when he came back, he said everything looked fine."

"Yes, ma'am. I'm glad."

She frowned. "What on earth happened to your head?"

He reached, unconsciously, and tugged at the bandage. "Oh . . . it's nothing."

She rode sidesaddle, and dismounted now to let her own horse drink. "What brings you here, Daniel? It is all right if I call you Daniel, isn't it?"

"Yes, ma'am."

"How did you get your name? Daniel, I mean. I'm not sure I want to know how you came to be called Killstraight."

"There's nothing barbaric about Killstraight," he said with a smile. "No blood-and-thunder tale, and it's not a name I really deserve." The smile had faded. "As for Daniel, I picked it," he said. "It was on the blackboard. That is how we got all of our names. At the school in Pennsylvania."

"It is a strong name," she said. "The prophet Daniel is one of my favorite stories from the Old Testament. Are you familiar with it?"

His voice revealed no mirth. "I lived among the Babylonians," he said, watching her eyes reveal surprise, then sadness.

He remembered the stories they had taught at the Industrial School on Sundays. Remembered them well. He had pictured School Father Pratt as Nebuchadnezzar. In the story he had heard, Daniel, the young prisoner, had been given a new name, Belshazzar. He and the other youths from that Israelite tribe had been sent away to learn the ways of the Babylonians, to pray to the Babylonian gods, to speak the tongue of the Babylonians, and he remembered young Daniel telling his friends that they must not forget who they were, that they must remember the teachings of their parents, not those of the Babylonians.

He hadn't meant to tell Randi Jordan any of this, but the words kept coming out, and she listened, eyes glistening with tears, dropping the bay's reins.

"I told one of my school mothers this," he said, trying to keep the bitterness out of his voice, "asked her if she couldn't see . . . 'You tell me the Babylonians were wrong, that David was a hero, yet you do the same to The People, and the other tribes. You give us your own names, make us learn your tongue, make us forget our own ways, make us worship your god.' I did not understand, she told me. My ways were pagan. The Comanche, the Lakota, the others, we were the Babylonians. I still do not understand all of this."

Randi stepped into the creek, gathered the reins she had dropped, and mounted the bay. "I have never thought of it that way, Daniel. Perhaps, though, God's hand directed you to choose that name. Perhaps you are, in your own way, a prophet."

Shaking his head, Daniel laughed. "It was not God's hand," he said. "It was my own. And I picked it because the Lakota girl before me would not do as the school fathers and school mothers told her, not until a school mother slapped her knuckles hard with a ruler. Three times. Then she chose her name. I did not want my knuckles to bleed, so I chose the name. But I am no prophet. I see no writings on the wall, and have not been thrown into a pit with lions."

Suddenly he frowned, the nightmarish vision of Jimmy Comes Last before him. "And I cannot interpret my own dreams."

"Maybe," she said. "Or maybe you have." Her next words startled him almost as much as she had when she had surprised him a few minutes earlier. "Will you escort me back to the mission, Daniel?"

He liked her. Hell, who wouldn't?

Certainly he found her appearance pleasing. Ben Buffalo Bone had told him that, but his attraction to Randi Jordan went beyond the physical. She had listened to him, seemed to understand—better than most pale eyes would—what he was trying to explain to her. Anyway, she hadn't threatened to slap his knuckles, hadn't accused him of blasphemy.

"Most Comanches and Kiowas that come to the mission school. . . ." She laughed as they rode south.

"Well, when I try to talk to them, it's like they think I am a dentist, or some other monster. You seem different than most Comanches."

His head nodded sadly. "There are times when I do not even feel like Comanche."

"Because you were away for . . . how long?"

"Seven years. But it goes before that. My mother was Mescalero. An Apache. Isa Nanaka . . . he says I must find my own way."

"That's true for all of us, I believe."

She was wise, too. "Yes," he said, suddenly wanting to steer the conversation away from him. "And what of you?"

"Me?" Her laugh sounded so warm. "I followed my Mother Henryetta and Father Wayne. From one tribe to another, it seems like. I was born in Missouri. I heard Father Wayne preach to Santees and Sac and Fox, Iowas and Kickapoos, Pottawatomies and Osage, Caddos and Wichitas, and, finally, Kiowas, Apaches, and Comanches. We lost Mother Henryetta five years ago, and Father Wayne was called to Glory the summer before last. A Saint Louis newspaper had a really nice story about Father Wayne. I'll show it to you when we get back to the school. Anyway, I had nowhere else to go, so I stayed here. A preacher came shortly after, but he left two months ago. Some people cannot adapt to life out here, but I love it. Most times. At some point, they'll send another preacher, but I hope I can stay on to teach the children. That, I guess, is my calling."

He figured he had better do some police work while he was seeing her back to the mission school, so he asked if she had seen any cowhands in the area, cattle other than J. C. C. McBride's, told her he was after free grazers. "Yes," she said sadly, "I know of those free grazers, but I can't say I've seen anyone who didn't work for Mister McBride. He's a friend to the Indians, Daniel."

A dread came upon him when he saw the steeple. He knew he'd have to leave her, and, for some reason, he had enjoyed the conversation. Even enjoyed talking, despite the bad memories, emptying his heart of the pain. The dread intensified when he saw the buckskin horse ground-reined in front of the mission school.

"Why Shad Carter!" Randi exclaimed as the Bar TA Slash cowhand stepped from behind a pile of warping lumber and crushed out a cigarette with his boot heel. "What brings you out here again so soon?"

"Cattle," he answered bluntly, his eyes glaring at Daniel.

"Shad. . . ." She tested his name like a musical note. "That's funny. Shadrach, Meshach, and Abednego. Daniel and I were just talking about the Bible. Were you named after Shadrach of the Old Testament?"

"I was named after some kin of my ma's," he said. Suddenly a grin stretched across his face, and he tipped back his hat. "I heard you almost got kilt over in Creek land."

"Choctaw," Daniel corrected. Then, just to be ornery, he asked: "Where were you, Carter?"

"Nursin' Mister McBride's longhorns. To keep you savages from starvin'."

"You don't know Jasper Cross?" he asked, thinking, wanting to look inside his Old Glory tablet to make sure he had the name right. "Or Murt Jones?"

He had tossed out those names looking for some reaction, but Shad Carter gave him none. He merely shrugged. "I don't get around much, Comanch'."

Rein in, he told himself. *Don't go around jumping to conclusions, Gunter would tell me. This is a thirty-a-month cowhand, not a man-killer, though he acts like he wants to be one. He just doesn't like Indians. Suspicion him, and you'd have to suspicion every drover south of the Red River. Marshal Noble wants facts, evidence, not Comanche notions.*

"Is that what happened to your head?" Concern filled Randi's voice. "You said it was nothing. What happened, Daniel? What's this all about? Who's Jasper Cross? Who is Murt Jones?"

"Jones is a renegade, Randi," Shad Carter answered. "Bushwhackin' bandit over in the Choctaw Nation. That's right, Comanche, I've heard of him. Sakes alive, every man betwixt Sherman and Sedalia has heard of Murt Jones. But it don't mean I rode with him, had a thing to do with him."

"What happened?" Randi asked again.

"We were escorting Comanche prisoners to Fort Smith," Daniel said, keeping his eyes on Shad Carter. "Ambushed by Murt Jones and his gang. We don't really know why. They killed Tach, another Metal Shirt. Two prisoners were killed, too, before a Cherokee came along and saved us."

Gently she touched his bandage. "And this is where . . . ?"

He felt embarrassed, didn't answer her. Couldn't answer her. Shad Carter looked bitter.

"Shouldn't you run along, Comanch'," Carter said, and not as a question. "Red nigger like you got plenty to do."

"Shad!" Randi demanded. "You can be so rude."

"No," Daniel said, deciding he would play peacekeeper. "No, he's right. I need to check the pastures, make sure nobody's eating Mister McBride's grass."

He started backing Skunk away, then decided to toss one more name out at Shad Carter, hoping for a reaction, damning Hugh Gunter's and Harvey P. Noble's thoughts on hunches.

"What about Thomas Benton?" Daniel asked. "And his wife Karen? You know them?" He corrected. "Knew them?"

Only . . . the reaction wasn't what he expected.

Chapter Fourteen

In the stall next to Daniel's bedroll, Skunk snorted and stamped his hoofs on the floor.

"Shut up," Daniel said, unfolding his arms, rolling onto his side, pulling the blanket over his head, trying to remember everything Randi Jordan had told him. When the horse broke wind, Daniel groaned, then tossed off his covers and sat up, searching in the moonlight for his Old Glory writing tablet and pencil.

"Oh," Randi had cried out when he had mentioned the Bentons. "That was ghastly, just awful! Poor Tom."

Tom. Not Thomas. Not Mr. Benton. She hadn't mentioned his wife's name, either.

Daniel scratched a few notes, trying to picture the scene.

"You knew him?" Daniel had asked.

"Yes. It was terrible, his death. Just dreadful." She was almost crying. "And all the work he was doing. Doing for you, Daniel. For all the Indian peoples."

Now, remembering this, he flipped back several pages in his tablet. Over at Gibson Station, Doc Campbell had mentioned Benton's work. When Marshal Noble had brought up Mrs. Benton's fidelity, the old sawbones had said something like: "Bluebirds have been saying things like that since Benton started working." No, not working. Work. Daniel had asked—"What work?"—but Marshal Noble had fired out another question, leading the conversation away from Benton's work, and Daniel had forgotten to ask about it, until Randi Jordan had brought it up again.

He turned the pages again, back to where he had started making notes a moment earlier, knowing he should have written these things down earlier, when he had first left Randi and Shad Carter, not waited until the dead of night.

R. Jordan knew Benton, he wrote. *Calls him "passionate crusader." Shad C. scoffed at that term. Benton had written letters to newspapers, Secretary of the Interior, commander at Fort Sill, Indian agents, Eastern churches. Something called Indian Rights Association. R. mentions grass money, squawmen, teaching business to Indians. Benton big supporter of Dawes. Started with Creek, Cherokee, Choctaw. Then aimed at Comanche reserve, Cheyenne, Arapahoe, others.*

He reread his notes, adding below the poor penmanship, twice underlining the question he hadn't thought to ask Randi Jordan:

Who is Dawes?

"Some policeman, some detective you are," he told himself, flinging the tablet aside.

As if in agreement, Skunk whinnied.

"Have you heard of a man named Dawes?" Daniel asked Ephraim Rueben the next morning.

He had stripped off his shirt, sweating, baking in the sun outside the corral as Ben Buffalo Bone and he worked with a farrier named Shelton, shoeing agency horses and mules. He never understood why the white men put iron shoes on the hoofs of their horses, but did not argue. This would be good training, Agent Rueben explained, learning a trade, shoeing horses, a skill Ben Buffalo Bone and Daniel

Killstraight could use to help their own people, shoe the horses of even Quanah Parker, earn a few bits doing it.

"Quanah's horses are unshod," Ben Buffalo Bone whispered.

"Uhn-huh." Daniel figured Rueben's real reason was that if two Comanche Metal Shirts could learn to shoe horses, Rueben wouldn't have to pay the farrier from Fort Sill.

Now, they had taken a noon break, drinking water from the well, enjoying the shade while eating jerky, and Rueben had walked over for polite conversation. So Daniel, the name troubling him all morning, had decided to ask the question. If anyone knew about this Dawes, it would be Rueben, he told himself, and he had to trust someone, someone in a position of authority.

"Dawes." The agent swallowed. "You mean Senator Dawes?"

Daniel straightened his leg. Senator? It made sense. "Yes," he said, then, uncertain, "I mean, I think so."

"Damnyankee," the farrier said, and spit tobacco juice on a beetle.

"Have any Comanches been asking you about Senator Dawes?" Rueben frowned.

"His name came up," Daniel answered, "the other day. Ran ... Rand ... Miss Randall Jordan down at the mission school mentioned his name. I hadn't heard his name till then." He wondered how much he could trust the agent, a pale eyes. "She said Thomas Benton had done some work for Dawes."

"Benton?" Rueben stared at Daniel, then at Ben Buffalo Bone, who shrugged and grinned, not understanding, then back at Daniel. "What are you interested in Thomas Benton for?"

"Actually," Daniel said, "it was Dawes I was wondering about."

"Damnyankee," the farrier said. "He'll ruin this country, sure as hell."

The agent sighed, and lit his pipe. "There's a faction in Congress, led by Senator Henry Dawes of Massachusetts." Rueben paused, thinking, getting the words right while he puffed. "What Dawes, and few others. . . ."

"Damnyankees," the farrier repeated.

"What a few others want is to survey the reservation land, then divide it into, oh, I guess the word is allotments. Each Indian would receive his own land. There would be no reservation to speak of. You would own your own land."

He couldn't quite see The People doing this. Owning land? The People did not own land. Horses, yes, but land? Land belonged to all of The People, and the other tribes, or had . . . before the pale eyes came and took it away from them.

"Gov'ment made a mess of this country afore." The farrier swore under his breath and spit tobacco juice again. "Homestead Act. Send a bunch of pilgrims out here to farm. But you can't farm on no hunnert an' sixty acres. No, sir. Not in this country. And turnin' Injuns into farmers, homesteaders, that ain't nothin' but horseshit."

"Well, I'm not for it." Rueben tapped his pipe against the well bucket. "I might not agree with all of Mister Shelton's choice of words . . ."—he cast a friendly grin at the farrier—"but I think passage of this act would be a terrible mistake."

Daniel nodded. *Yes, Agent Rueben,* he thought, *you would think so. You'd be out of a job.* Quickly he let the theory bounce around his brain: Benton works for

Dawes, trying to end the reservation. Rueben goes to Gibson Station, tries to talk Benton out of working for Dawes. They argue. The Bentons are murdered, and Rueben leads the law to Jimmy Comes Last.

For about two seconds, he let that sink in, before saying to himself: "You idiot."

"What's that?" Rueben asked.

"Nothing." Hugh Gunter would laugh in Daniel's face if he were to present that theory. Facts, he told himself. Find facts. A bunch of people would be against this plan Dawes had, pale eyes as well as Indians. Ask some others. And find out exactly what Tom Benton was doing for Senator Dawes.

Thursday was trial day.

They met at the agency headquarters, holding court outside because inside would have been too hot, and most of The People found it uncomfortable in a square building made of logs or stone. Daniel found a place, luckily, in the shade of the porch, watching Comanches, Kiowas, and a few Apaches sit on blankets in the yard. Ben Buffalo Bone and two other Metal Shirts stood guard, while Sergeant Sitting Still walked among the defendants, accusers, witnesses, and a few spectators from Fort Sill. Finally Agent Ephraim Rueben stepped outside, followed by Quanah Parker.

"This is the Court of Indian Offenses," Rueben announced, "the honorable Quanah of the Comanches presiding."

Quanah leaned against a hitching post, and Rueben explained the first case would be against Long Feather of the Kiowas, charged with stealing a horse belonging to the Apache called Donato.

"I hear no case," Quanah said, and one of the Fort

Sill men almost swallowed his tobacco. Two Comanches broke out in laughter.

"You must . . . ," Rueben began.

"To steal horse way of all Indians," Quanah said, and repeated his decision in Comanche.

"Quanah, horse theft is a crime," the agent pleaded. "Down in Texas, I've seen men hanged. . . ."

"Horse theft," Quanah said, "way of life." He spoke again in Comanche, adding to his decision, saying it was not only a way of life, but an art, honorable. He would hear no such case, not against a Comanche, or any other Indian, and that, if forced to hand out a sentence, he would judge the Apache, Donato, quite harshly for letting a Kiowa steal his horse and not trying to get it back the way any warrior would.

Rueben and the other pale eyes understood none of that, but they certainly comprehended the crowd's laughter. Even Daniel had chuckled.

So the court proceeded. Two Apaches accused of brewing *tizwin*, the Apache beer brewed from mescal, were sentenced to a week-long detail under the supervision of an Apache Metal Shirt, and a Comanche charged with theft, from another Comanche, earned Quanah's wrath. Daniel and Ben Buffalo Bone nodded in agreement with the two-month sentence. The People did not steal from each other, or hadn't, not often, until surrendering to the pale eyes. Two other cases involving horse theft were also dismissed, much to Rueben's frustration.

When court was adjourned, Daniel made his way toward Quanah, who greeted him warmly.

"I. . . ." Daniel tried to find the right words. "I would like to speak of something to you, privately."

With a somber nod, Quanah walked to a lean-to,

and Daniel followed. They talked about the weather,
Quanah's wives, and the Court of Indian Offenses
for a few minutes, talked of old Isa Nanaka, of
Daniel's fight with the bushwhackers led by Murt
Jones, and of pony herds and Skunk, before Daniel
broached the subject of Senator Henry Dawes and a
Creek squawman named Thomas Benton.

"It is difficult to understand what is right for The
People, and what is wrong," Quanah said. "We could
reap much honor, much money, controlling our-
selves. Or we could reap ruination." He shook his
head. "There are times when I wish Bad Hand and
the other Long Knives had not named me chief of
all The People."

"Agent Rueben, he says Dawes is wrong. But this
Benton . . . he must have thought it would be good,
and he was an Indian."

"Creek." Frowning hard, Quanah shook his head.
"It is not the same as being of The People. And Benton was a pale eyes who married a Creek woman."

Daniel respectfully agreed.

"The People must stand on our own feet, eventually," Quanah said. "This is what this man Dawes
said."

"You have spoken to Dawes?"

"Yes. I have heard his words, and I have heard
the words of others, those who say Dawes is wrong.
We shall see. I am told the men who work for the
pale eyes President, who they tell us is called the
Great White Father, as if any *taibo* could be great,
they must decide on this. It may come to pass. It may
not." He held out his palms in a sign of uncertainty.

"I am told the man named Benton worked for this
Dawes."

The frown hardened, and minutes passed before

Quanah spoke again. At first, Daniel thought Quanah would scold him, chastise him. "I do not wish to be impolite, to speak of one who has gone to The Land Beyond The Sun. To speak the name of one whose death has caused much grief among my people." He meant Naséca's heartbreak. "But you have been away for a long time, you have lived with the pale eyes, and you are seeking to find your own path. So I will speak of this man.

"Yes, I met this man." Bowing to Comanche custom, he still wouldn't speak Tom Benton's name. "Two times. No, three." Without warning, Quanah smiled. "He reminded me of Isa Nanaka, always telling the same story over and over again." He chuckled, shifted his legs, and continued. "The bull buffalo Isa Nanaka would kill on a hunt kept growing the more times he told this story. Growing and growing and growing. Well, this was the way of. . . ." Quanah swallowed. " 'Pale eyes are cheating us,' he would say. Stealing from us. Taking advantage of us. This man, this man who was rubbed out with his wife, he said he would stop this."

"How?"

Shaking his head, Quanah started walking away. "I do not know. He blamed the cattlemen, the Texans, even the agents we have had in the past. And many have cheated us. I do not know how this man thought he could protect us, except by helping this man Dawes put an end to the reservations, and I do not know what this man was trying to find out, but this could be why he was rubbed out."

Ten yards away, Quanah stopped and turned. "Or it could mean nothing. And there are other stories I have heard of this dead man, stories I will not tell you because I do not know if they are true. I hope

they are not true. You must learn these on your own.
It could be that the pale eyes were right, and that. . . .'
He didn't finish. Agent Rueben was calling him into
the office, but Daniel thought he understood. It was
the same thing Hugh Gunter had told him.

It could be that Jimmy Comes Last, gripped by
Creek whiskey, had killed the Bentons.

On Sunday, Daniel rode to Naséca's, only to find the
lodge empty. *Visiting*, he thought. *Wasted trip.* Only
after he had mounted Skunk and started toward
the creek did he think of something else, so he
turned around and rode to the burned lodge, the
lodge that had belonged to Jimmy Comes Last.
He dropped to the ground, and wandered about the
ruin, the charred pieces of wood, the remaining ash
and trash that hadn't been scattered by wind or
washed away by rain.

With the toe of his moccasin, he pushed over a
thigh-size patch of blackened leather, saw something else, and knelt, fingering a piece of . . . what?
Paper. Burned paper, and, through the blackness, he
could make out letters. English. But Jimmy Comes
Last could not read or write. He couldn't read the
word, and then the bit crumpled in his hand, and
the wind took it away.

He muttered a curse, wiped his fingers on his
trousers, and gathered the hackamore. Instead of
riding away, however, he walked to Jimmy Comes
Last's grave. The bones of the horse Naséca had
killed had been scattered, the grave starting to sink,
and an uneasiness settled about him as he walked
around the grave, looking at the bones and bits of
rotting flesh and skin the ants and coyotes had not
picked clean. Partly buried under dirt and leaves, he

found one patch, lifted it, studied it for a moment before tossing it back to the ground. Worthless. He wasn't even sure what he had hoped to find. Nothing. There was nothing here, but still he looked, fingering bones and hide. He was about to give up when he saw another piece of horsehide, baked in the sun, chewed by coyotes, pecked by ravens, but now almost covered with rotting leaves and dirt. He brushed the dirt away, and his fingers traced the brand.

Luck, he told himself, *finding the branded hide. What would Jimmy Comes Last be doing with a branded horse? The People do not mark their mounts in such a way. Maybe this was why Jimmy had died.*

Frowning, he pitched the dead skin back to the earth.

Or not. Jimmy could have stolen the horse. The People once had many horses with their hides marked by hot iron. Quanah had explained as much during the Court of Indian Offenses. They stole horses. For honor. For glory. For wealth.

Besides, he had hoped the brand would have been the Lazy B. Maybe the Bar TA Slash, even the US mark of the Long Knives, something that would give him a theory, something he could pursue, but the brand, the Circle 9, meant nothing to him.

He swore again, climbed into the saddle, and kicked Skunk into a lope.

Chapter Fifteen

He spotted the dust long before he heard or saw the longhorns and Texas drovers. Daniel had just deposited a Kwahadi boy, maybe twelve, no more than fourteen years old, in the stockade for what Agent Rueben would call drunk and disorderly conduct. He had made the arrest at Sergeant Sitting Still's lodge—the sergeant off scouting the northern reservation—and the kid had almost taken Daniel's head off with a singletree after Daniel had poured the remaining Creek whiskey from the bottle.

Hearing Ben Buffalo Bone's call for assistance, Daniel trotted over to the large corral to help his friend swing open the gate, and wave the beef on the hoof inside. The cattle bawled, the cowhands yipped and swore, as Daniel choked on the dust while the riders pushed the leathery, worn-out animals through the opening.

One of Agent Rueben's assistants shouted out a head count, and a cowhand told the Indians to shut the gate. Daniel was glad to get away from the noise, the air heavy with dirt. He blinked constantly until he reached the water trough. Then, he and Ben Buffalo Bone washed their faces and spit out tepid water.

"Reckon you Injuns'll have a high time tomorrow," a cowhand drawled, and Daniel studied the men, glad he didn't see Shad Carter among the crew. He recognized Cotton Henry, but the young drover was too busy talking to Rueben's assistant to notice him.

"Well, if it ain't that book-learnt Comanch'," a voice came from behind him, and Daniel turned, dabbing the droplets of water from his face, to see J. C. C. McBride rolling a cigar in his fingers, followed by Rueben. Likely the rancher had ridden in ahead of the herd.

"Hello," Daniel said, and spoke the Comanche name, "Those Who Always Follow Our Trails."

The rancher cackled, and struck a match on the side of the building. "We brung you some prime Bar TA Slash beef, Killstraight," he said after he had the cigar going to his satisfaction. "Hear tell that you almost got sent off to the happy hunting ground."

Daniel started to reach for his head, but stopped. Sometimes he felt as if the bandage were still itching him, but he had removed it a few weeks back. The head didn't hurt so much any more, the gash carved by Gunter's heavy rifle barrel had all but healed, and his hair was growing longer.

"I got lucky."

"Well, I've always put a mighty high value on luck. They catch the rowdies that waylaid you?"

"One was killed." He decided to test the name for a reaction. "Jasper Cross."

The rancher exhaled, shaking his head. "Never heard of him."

Another test. "He rode with Murt Jones."

This time, J. C. C. McBride removed the cigar, tapping ash to the ground, his eyes widening, his lips curling into a Texas grin. "Now, him I know. Chased that *hombre* many a time when he was raising Cain down in Texas and we was Those Who Always Follow Your Damned Comanche-Thieving Trails. You remember him, don't you, Ephraim?" He returned the cigar, chewing the end.

The agent's head bobbed. "A hard rock. But he'll answer to the law." Excusing himself, Rueben walked to the corral. Probably to get a receipt signed.

"Did you know a Thomas Benton?" Daniel asked.

Shaking his head, McBride took out the cigar and spit out a mouthful of saliva. "He another one of Murt's renegades?"

"No. White man living with the Creeks. He was killed a while back at Gibson Station."

"The Nations can be a wicked, woolly place." McBride puffed on the cigar.

"How about Senator Dawes?"

Again the cigar came out, and the rancher gave a quizzical stare. "You're full of questions today, Killstraight. Nope, I ain't had the pleasure of drawing a bead on Senator Dawes or any of those other jaspers who think they know what's best for us Westerners, and you Injuns." The smile faded. "You got a reason for this interview?"

Daniel shrugged. "I've been away for a long time. Dawes seems interested in what's going on in Indian Territory. Thomas Benton was interested in the senator's work."

Using his cigar as a pointer, McBride gestured toward the corral. "Best think a minute, boy, before you start some heathen dance and proclaim Dawes your savior. That beef you're about to eat? The government feeds you Comanches. Think your people can feed themselves? Ain't no buffalo left to speak of on the ranges. You Injuns got a good deal here. You carve up this land to homesteads, and all of the Comanches are gonna end up piss poor and starving. That what you want?"

He could see McBride's point. Maybe he even agreed with it, thinking about that Kwahadi boy he had locked up. Give that kid 160 acres and what would he do? Sell it for a bottle of Creek whiskey. Then what? He'd have no money, no land, just a thirst to get drunk, so he'd steal again, dishonor himself, disgrace The People. Daniel tried to match McBride's stare, but knew he couldn't. Instead, he tilted his head toward the corrals. "The government pays you for that beef, though," he said. "Good business for you."

McBride's stone face softened, and he laughed again, shaking his head at Daniel's persistence before sticking the cigar into his mouth. Through clenched teeth, he spoke. "Yeah. But not what Shad Carter'll get for the herd of mine he's driving to Dodge."

The agent had returned, folding a piece of paper into his coat pocket. Cotton Henry rode behind him, even though the distance from the corral to the building covered no more than twenty yards. Cowboys were like that. They'd ride a yard before they'd walk. So would most Comanches.

"Thank you, J.C.C." Rueben shook McBride's hand.

"I feed your Injuns out of the goodness of my heart," the rancher said, speaking to Daniel, not the agent.

On Sunday, he rode to rid himself of the stench of ration day, the cacophony of voices, the taste of dust and blood, the memories. He hated ration day, seeing some of The People turn into beggars, others trying to hold on to their traditions, their pride, watching the pale eyes look upon the scene with contempt.

He rode to visit Isa Nanaka.

It felt good to smoke the pipe with the warrior. Felt even better just to see his father's friend, alive, though looking so old, worn-out, so wasted from the lung sickness. It felt good to be away from the agency, here in the sacred Wichita Mountains, and felt good because here, visiting the warrior known as Wolf's Howl, he did not have to think about Jimmy Comes Last, a senator named Dawes, a murdered man and wife. Didn't have to think at all. Just watch, talk, and remember.

"I see your talent lies not only in making lances for The People," Daniel said lightly.

Toothlessly Isa Nanaka grinned, his gnarled, ancient fingers working on the leather. Old? How old was Isa Nanaka. Forty? Forty-five? Not really old, but he seemed like such a relic, flesh and organs ravaged by the disease, by the destruction of The People, by his time spent in the damp walls of Fort Marion in Florida. His smile was his only reply, and he kept working, tightening the leather on the wood.

Lances, coup sticks, bows, arrows. Weapons were important to The People, but Daniel knew of nothing as powerful as a warrior's *chimal*. The shield was everything, a blend of a warrior's *puha*, his protection, physically, and spiritually.

The leather came from buckskin—buffalo hide too scarce on the reservation, or anywhere else, these days—a rich color of the clay north of here, decorated with the drawings of talons. On the ground lay hawk feathers strung with sinew and bear claws, other paints, to be added later.

Grunting, then spitting, Isa Nanaka bent over and tore a book in half, spilling a few pages, and Daniel cringed as the warrior stuck the pages inside the tough hide. Long ago, The People had filled the insides of their shields with horsehair, but pale eyes paper worked well enough. A *chimal* wouldn't stop a bullet, but it might deflect an arrow.

"Does this destruction detest you?" Isa Nanaka asked without looking away from his project.

Daniel smiled back. He could picture School Father Pratt frothing like a mad wolf over Isa Nanaka's actions. Slowly Daniel picked up the pages that had fallen at his moccasins and handed them to his father's friend. "There are those among the pale eyes who believe in the power of the Bible," he said. "I guess I have lived with them too long."

"Then the power of this book might protect a warrior of The People."

Daniel looked at the page in his hand. He only managed to read a sentence before Isa Nanaka snatched the paper and shoved it inside the shield.

In the first year of Belshazzar, king of Babylon, Daniel had a dream and visions of his head upon his bed; then he wrote the dream, and told the sum of the matters.

"I am not a Christian," Isa Nanaka said. "I am Comanche."

"Can one not be both?" Daniel asked.

"Perhaps." He shook his head. "No, yes. The answer is not perhaps, but yes. Yet the true power lies in that of The People. How is your journey?"

"I am not sure."

"You have come far." Isa Nanaka's head bobbed, and he gave Daniel a look of satisfaction.

Yet Daniel remained skeptical. "I am not sure."

"Far. Not much farther to go." The warrior tilted his head, studying his work, found a *Farmer's Home Journal*, and began tearing its pages, stuffing them inside the shield. "I have done all that I can do for you," he said. "The rest you must find on your own. Come, we shall smoke again."

He bid farewell, mounted Skunk, and rode away from the Wichita Mountains, thinking about that passage from the Bible. Book of Daniel. Chapter Seven. Dropped intentionally by Isa Nanaka? Or by the pale eyes God? *Puha? Coincidence? Well,* he thought as he rode, *it's not like I can interpret any dreams, solve any crimes.*

Yet he rode not back toward Ben Buffalo Bone's, but south and east, giving Skunk his head, letting him lope, riding toward the mission school, and Randi Jordan. The churchgoers would be gone by the time he reached the mission, and he didn't know what he would ask her, what she could tell him about Senator Dawes and Thomas Benton. He'd lope for a while, then slow Skunk, thinking about Isa Nanaka, thinking about the shield, thinking about the Bible, and thinking how much he enjoyed riding a horse.

When he neared the mission road, he kicked Skunk into a trot, then gallop, and rode, smiling, into the mission yard, reining in at the sight of cowboys filing out of the mission school. Randi Jordan followed them, shielding her eyes from the dust.

"Hello, Daniel," Randi said after the dust had settled.

"Ma'am," he said, barely audible, fuming. *Every time I visit Randi, I find more drovers here than Indian children.*

"Kiowas chasin' you?" one of the cowhands said. Daniel remembered that one, a middle-aged fellow in a bowler, cleaning the lenses of his pince-nez glasses with the frayed ends of his calico bandanna. He had been with Cotton Henry and Shad Carter when Daniel had first visited the mission school with Ben Buffalo Bone. He couldn't remember the man's name. Likely the man had never introduced himself.

"He's Comanch'."

Daniel turned to the cowhand who had spoken. He knew this one. Wouldn't forget Cotton Henry, ever, not after watching Jimmy Comes Last hang.

"You mean he's the carpenter." The cowhand in the bowler set his glasses on his nose. "I remember him."

"Whatever he is, he's got a pretty fast horse," another one said, his voice a dare. "I'd say that hoss is faster than your chestnut, Cotton."

"Like he. . . ." Swallowing the oath, Cotton Henry cast an embarrassed glance toward Randi.

"Boys, boys, boys," an older cowhand said. "You boys be talkin' 'bout holdin' a hoss race, on the Sabbath." He clucked his tongue.

Every one of them turned to stare at Randi Jordan.

"Oh," she said, then giggled, trying to cover her mouth. "Well. I . . . well, I guess . . . as long as there is no wagering."

"Racin' for pride, ma'am," Pince-Nez said. "If the Injun carpenter don't show yeller."

"Now, behave yourselves," Randi scolded. "Daniel, you don't have to race Mister Henry if you don't want to." Her face warmed him. "I'm glad you came to visit. I've been thinking about you, wondering how you've been. I see your bandage is gone."

"I have been fine, ma'am." Skunk snorted, and Daniel patted his neck, and slid from the saddle, handing one of the cowhands the hackamore. "You get lots of visitors."

"On our way back to Texas," Cotton Henry explained. "Thought we might help the lady out, but she don't hold no truck to workin' on the Lord's day."

"It's a day of rest," she said.

"And runnin' horses," added the one who had started the dare.

"What distance?" Daniel asked, and one of the cowhands slapped his chaps, excited by the prospects of a horse race.

Cotton Henry had moved over to look at Skunk, and Daniel sought the chestnut. Looked like a good horse, and it hadn't been loping along in the afternoon sun all the way from the Wichitas. A tad under fifteen hands, short-coupled, lot of muscle, powerful legs.

"Well," the daring cowboy was saying, "I'd reckon if Chet can figger the distance, we'd try, maybe, two furlongs."

Quarter mile. Daniel knew Skunk, even on his best day, could never outrun the chestnut at that distance, or anything shorter. "I was thinking more about a mile."

"You ain't ridin' no thoroughbred, buck," another cowhand said. "And we ain't got all day. Need to swim the Red before full dark."

"Five furlongs," Daniel suggested.

"Can't do nothin' more than two," Cotton Henry said.

"Oh, come on," Pince-Nez said. "You got to haggle some, Cotton. Look at that Injun. I've seen hogs skinnier than he is. Chubby ol' pork chop like that, in some poor-looking saddle. If you and Livermore can't outrun him, you ought to cry."

"It's a pinto, by Gawd," the excited drover said, before quickly looking sheepishly at Randi, pulling off his hat, and apologizing. Cowboys, Daniel had heard, had a strong prejudice against paint horses. The People, on the other hand, knew better than to judge a horse on color.

"Three furlongs," the daring cowboy suggested.

Daniel was about to counter at three and a half when he saw the brand burned into the chestnut's hide, and his stomach soured.

It was the Circle 9.

Chapter Sixteen

"Killstraight, got a chore for you!"

Ephraim Rueben's voice made Daniel cringe, and he flipped through the pages of his writing tablet, which he had been reading in the shade, slid the tablet into a parfleche bag Ben Buffalo Bone's sister had given him to replace his battered war bag and old carpetbag. He pulled himself up.

The agent stood on the porch, smoking a cigar with another familiar face. J. C. C. McBride bit off the end of his cigar, spit, and grinned as Daniel approached the white men.

"Hear tell you ran roughshod over one of my boys," the rancher remarked.

Daniel answered with a nod, and waited, remembering.

It had been a pretty good race. Cotton Henry's chestnut Quarter horse had experience running; so did the rider. Over the cheers of the Bar TA Slash riders, Henry exploded to a quick lead, kicking up clouds of dust while Daniel fought the hackamore to keep Skunk under control. The paint horse wanted to run its heart out, but Daniel knew better. He let the cowhand rake his spurs, let the chestnut pull ahead, trying to ignore the laughter and taunts from the watching cowhands.

"Come on, Daniel!"

Well, at least one person cheered for him. He smiled at Randi Jordan's voice.

The cowhand in the eyeglasses had marked the course, down the path, through the little creek, circle the dead elm tree in the pasture, then sprint back to the road, crossing the finish line in front of the mission schoolhouse under construction. "That's a good four furlongs," Pince-Nez had said with a smirk. More like a tad over three, Daniel had thought, but he had agreed anyway.

By the time they reined their horses off the road and splashed across the creek, Henry's chestnut had shot out ahead by three lengths. Daniel couldn't hear the shouts now, just the blood rushing to his head, the pounding of hoofs, the wind blowing past his ears. He wished his father could have seen this. Marsh Hawk had loved racing horses almost as much as he had enjoyed stealing them.

Ahead of him, Henry spurred the chestnut ahead, circling the dead tree, but he made his turn too wide, and the horse stumbled in the thick earth. The cowhand knew how to ride, though. Daniel would concede that. *Pretty good horseman,* he thought. *No, a fine rider. Almost as though he was born in the saddle. Like The People.*

Cowhand and chestnut recovered, made the turn, kept charging. A lesser rider might have fallen. An average horseman would have lost much ground, but Henry rounded the tree still leading Daniel by two lengths. They were already crossing the shallow creek when Daniel made his turn, keeping Skunk close, never losing much stride.

Cheers sounded again in his head, and he saw the crowd waiting in the distance. Randi Jordan clasped her hands, jumping up and down like a schoolgirl. Cotton Henry was whipping the chestnut with his reins, still digging his spurs.

"Nabohcutz, you are the wind," Daniel whispered in Comanche as he leaned forward, and gave the gelding his head.

He laughed as the horse lunged, loving the feel, the sound, his heart racing. Skunk closed in rapidly, and at least one of the cowboys had forgotten about Randi's presence and began swearing wildly. So was Cotton Henry, only quietly, pounding the chestnut as Skunk pulled even with the cow pony. Daniel's smile vanished. He might have waited too long. He focused on the road, the mission school, heard Randi's shouts. A moment later, they crossed the finish line.

"Hear tell there was almost a fight," the rancher said now as he fired up his cigar.

Daniel shrugged. There might have been a fight, had Randi not been there. A few of the cowhands argued over the outcome, and even Daniel had to admit it had been close, although he felt pretty sure he had won by a nose.

"Daniel did it!" Randi had shouted, and hugged him tightly after he slid off Skunk. Suddenly embarrassed, he had let Skunk tug him away from the young woman.

"No!" one of the cowboys had said. "Ain't no way. . . ."

"He won," Randi had insisted. "It was close. My gosh!" She had to catch her breath. "I've never seen such a race."

"Well, I say the Injun didn't win," Pince-Nez had argued. "No. Not some red nigger on a blame pinto!"

It was Cotton Henry who had ended the argument. Thinking back, Daniel now realized the cowhand, not Randi Jordan, had stopped any fight.

"The Comanche won," Henry had said. "And watch your language, Peavy." Henry's voice suddenly lost its edge, and, exhaling, he turned toward Daniel while forcing a smile. "Good race," he had said, and started to offer his hand, but couldn't quite go through with it.

"Got lucky," Daniel now told McBride, which is what he had told Cotton Henry, too.

McBride turned toward the agent. "Ought to have fired the boy." Daniel couldn't tell if the rancher were joking. "I don't like losing."

"You did not lose," Daniel said, and waited for both of the pale eyes to remove their cigars and stare. "You sold the horse to the agency. It was your horse I rode."

Shaking his head, McBride guffawed so hard he almost sent his cigar into the dirt. "Killstraight," he said when he had recovered, "I could almost grow to like you, even if you is Comanch'."

No, you couldn't, Daniel thought. He faced Rueben. "You need me, sir?"

Yet McBride wasn't about to be dismissed. "What was you doing down yonder, Killstraight? You ain't sweet on that church lady, is you?"

"Just riding," Daniel answered.

"I got some beef grazing down that way."

"You have much cattle grazing," Daniel agreed.

"But I pay." There was a challenge in his voice, which Daniel didn't understand.

"I know that," he answered hesitantly.

"But you been asking a lot of questions. Asked that girl at the mission. Asked Ephraim here. Asked me. Only you haven't asked me none today."

"All right," Daniel said. "The horse your man Cotton Henry rode, the one that I raced, and beat, it was wearing a Circle Nine brand. All the other horses . . . I checked them . . . carried the Bar TA Slash of your cows."

"So?"

He waited, trying to form the question, unsure how much to reveal, and at last decided to empty his gut. "When we brought Jimmy Comes Last home to be buried, Naséca, his mother, killed a horse at his grave."

"Damn' waste." Rueben spit. "I don't know why you people think you have to do that."

"It is our way," Daniel said, keeping his eyes on McBride. "A few days ago, I came to Jimmy's grave. There was not much left of the horse after all this time, but I found some bones, some hide and hair, and I found a piece of hide that had been branded with the Circle Nine."

"Do you have that piece of evidence?" McBride asked, his voice accented with sarcasm.

Daniel blinked, nervous. "No." He felt stupid. He hadn't considered it evidence, hadn't considered it anything, not really, not until he had seen the same brand on Henry's chestnut.

McBride laughed. "Hell, what makes you sure it was the Circle Nine? For all you know, if it was just a hunk of hide, it could have been the Circle Six, ain't that right?"

Daniel couldn't answer. "Either brand mean a thing to you?" he asked.

The rancher shook his head.

"A dead horse, a brand, what do they have to do with anything?" Rueben pitched his cigar on the ground, didn't bother crushing it out with his boot heel. "What does that dead Indian have to do with anything? He killed two people and was hanged for it. He was a drunk. Worthless."

"Then why did you hire him as a Metal Shirt?" Daniel asked bitterly.

"Don't take that tone with me, Killstraight. Don't you ever sass me, boy, or you'll rue the day. You're a snot-nosed Comanche kid, fresh from Pratt's school. You've seen the type of policemen I'm forced to hire. There are mighty slim pickings on this reserve, young man. I do the best I can with what I can get. And why are you so interested in a dead murderer?"

"I don't think he killed anyone," Daniel shot back, and let the silence fill the afternoon.

"How's that?" Rueben finally asked.

Daniel took a deep breath, exhaled, shuffled his feet, and answered. "I talked to a doctor at Gibson Station," he said. "When I was laid up after that Murt Jones affair." Another breath, holding it, hesitating. He had to finish, though, had to tell them everything. "The doctor examined the dead bodies. The woman . . . well . . . it is not the way of The People to touch a woman when she is . . . that way."

"Like hell." McBride's words came out savagely, and he flung the cigar past Daniel's ear. "You're forgetting, boy, forgetting that I was trying to stay alive in Texas long before you bucks gave up and let the U.S. government wet-nurse you. Maybe you're too young to remember the old ways. But I buried many women, butchered by the likes of you murdering Comanch', seen pals hacked to pieces, homes burnt, men scalped, friends I couldn't recognize after what all had been done to them. I buried . . ." Abruptly he stopped, regained some composure, and shook his head. "A Comanch' would ravage anyone, anytime. From what I've seen. As a rancher. As a Ranger. As a Texian."

Slowly Daniel's head shook. "It is taboo. Jimmy would not have done that."

"He did anything," Rueben interjected, "for whiskey."

"It is not our way," Daniel repeated.

"Well, he's dead, ain't he?" McBride laughed. He stepped off the porch and tapped the badge pinned on Daniel's shirt. "You taking that chunk of tin a little far, ain't you, Killstraight? You're a Metal Shirt boy. You ain't no solicitor, no Pinkerton man."

"He's right," Rueben said. "You have a theory, maybe a brand. And the brand, well, what does it prove? Jimmy Comes Last could have stolen the horse. Could have traded for it, or bought it. Besides, what does a brand have to do with two dead people at Gibson Station? I'll tell you what . . . nothing. Not one damn' thing. What else do you have?"

"Other than two dead Indians and a trouble-maker?" McBride added acidly.

"A promise," Daniel said softly.

"What's that?" both men asked.

"Nothing," Daniel said, which was exactly what he had. Nothing. No evidence. Nothing to go on. "What can you tell me about the brand on Cotton Henry's horse?" he asked.

"You'd have to ask him," McBride said, and headed to his horse. "I got better things to do than go around reading the brands on the mounts my boys ride."

They watched him ride off, toward the Camp Supply Road, and Daniel faced the agent once more. "You need me, sir?" he asked.

* * *

East of the Cache Creek confluence, Skunk's hoofs *clopped* along the old path that meandered beside the Red River's overgrown banks. The air felt stifling, and he had seen nothing since noon, except horseflies, wasps, and mosquitoes. Too hot for anything else. Sweat glued the shirt to his back, his bangs to his forehead.

No one would be out. Not in this furnace. Not even Creek whiskey-runners, which is why Agent Rueben had sent him down here.

Yet riding, sweating and bored, at least he wasn't doing one of Rueben's chores, repairing the roof, raking the yard, learning how to shoe horses like a pale eyes. He had time to think. Think and sweat. That's about all one could do.

What did he have, for evidence? Nothing. Even if he had evidence, what did it prove? Daniel had no theory, no idea. The Bentons had been butchered, and Jimmy Comes Last had hanged for the crime, hadn't even denied his guilt. A drunk, Rueben had called him, and that's what he was, Daniel reluctantly admitted. Like that Kwahadi kid he had arrested at Sergeant Sitting Still's lodge. He could easily picture Jimmy in the boy's place. Drunk, violent, angry. Picking up the singletree and trying to kill anyone who'd dare empty his whiskey bottle.

Sitting up a little straighter, Daniel wiped the sweat off his brow, trying to picture the Kwahadi boy, recalling everything, every blade of grass. The boy had been singing, drunkenly sitting in front of the teepee's flap, trapping Sergeant Sitting Still's wife and children inside. Daniel had dismounted, tried to talk to the boy, but the kid was so . . . roostered, the pale eyes would have called it . . . he heard nothing. Just sat, swaying, singing some song until Daniel found the bottle and emptied the remaining swallows. Rage consumed the kid, and Daniel had nearly gotten his skull bashed in.

"By a singletree," he said to himself, wishing he had brought the Old Glory writing tablet with him. "What was he doing with a singletree?" Daniel rubbed his jaw. He had seen no wagon, but now he remembered harness hanging in the brush arbor near the sergeant's lodge. He thought back to the butchered beef in the pasture from so long ago, the wagon tracks pointing north. Hadn't it been the sergeant who refused to stop and look for the revolver the free grazer had dropped? He'd have to check his notes when he got back home.

The drunk boy was Kwahadi. Sitting Still was Kotsoteka, same as Ben Buffalo Bone, same as many Comanches on the reservation. Why would a Kwahadi kid plant himself in front of a Kotsoteka lodge?

Slumping forward, he tried to come up with some premise, losing himself in the heat and in his suspicions.

A hawk's cry pierced the sky, and Daniel shot upright in the saddle, searching for the raptor, feeling the *buzz* of the bullet that sang past his nose just as the gunshot registered. He fell backward, somersaulting over Skunk's back as his horse charged forward. Daniel landed hard, rolled, heard a second shot, tasted dirt that the bullet kicked into his mouth. Grabbing for the Remington, he pulled himself to his knees and dived through briars and brambles, forcing himself partway down the embankment.

Another shot. Followed by two more and a pale eyes curse. Only not at him. Hoofs beat down the road, and Daniel knew. They weren't shooting at him now, but at Skunk.

"You sons of bitches!" he screamed, fighting his way through the thick growth, not even bothering to aim as he fired. He pulled the trigger, felt the sting and heat of the weapon. He couldn't hit anyone, but didn't care. The bullets would make whoever it was shooting at him keep his head down. Or heads down. How many were out there?

He glanced down the road. Skunk had rounded the bend. Safe. He yelled at his horse, told Skunk to keep running, then ducked as a bullet clipped a branch above his head.

Now what?

He slid as bullets ripped through the brush. More than one man, that was for certain. His arms bled from the thorns, and sweat flowed into the wounds like acid. He was running now, or trying to, fighting through brush, chopping at vines and greenery as if the Remington were a machete. A bullet tugged at his collar, and a second later he felt himself falling, turning, dropping the final six feet.

The monstrous Red River rushed up to slam into him, then swallowed him whole.

Chapter Seventeen

He woke to croaking bullfrogs and soft, gurgling water, to the putrid smell of decaying plants and Red River mud.

Something hard pressed against his right arm, and he gripped a heavy, cold, wet object in his fist. A raven *cawed*. The air still felt hot, but his legs were freezing. Once he wiped hair, leaves, and water from his eyes, he saw the driftwood, part of a tree that he vaguely recalled grabbing after plunging into the swift-flowing river. He lifted his arm, still clutching the heavy weight, and realized it was his Remington. Stupid. He had never let go. Might have drowned. Probably would have drowned if he hadn't somehow managed to grab the tree trunk as it rifled downstream. Drowned, or been shot dead by those assassins.

Daniel pulled his legs out of the water. It was getting late in the afternoon. The banks here were not so dense, not so steep. Wherever here was. Sitting up, he examined the revolver. Useless now. The paper cartridges of that antiquated weapon had to be soaked through, if he hadn't fired all five rounds. He couldn't remember. Dipping the pistol in the river, washing off the mud and leaves, he tried to figure out his next move.

Were the men still chasing him?

Who were they?

Why did someone want him dead?

He had been back on the reservation for a few months, and during that time he had been shot at three times. By free grazers, by Murt Jones and his gang of cutthroats, and by whoever had tried to kill him on the river road. The first time he could understand. Texas cowboys fleeing the law. Maybe he could find some reasoning to the ambush in the Choctaw Nation where a desperado might kill a man for the gold in his fillings. But this time? These men were after him, wanted him dead, had even sent a few shots after his horse when Skunk galloped away in fright. That meant they weren't after his horse, weren't horse thieves, but were out to make sure the horse didn't attract the attention of some passerby.

Daniel rose, weaving, shoving the dripping revolver into his holster, brushing the sticks and mud out of his hair. Thinking of his horse, he called out Skunk's name in Comanche, waited, nervous, and tried it again, louder this time.

"Nabohcutz?"

Nothing.

Slowly he climbed up the bank, slipping on the wet leaves once, then trying again. He *squeaked* as he walked. Reaching the top, he leaned against a small tree to rest, gather his bearings, look around, think.

Maybe those assassins had been jealous Bar TA Slash cowboys. Maybe they were shooting at Skunk, angry because the paint horse had showed up Cotton Henry's chestnut. No. Too thin. Besides, that first shot had been meant for Daniel, as had several more. So maybe the cowhands wanted to kill Daniel. Get even for the horse race. No. Cotton Henry and that crowd back at the mission school didn't strike him as murderers. Besides, thirty-a-month cowhands typically didn't resort to killing horses, or even Comanches.

He looked down at the river again, then said: "Shit." It was the choice curse word of miners and farmers in Pennsylvania. Once, he had even heard one of the Carlisle school mothers use it.

"The river. . . ."

He stood on the wrong side. He was in Texas.

Not that he could do anything about it. Swimming was a talent he had never truly mastered. So he walked, hoping he was going in the right direction.

The sunburned gent with the tobacco-streaked gray beard at Hill's Ferry eyed him suspiciously, but took him across the river without making him pay the nickel fare. Maybe because of the badge pinned to his shirt. Maybe because he had already had a paying customer in a medicine show wagon. Maybe because, like most Texians, he'd rather have a Comanche on the north side of the river than down here.

Neither the slick-haired grafter in the claret-colored brocade vest nor his short Negro driver offered Daniel a ride once they reached Indian Territory—they avoided looking at him, in fact—and soon two jennies had pulled the wagon and its riders out of sight.

Daniel walked.

The sun set.

He kept moving, thinking, wishing he had that Old Glory tablet so he could jot down his thoughts.

Later, when moon and exhaustion began to rise, he left the road, and found a small sinkhole, dry but not too rocky, which would serve as a bed and hiding place. He still worried about the men who had way-laid him, although he had to figure they had given up the chase by now. Maybe they thought he had drowned.

He didn't sleep well.

Voices sang out, loud, not quite in time with the pi-ano, sang out with the enthusiasm he had heard at the pale eyes' churches. It didn't surprise Daniel. The People loved to sing, even if he doubted that the children understood the pale eyes' words.

This for sin could not atone,
Thou must save and Thou alone;
In my hand no price I bring,
Simply to Thy cross I cling.

He reached the mission church before Randi Jordan directed about three dozen Indian youngsters—Comanche, Apache, and Kiowa—to the last verse.

While I draw this fleeting breath,
When mine eyelids close in death,
When I rise to worlds un. . . .

Randi, who had been singing with her students, dropped her hands and stared. She choked off the last word syllable, "known."

The children turned quickly, and one Kiowa girl gasped at the creature blocking the doorway, left open to cause a draft.

Caked in dust, already sweating from the after-noon heat, Daniel realized he must look like some monster after walking all morning, but a Comanche boy—one of Twice Bent Nose's teenage sons—recognized the man.

"It is Killstraight," he said, and laughed. "Where is your horse? Ha!"

Others joined Twice Bent Nose's boy's laughter.

Running his fingers through his knotted hair, Daniel managed a smile as he wearily staggered into the coolness of the church. Pinned on the wall was a newspaper clipping from the *Globe-Democrat*, about Randi's father, and another, shorter, article from some other newspaper. He didn't stop to read them. He had worn a hole through one of the soles of his moccasins, and a pebble kept tormenting his heel. He sat on the back pew and massaged both feet.

"I did not mean to startle you," he said, keeping his eyes on Randi Jordan. "Did not mean to interrupt."

She had recovered, closing the hymnal, Bible, whatever book she held in her hand, and moved toward him, telling a Kiowa boy to fetch water.

"What on earth happened to you, Daniel?" she asked. "Where is your horse? You didn't walk all the way from . . . ? Are you hurt?"

"He come to see you, Miss Randi!" an Apache girl said, prompting a chorus of snickers, before a Penateka girl teased: "Soon, he will bring his flute and play songs for you."

"Children, go out and play!" Her face flushed, Randi Jordan looked as embarrassed as Daniel felt.

Screaming—Indian children weren't that much different than others he had seen—the class stampeded through the open doors, leaving Daniel working to dislodge the pebble in his moccasin, and

Randi Jordan staring at the floors while wringing her hands.

The chore boy ran back inside, handed Daniel a ladle of water, most of which had sloshed onto the floor between the well bucket and Daniel's pew, and shot out a question: "Me go play, too?"

"Yes," Randi said, and the boy vanished.

"What happened?" she asked.

It took him fifteen minutes to tell the story, the most he could remember talking since his childhood on the Llano Estacado. She looked at him the entire time he talked with those penetrating eyes, sad, he thought, concerned, lovely.

"You think this has something to do with the murder of Mister Benton," she said when he had finished. It wasn't a question.

"I think it has something to do with Mister Rueben," he answered.

She sat straighter. "The agent?"

Daniel nodded. He hadn't meant to toss his opinion out in the open, but the more he had thought about all the events since he had come home, the more Ephraim Rueben kept popping up in his mind. Agent Rueben had sent him chasing the free grazers. Agent Rueben had sent him to escort the prisoners to Fort Smith. Agent Rueben had sent him to the Red River. Sent him . . . to be killed?

"But why?"

Instead of replying, he had a question of his own. "What was Benton, the Creek squawman . . . why was he here? How did he know you?"

Tilting her head, she seemed to consider him differently, wondering about him. "He. . . ." She hesitated.

"It had something to do with Senator Dawes. Evidence. That's what he said. Showing how the Indians were being mistreated, misled. Malfeasance, he called it. Cheating. Cheating you Indians."

You Indians. He couldn't stop his shoulders from sagging at her choice of words. Words like a bridge. Or no bridge, washed away, separating them. White and red.

"But Mister Benton was killed by a Comanche," she said.

A nod.

"It makes no sense."

A shrug. Hearing the hoofbeats, he rose, moving gingerly but quickly to the doorway. Through the dust, he made out the horses first, next a couple of the riders, and slowly exhaled. He hadn't realized he had been holding his breath. Relieved, Daniel walked outside and held up his hand in greeting.

"*Bávi!*" Daniel called out to Ben Buffalo Bone in Comanche. "It is good to see you."

"My brother, it is good to see you, too." A grin cracked his friend's sweaty, dirty face. "But it hurts my pride to see my brother walking our land like some *janibaraibo.*"

"I am not a farmer," Daniel said.

"But you have no horse, *bávi.*" His eyes twinkled. "Surely, you, a Metal Shirt for The People, surely you did not lose your horse."

Daniel glanced at the children, all staring, mouths open. He felt Randi's presence behind him. Finally he walked to Ben Buffalo Bone, rubbing the horse's neck, then moved down to the paint horse his friend pulled behind him. Seeing Skunk, alive, pleased him almost as much as seeing Comanches. Skunk nuzzled him.

"It is good to see you, too," he whispered to the horse. "This is a good animal," Daniel told Ben Buffalo Bone. "I will take him."

"Be careful," Twice Bent Nose said lightly. "You might get tossed off . . . again."

"I was shot at on the Red River," Daniel told them, and the faces of his companions hardened. "Yesterday. Skunk got away."

"He came to our lodge yesterday evening," Ben Buffalo Bone said, sliding from the saddle. "Truly I worried about you. But I thought you might have been thrown, not ambushed."

"You have . . ."—Twice Bent Nose struggled, searching his memories—"what . . . what the pale eyes call . . . a . . . knack . . . for getting shot at."

Nodding, Daniel turned back to Randi. "It is all right," he said in English. "I will go home with my friends. Thank you for your kindness."

"Be careful," she said, forgetting her manners, not asking if Daniel's rescuers wanted water. Clapping her hands, she called for the children to come back inside, and their voices sang out in some hymn by the time the three Comanche policemen were riding down the path to the main road.

The aroma of broiled beef reminded him that he hadn't eaten in . . . when? He couldn't remember having anything but a drink of water at the mission school, not even food on the ride home. They rode into Ben Buffalo Bone's lodge late that afternoon, and Daniel's eyes widened at the sight of old Naséca, squatting in front of the cook fire, instructing Ben Buffalo Bone's sister on the art of cooking *pimoró*. She stood instantly, and ran toward Daniel, crying in Comanche that he was alive, that they—everyone—had feared him dead. Tears streamed down her face, and she gripped his hand. The strength of her grip surprised him.

Other members of Ben Buffalo Bone's family filed out of the lodge.

"What happened?" asked Rain Shower, Ben's oldest sister. She had altered Daniel's moccasins, originally made for Naséca's son, to make them fit. He hated to tell her she'd need to repair them again.

"It is a story only he can tell!" Twice Bent Nose called out. "And he will tell it. He fought a giant monster in the big river, killing it with his own hands, then crawled out of the mud and slime and found a white buffalo. He rode the white buffalo across the river, then the white buffalo offered him his liver, and he ate it, raw. He counted many coup. Took many scalps. Bedded many women. Hear me! We will sing his songs and feast tonight. It will be like the old days!"

His stomach stuffed from beef, corn, and pale eyes coffee, he moved from the fire, where Twice Bent Nose was telling another lie. He hadn't known what to think of Twice Bent Nose at first, thought he might be more like Sergeant Sitting Still than Ben Buffalo Bone or Isa Nanaka, but the Metal Shirt was truly one of The People.

No one tried to stop Daniel as he slowly walked toward the building that served as a barn and his home. They knew he was tired, and the children knew no one could tell a story like Twice Bent Nose.

Inside, a full moon shone directly on the shield hanging on the wall near his bedroll. Daniel stopped, staring at it, amazed, wondering, remembering.

It was the shield Isa Nanaka had been working on.

Tentatively Daniel touched it, his fingers gently tracing the buckskin, brushing the hawk feathers and bear claws that decorated the weapon, its guts, Daniel remembered, stuffed with the pages of the Bible, the pale eyes power. Drawings of talons covered the shield, and Daniel, suddenly remembering, choked out a sob, and felt a tear dart down his cheek.

His father had carried a *chimal* much like this one.

"No one will ever have Isa Nanaka's way."

Daniel turned, wiping his eyes, and waited for Naséca to step closer. Hesitantly she held out her hand, and touched the shield as if she thought it might burn her fingers. "He is a master, an artist, the last of The People who know the old ways."

"My father...." Daniel paused, hoping for strength. A horse stalled nearby whinnied. "He carried a *chimal* like this one."

"I remember. The man of whom you speak never forgot the ways of The People, either." She turned. "You should learn the ways from Isa Nanaka, before he goes to The Land Beyond The Sun."

"I have not such a gift," Daniel confessed.

"My son did before...." She looked down at her dirty moccasins. "Isa Nanaka tried to teach him the way."

Even before she had finished talking, she was running, fleeing the pale eyes house, fleeing the fire and the moon and Twice Bent Nose's lies, leaving Daniel alone with a beautiful shield and no answers for all the questions in the Old Glory tablet beside his bedroll.

Chapter Eighteen

The next morning, Ephraim Rueben rubbed his beard and stared while Daniel told him all that had happened along the Red River. Once Daniel had finished, the agent shook his head, incredulously, struck a match, and started to light his pipe, pulling the Lucifer away at the last moment and shaking it out.

"You didn't see these men, those who shot at you?"

"No, sir."

"And no one else saw this savage ambuscade?"

His head shook. "I was alone."

"Not much to go on." He struck another match. "I'm glad you're alive, Killstraight. But this whole thing is perplexing."

He waited till the agent put the match on the pipe tobacco, then said: "But I heard that name again."

The match pulled away from the pipe, and Rueben's head jerked up. "What name?"

"Murt."

They stared at each other until the flame burned Rueben's finger, and he cursed, tossed the match away, and rose. "Murt . . . are you sure, Killstraight?"

"Yes, sir. There were at least two men. One of them yelled something about Murt. Right before I hit the river."

"Murt . . . Murt Jones." Rueben looked as if he had been poleaxed.

"I reckon so. Twice I've heard that name when

someone was shooting at me. Odd. I'd never heard of Murt Jones till I came back home."

Daniel studied the agent. Of course, he had heard no such thing along the Red River. Hadn't heard a thing over the roar of rifle fire and horse hoofs. He wasn't used to telling a lie, wasn't sure he could pull it off, but the agent seemed to accept it. Daniel spoke again. "I thought Murt Jones operated mainly in Choctaw and Creek country . . . since you Rangers chased him out of Texas." He had to say it again before the agent looked up.

"He has been seen, or allegedly seen, in Kansas. Caldwell. Wichita. Places like that. And over in Missouri. Saint Louis, mostly." Finally the agent got his pipe lit. " 'Course," he said, recovering, "if you only heard that one name, Murt, it could have been someone else. Maybe Murt Smith." The agent smiled at his humor.

"Perhaps," Daniel said, stone-faced.

"I'll write up your report, send letters to Wichita Falls and Fort Smith. If Murt Jones is operating in this area, the law should know."

When Daniel left the agent's cabin, he didn't know if he had accomplished anything. Learned anything? Not really. Murt Jones on the reservation made Rueben nervous. Well, it made Daniel nervous, too. It would make most people nervous. And, really, what would a man like Murt Jones be doing this far west of his stomping grounds? Why would Murt Jones want Daniel dead? Daniel kicked a clod of dirt, shaking his head, muttering a pale eyes curse. His charade, chicanery, falsehood, whatever you wanted to call it, had been pointless. Agent Rueben had not revealed his hand, likely had no cards to show. Maybe those attacks had been random.

Maybe he was just unlucky. He had never had much luck to begin with. Well, at least he was alive, which was more than Tach, William Barking Dog, or Beats His Horse could claim.

Or Jimmy Comes Last.

He spent the next few weeks digging a ditch, and doing other mundane chores, reading the notes in his Old Glory tablet when he had a moment, trying to find something he had overlooked, something that might suddenly make sense.

A few days before ration day, he found himself riding north to solve another pointless dispute over a horse between two Kotosekas. By the time he got back, a surrey sat out front of the agency headquarters, and Randi Jordan and Ephraim Rueben stood under the shade of an elm, talking.

Pretending he hadn't noticed the agent's visitor, he turned Skunk out in the corral, and washed his face in the trough.

"Daniel!"

He heard her footsteps, and straightened, patting his face dry, watching her walk toward him. From the corner of the cabin, Rueben stared through the pipe smoke. "I was looking for you," Randi said.

"How are you?" He couldn't think of anything else.

"I'm fine."

A long pause followed, neither knowing what to say. Rueben tapped his pipe against the wall, and went back inside.

"I feel . . . ," she began. "I guess . . . I must have acted rather curt with you the last time you were at the school. I mean. . . ." She sighed, shook her head. "I don't know what I mean."

He grinned. "I know that feeling."

"Tom stopped by the mission often before. . . ." She looked up. "Thomas Benton. Before he was killed. I . . . I . . . I never knew he had a wife at Gibson Station."

Such information made him uncomfortable. He didn't need to know this. Or did he?

"He seemed devoted to the cause of you Indians."

You Indians. There it was again. Maybe she didn't know better.

"I don't know," she said, speaking rapidly. "I thought at first I liked him. But I don't know much about men. And I don't know much about what he wanted to find."

Now Daniel was interested. "He never talked about his work?"

Her head shook fast. "No. Just what I've told you. But . . . the last time I saw him, he was happy." Her head dropped. "Well, he was in his cups. I didn't know he drank intoxicating spirits. Not until then. He said he had found what he needed. Up north." She lifted her head. Tears filled her eyes. "That's all he said. Up north. I thought you should know."

He apologized for bringing up bad memories. Perhaps The People's way was best. You didn't speak of the dead, didn't bring up those remembrances, didn't invite the ghosts to torment you.

"It's best to get these things out in the open," she said. "Tom Benton was . . . wasn't . . . well, never mind. Water under the bridge."

"Up north." Daniel tested the words. *North? Where? North of the mission school? North into the Wichita Agency? At the Cheyenne or Arapaho encampments? Fort Reno or Camp Supply? Kansas?*

"That's all Tom said. Thomas, I mean. Mister Benton."

"Thanks for telling me this," Daniel said. He made himself smile. "It is good to see you."

She turned, walking to the surrey, stopped, faced him again. The tears were gone. "Good luck, Daniel."

He thought about her as he rode back home, thought about her when Ben Buffalo Bone's sister asked him if he needed anything, and, when he didn't respond, Ben's sister told him: "You think of only that white woman."

Daniel studied Rain Shower, unable to speak.

"Maybe you should speak to the big man from Washington," she said.

She was a lovely girl, hair the color of a raven's wing, parted in the middle, dark eyebrows, round face. Yellow paint below her lids highlighted her black eyes, and she had painted reddish-orange circles on her cheeks. Heavy bracelets of copper with red and yellow stones adorned her wrists, and a bone necklace decorated with German silver crosses fell between the outline of her small breasts against the yellow buckskin dress she wore. He hadn't really noticed her before. A handsome girl. No . . . a woman.

"What big man?" he asked.

"Dawes."

Forcing a smile, he shook his head. "Not much chance of that."

"Yes," she said, "there is. He's visiting Quanah this afternoon. At the Star House."

Henry L. Dawes looked like a senator, and even over the aroma of Comanche pipe smoke, he smelled of power. Sitting in one of Quanah's leather chairs, he wore a handsome suit of black wool, silk bow tie perfectly knotted, and a fine white shirt. His eyes were set close to a prominent nose, gray hair thinning on the top of his head, a strong gray mustache and beard, well-groomed, much thicker than the rest of his hair. He didn't seem to sweat, didn't have a speck of dust on him. He shook Daniel's hand forcefully, his eyes afire, energetic, and he had to be sixty, if not seventy, years old.

"I am sorry to interrupt," Daniel said in English, but the senator waved off his apology.

"Nonsense," he said in a Massachusetts whine. "Nonsense. Quanah and I had finished our conversation, and I am sick of talking politics, sick of hearing those blasted Democrats bemoan me as an Indian lover. The General Allotment Act will pass, gentlemen. It must pass. For the sake of all Indians. It will free you from corruption, from the white man's grip."

For better than a decade, Dawes had been in the Senate, and before that he had served eighteen years in the House of Representatives. He had been an Abolitionist, a firm believer in Reconstruction, had helped develop daily weather reports, and, since joining the Senate, had served as chairman of the Committee on Indian Affairs.

Although his heart was good, Daniel still didn't know if Dawes's plan would work, would benefit The People. But he knew nothing of politics. He didn't know much more about police work.

When Dawes had finished his speech—Daniel came to believe that the senator never really tired of talking politics—he opened a silver case, brought out three cigars, and passed them around. Once the senator was smoking, he leaned back in the chair in Quanah's office and asked: "Now, what can I do for you, young man?"

Daniel set the cigar on the table, unlit, and glanced at some of the notes he had written in the tablet.

"Are you a newspaper reporter?" Dawes asked. "They have a paper, you know, in the Cherokee Nation."

"No, sir. I am a policeman." He tapped his badge with the pencil.

"I see."

He didn't know where to begin. "Have you ever heard of . . . ?"

"You're not investigating me, are you, lad, for some crime?"

Daniel looked up, his throat dry until he saw the twinkle in the lawmaker's eyes. He smiled. "No, sir. Nothing like that. Have you ever heard of a man named Murt Jones?"

"No. No, I haven't."

He didn't think Dawes would have.

"Bad man," Quanah said. "Pale eyes. Bad man. *Muy mal.*"

"Probably not as bad as some men I've had to work with in Washington City, gentlemen."

"Have you ever heard of a Thomas Benton? Or Tom Benton?"

"Him I know." The senator nodded, taking out his cigar for a moment. His verbosity had suddenly evaporated.

"Creek," Quanah said. "Squawman."

"Yes." Dawes drew hard on the cigar.

"I have been told that this Benton was working with you. That he wanted to clean up the reservation."

The senator blew a cloud of smoke toward a mounted deer's head. "Who told you that?"

Daniel tried to remember. "I have heard it . . . often. From many."

Dawes shook his head. "Benton was not working for me."

"But. . . ."

A raised hand stopped Daniel from interruption.

"He was not a man in my employ. I found him to be an unsavory boor. A lout. Not a pleasant man. Oh, perhaps he was interested in his wife's people, the Creeks, perhaps he was interested in ridding the reservation of free grazers, of horse thieves, of whiskey-runners, and when I met him . . . just once, mind you, at that mission school of yours . . . he certainly asked a lot about my work. But I don't think Benton was interested in anything or anyone other than himself."

Daniel stopped writing. Now what? Where? He tried to form a question, but couldn't think of anything to ask. He had always pictured Thomas Benton as the hero, a white man gone Injun, as the *taibos* might say, and had been murdered for helping The People, the Creeks, the Cherokees, Kiowas—all tribes confined to Indian Territory.

"Do you know the Comanche agent?"

"Your English is quite remarkable, young man. I visited the school down at Hampton once, where the Negro and the Indian are being educated, but have not gone to Captain Pratt's school in Pennsylvania. Perhaps I shall, especially if the students are as refined as you are. You are a credit to your race. You will help your people. I applaud you, sir."

Quanah nodded. Daniel repeated his question.

"The current one?" Dawes tapped away ash from the cigar. "This agency tends to go through agents rather rapidly. Many of them are kicked out for mal-feasance. Yes, I have met Ephraim Rueben four times, if memory serves. Twice in Washington. Another interview at the agency here. Once, briefly, by hap-penstance in Wichita, Kansas. I don't know him well. I hope he is not corrupt as the other agents have been. But I hope, nay, I promise, that I will find justice for your people. You will not be under the thumb of our government. You will be free. And this blight of a reservation system will be relegated to the pages of tragic history."

When Dawes halted his speech for a taste of to-bacco, Daniel took advantage of the opening. "Ben-ton was after free grazers, I believe." He stopped. Free grazers. Up north, Randi Jordan had said. His head snapped toward Quanah, and he asked in Co-manche: "Who leases the pastures north? North, be-tween Fort Sill and the Wichita Agency?"

Quanah laid his cigar on his ashtray. "We lease to two ranchers. Others sometimes pay a tribute to graze while passing through this country," he said. "The ranchers are McBride and Tompkins, Jeddah Tompkins. McBride leases pastures just across the Red River. Mister Tompkins leases our large pasture for two thousand head north of West Cache Creek. This Tompkins, he is the only one north. Our other pastures are for The People."

"Is Mister Tompkins's brand the Circle Nine?" Another thought popped into his head. "Or the Lazy B?"

Quanah shrugged. "He is a big rancher," he re-plied. "He marks his cattle many ways."

Chapter Nineteen

He found the cattle grazing along the endless expanse of plain toward the northwest corner of the reservation. Daniel assumed these cattle—white-faced, big animals, with short horns and reddish coats—belonged to Jeddah Tompkins. They bawled noisily, more skittish than longhorns, but fatter, like a baby buffalo. He pulled on the hackamore, halting Skunk, and reached inside the parfleche he carried, withdrawing the Old Glory tablet. From the top of his ear, he withdrew his pencil—a carpenter at Carlisle had taught him that trick—and wrote down the brand.

Rafter T.

He felt disappointed. A Circle 9 would have given him something to work on, but Quanah had told him Tompkins had many cattle, many brands, so he kept riding and jotting down the brands on the paper. Most of them were Rafter T. Others carried the Diamond J Bar. Some had some design he couldn't read, but did his best to copy on the tablet despite the wind. Other brands looked blotched. No Circle 9, though. No Lazy B.

He shoved the tablet into the parfleche, closed the lid, and chewed on the pencil. What was he doing here anyway? Pretending he was a peace officer, chasing clues he wouldn't know the meaning of even if he found something. Pretending he was Kwahadi

Comanche, when, in truth, he didn't know what he was, who he was.

Disgusted with himself, he nudged Skunk into a walk, started to head back toward home, but on a whim decided to ride east, along the northern edge of Comanche land. Thomas Benton had found his answer up north. Maybe Daniel could learn that answer, too.

He liked this country, its spartan landscape, the solitude, the wind. The red clay, and high grass, green from summer rains. Trees as few as buffalo. A man could see forever.

What Daniel saw were wagon tracks.

In a little gully, he came upon them suddenly. After swinging down from Skunk, he studied the sign. The tracks pointed northeast, had come from the southwest, and from the horse dung he found and broke open, not that long ago. If the wagon kept to this course, it would cross Cache Creek, skirt south of the Delaware Agency and over the Washita River, maybe ford the Canadian near the Negro Settlement in the Oklahoma Country, keep traveling east into Creek Country.

Of course, that was only a hunch, but Daniel couldn't shed the thought that this wagon belonged to some whiskey-runner. He unholstered his Remington to check the loads, and swung back into the saddle.

For an hour and a half, he followed the trail, sweating now, worried, but feeling like a true Metal Shirt. When Skunk snorted, fought the hackamore, Daniel dismounted, knowing the horse smelled something. He rubbed the horse's neck before ground-reining the animal, and, in a crouch, followed the tracks up an embankment, stopping before the crest, then flopping to his belly and slithering through the grass, revolver in his right hand.

The stench of blood and offal reached him first, reminding Daniel of ration day. A moment later, he heard the grunts of a man at work. Slowly Daniel lifted his head.

He remembered that type of wagon from his days working for that farmer in Pennsylvania, with a bottom box of white pine and weighing about 2,500 pounds. Good for hauling barley or oats, or potatoes, which Daniel had had his fill of in Franklin County. But it would do to haul stolen beef. This wagon looked about as abused as the potato farmer's had.

Absorbed in his bloody work, the butcher had his back to Daniel, and a hard scan of the area revealed no one else. Daniel rose, and moved slowly to the Comanche man sawing through the bones of the spotted longhorn. He waited until the man set down the saw and started to reach for a large knife before he thumbed back the Remington's hammer.

The Indian stopped at the metallic *click.*

Raising the pistol, Daniel spoke in Comanche. "Stand up, Noihqueyúcat," he told Sergeant Sitting Still. "Leave the knife on the ground, and lift your hands high."

The sergeant's face remained rigid, his eyes burning when he realized he had been caught by Daniel Killstraight.

"Pale eyes do not like their cattle to be killed without payment," Daniel said.

Sitting Still remained silent until Daniel gestured with the revolver.

"It was dead when I found it," he said. "We should not let it go to waste."

Daniel spotted the remains of a campfire, and

pony tracks. The sergeant had met someone here, and that hunch still nagged him. "Stay where you are," Daniel said, and walked to the wagon. Behind the driver's box, he found four large clay jugs. He didn't have to pull a cork to learn what was inside. Now he knew why that Kwahadi boy had been drunk at Sergeant Sitting Still's lodge. That's why there had been a singletree there.

"Where do you hide the wagon?"

This time, Sergeant Sitting Still remained a rock.

"You work with the Creeks." He had probably just missed the little transaction. He'd have to be careful, quiet. If the Creeks returned, he'd be in trouble. From the tracks, there had been at least four of them.

Daniel remembered some notes he had jotted down in his Old Glory tablet, and he sounded out his theory. "At the pasture down south, where we caught the free grazers, you did not want to stop when we came back. Did not want to look for that cowboy's pistol. You came back to butcher the cattle yourself. Did Naséca pay you for the quarter you left her?"

"I help The People," the sergeant said belligerently.

Daniel considered this. Maybe. Naséca had told him spirits left the beef at night. He had thought she had been protecting someone, or the beef had bought her silence, but maybe Sergeant Sitting Still had been looking after her, taking care of the old woman. Maybe he had not sold her the quarter. Perhaps even he had spoken the truth when he said the longhorn was dead. He'd like to think there was some good in this man's heart—Sitting Still was Comanche—but the farm wagon had revealed something else.

"Whiskey does not help The People," he said bitterly. "It poisons us."

With a fierce roar, Sergeant Sitting Still charged, whipping a second knife from a deer-hide sheath on his belt. Straightening, Daniel aimed the Remington, but remembered the Creeks. He turned sideways, lowering the hammer, spinning the weapon in his right hand, catching the barrel near the cylinder with two fingers and his thumb, the middle finger near the hammer, the other inside the trigger guard. Turning the gun sideways, now holding it entirely by the barrel, he pivoted, trying to avoid Sergeant Sitting Still's wild slash. He had underestimated the sergeant's fury, his reach, had to suck in his stomach to avoid having his guts spill onto the grass. The metal blade ripped Daniel's shirt, carved a furrow across his stomach, not deep, but painful. Daniel staggered, off balance, hadn't gotten a chance to use the Remington like a club.

He braced himself. Sitting Still fell back against the wagon, grinned suddenly, came again, raising the knife, crying out in Comanche. Daniel's left hand shot out, just grabbing the wrist that held the knife. He tried to swing the Remington, use it like a war axe, but the sergeant gripped Daniel's right hand. They were locked together, doing some strange dance. Sweating. Grunting. Eyes glaring at each other.

He couldn't match Sitting Still's strength, felt himself weakening. They moved slowly. Daniel's grip slid against the sergeant's wrist, wet with blood from the longhorn. He bit his lip, tried to summon extra strength, moved toward the dead steer. Sitting Still's grin widened.

The sergeant slipped. Slipped on the entrails of

the longhorn. They broke free, Sitting Still sliding onto the grass, Daniel staggering away but managing to keep his feet. He straightened. Sergeant Sitting Still jumped up, sprang at him again. Daniel started to his left, turning sideways, then jumped to his right as the sergeant went past him, slashing again, missing, the momentum carrying him toward the wagon.

Daniel brought the Remington down, as hard as he could, missing the head but slamming against the Comanche's spine. A grunt and an oath escaped the sergeant's mouth. He turned, fell against the wagon, near the rear wheel, bounced up, shoving the knife upward. Again, he missed with the blade, and this time Daniel swung the Remington's walnut grip harder. He meant to hit the top of Sitting Still's head, but instead caught the forehead and nose. Blood spurted. The sergeant fell.

He did not stir.

Dropping the Remington, Daniel collapsed to his knees, fighting for breath, pressing one hand against his stomach, sticky, warm with blood. His left arm kept him upright, barely, but not for long.

He fell onto the grass, rolled over on his back, and spoke again, this time in English.

"Shit."

The cavalry sergeant at Fort Sill withdrew a soggy, well-chewed cigar from his mouth, considered it, rejected it, and tossed it into the nearby spittoon.

"You're arrestin' your own sergeant?" he asked in a surprised Southern drawl. "That's Sittin' Still, boy."

"I know who it is." Daniel's voice carried an edge. "I want him locked up, Sergeant."

"Needs a surgeon," the sergeant said. "Maybe a dozen stitches. That face is a bloody mess."

"Fetch a doctor if you must. I just want him locked up."

"Reckon we can put him in the pit, if the lieutenant says it's all right. What'd he do, other than lose what must have been a pretty fair fight?"

"He was working with Creek whiskey-runners." Daniel held out a jug for evidence.

The sergeant took it, pulled out the cork with his teeth, and sniffed. A smile carved its way across his face, and he spit the cork into his free hand, and took a taste.

"That's Creek scamper juice, all right." The sergeant smacked his lips.

"Don't drink all my evidence," Daniel said, and forced a smile. *Be nice to this Long Knife. Hold your temper. You need Noihqueyúcat in jail.*

"You look like you could use our sawbones yourself." The soldier corked the jug.

"I'm all right."

"How many bottles of this rotgut you got?" He peered into the wagon bed, and grimaced. "And what the hell is that bloody cow carcass for?"

"More evidence," Daniel said.

"Well, whoever runs the Circle Nine brand'll be madder than a hornet, what with his steer butchered." The sergeant dropped the jug with the others. "Yonder comes the lieutenant. I'll fetch the post surgeon. And let Rueben know what's goin' on."

"No," Daniel said urgently. "Don't tell Rueben anything. Not yet."

"Boy, he's the agent." The sergeant tilted his head, trying to read Daniel's face.

"But I'd like to send a wire to Harvey P. Noble," Daniel said, smiling again. "Deputy marshal out of Fort Smith."

He left the farm wagon at the post corral, and made sure he got receipts from the officer of the day, for his prisoner, and for his evidence. Then he mounted Skunk, and rode home.

It was pushing midnight when he arrived at Ben Buffalo Bone's encampment. The lodges were quiet, but light flowed from the house the pale eyes had built. Either Ben or maybe his sister had turned up the lantern. He unsaddled Skunk, rubbed down the paint horse before turning the gelding out in the pasture, letting him graze for the night.

Daniel tossed the saddle and hackamore beside the door to the house, pulled his tablet from the parfleche, and walked inside, stopping abruptly at the sight of the tall man standing in the shadows, a heavy Winchester rifle cradled in nook of his arm.

At his feet lay a dead man.

Chapter Twenty

"*O-si-yo!*" Tall Hugh Gunter, the Cherokee, stepped into the yellowish light.

Daniel took a sharp breath, waited for his heart to start again, and looked at the dead man. A white man. Brown beard stubble. Shell belt and holster, no revolver, but a bowie knife still sheathed. Black-striped britches, dirty socks. No boots. Dried blood in both corners of his mouth, the front of his shirt matted with blood, a monstrous hole right below the center of his rib cage. Probably a smaller hole from where the bullet had struck the man, in his back.

"What . . . happened?"

"I killed him," Gunter said proudly.

"Why'd you bring him here?" Daniel looked up. "Who is he?"

"I brought him nowhere," Gunter said. "He was here already. He come calling you. And he is Murt Jones. Leastways, I think he is. Hope he is. If he isn't, I'll be in a heap of trouble." The Cherokee leaned the big rifle against the wall. He stared at Daniel, pausing to study Daniel's own rough appearance before asking: "What happened to you?"

They both had some explaining to do.

Daniel kept his short, then let the Cherokee talk.

"I rode up this evening," Gunter said. "Don't fear. All the folks here is all right. The fellow, your pal, what's his name? Ben Buffalo Bone? Well, he's not here. Got sent down to deliver some prisoners to

Wichita Falls this morning. At least, that's what the girl told me. Soon as this fracas was over, I sent her loping off to Texas. She can ride better than many men I've known."

Rain Shower? Gunter had to mean Ben Buffalo's sister. "What for? Why did you send her away? Without a pass!"

"To fetch Harvey Noble."

"Noble?" Daniel massaged his temples. "I asked a lieutenant to send a telegraph to Noble at Fort Smith."

The tall Cherokee grinned. "Good thing I'm here. It'll be a spell before Noble's back in Arkansas. No, he's down in Texas. Now, let me go on with my story here. Anyway, I took supper with your friends here, and they told me they didn't know when you'd be back, but for me to make myself at home at your home." Gunter shook his head. "Some lodgings you got here, Killstraight. You Comanch' know how to make a house feel homely."

Impatiently Daniel waited.

"So, shortly after nightfall, this gent comes in. Notice, he ain't wearing boots. Being real quiet. I found his boots by his horse, hobbled over behind the brush arbor. Horse had lost a shoe. Pretty lame. Maybe he wanted to steal your horse. Had a big old Colt's revolver in his hand when he snuck in here. It's my belief that he come to do you harm. Must have thought I was you. Well, I was awake, and so was Ridge here." He patted the stock of the big rifle. "He fired once. I told him to halt. He turned. I plugged him. That's about the size of it."

Daniel knelt beside the corpse, studying the face. The man, pallid, eyes closed tight, didn't look like some murderous outlaw, but dead men never looked anything but dead. Daniel shook his head. He had never seen the man before.

"You're sure this is Murt Jones?"

"No papers on him, but some cash money, and a map to this place. Nothing in his war bag to speak of. Tintype of his girl. Deck of cards. Razor. Not much money, neither. Ten dollars and eighteen cents. And a token to a bawdy house in Wichita." He winked. "Don't reckon he'll ever get to use it."

Daniel shook his head, and collapsed by the dead man, trying to sort it out.

"The map's a puzzle." Gunter fished the paper from his pocket and handed it to Daniel. "He was gunning for you, kid. First in Choctaw land. Now at your own place. Twice."

"Three times," Daniel said. "Maybe." *Most likely*, he thought, seeing the dead man here. He told Gunter what had happened along the Red River.

"And you're sure you've never laid eyes on him?"

"I've never seen him, until now." His head jerked up. "What are you doing here?"

"Saving your hide," Gunter said, but the grin quickly faded. "No. I brung you some bad news. It troubled me, what you said back at Gibson Station, about how you didn't think Jimmy Comes Last killed the Bentons. Troubled Harvey Noble more. Nobody wants to have to live with the notion that they put a noose around some innocent man's neck. We've been doing some investigating. That's why Harvey Noble's down in Wichita Falls. He told me to tell you he went ahead and checked that brand you saw."

"The Lazy B?"

"Uhn-huh. Nothing there, though. Or so Harvey

says. It's registered to a rancher named Murphey, down Decatur way. Harvey says he's as big a skinflint as they come, and this ain't the first time the Lazy B has been caught free grazing. Wouldn't be likely Murphey or the Lazy B boys would have a thing to do with the Bentons." He pointed his jaw at the dead man. "And certainly not Murt Jones."

"Is that your bad news?"

"No," Gunter said, and Daniel braced himself.

"You remember when we had that talk with Doc Campbell?" the Cherokee asked.

"Yes."

"Doc was drinking if you recollect."

Another nod.

"Whiskey ain't legal in the Nations."

"You didn't stop him. Nor did Marshal Noble."

"Oh, it didn't trouble me then. I've been known to pull a cork now and again myself. So has Harvey. But later I got to thinking. So I went back a week or so ago and braced the good doctor. He wasn't drinking doctoring whiskey, nothing like that, but fortyrod Creek bust-head. So I demanded to know where he got the stuff."

Daniel's gut rumbled. He already knew what Gunter would tell him.

"It was Tom Benton. He was running Creek whiskey, and not just in Creek country, but throughout the territory."

Tom Benton. Inside, Daniel cursed the squawman, who was becoming a bigger son of a bitch the more he learned about the dead man. Tom Benton, whiskey-runner. More evidence that would have helped hanged Jimmy Comes Last. Changed the prosecution's theory, but only slightly. Drunken Comanche storms into whiskey-runner's cabin, seeking whiskey. Fight breaks out. Enraged Comanche kills man and wife.

"I know you wanted to think your friend had nothing to do with it. . . ."

Daniel shook his head. "There's still the taboo," he said. "Of. . . ." He couldn't bring up Mrs. Benton. "Besides, Gibson Station is a long way from Cache Creek. How did Jimmy get there?"

Another thought caused Daniel to slump again. Maybe Jimmy was working with Sergeant Sitting Still. Maybe that's how he knew where to find the Benton cabin. Maybe the Bentons were supplying Sitting Still with whiskey, and, when the Bentons were killed, the sergeant found another operator. Maybe. . . .

"I ain't saying all the questions have answers," Gunter said. "And here's one that eats at my craw." He stuck a long finger at Murt Jones's dead face. "What's this gent doing with a map to your place? Why's Murt Jones after you, a Comanche kid?"

Daniel rubbed his stomach. He had tied part of a bedsheet around the knife wound, first heading north after his fight with Sitting Still, later again at Fort Sill. It needed changing once more.

"Ephraim Rueben knew where I was every time I got shot at," Daniel said.

"The agent?"

"Yes. He sent me to those places. Ordered me. And he gave me explicit instructions on where to camp when I was delivering those prisoners to Fort Smith."

The Cherokee wasn't convinced. "From what I know about that agent, that's just his way."

That was true. Daniel studied the map. Was it made by Rueben's hand? He couldn't tell.

He felt exhausted. Wanted to sleep.

"Thanks for. . . ." He looked back at the dead man.

"I'm getting mighty good at saving your bacon," Gunter said.

"You're better than any *chimal*," Daniel said, and stopped, letting the word bounce around his mouth, reaching for the wall, pulling himself to his feet. "Shield." He headed for the door. "Come on!" he called back to Gunter.

"Where we going?"

"To dig."

Coyotes *yipped* in the distance as the leaves rustled in the cooling wind. Skunk and the mule Hugh Gunter had ridden stomped their hoofs nervously, as Daniel shoved the spade into the earth near Naséca's lodge.

"I feel like a damned ghoul," Gunter said.

So do I, Daniel thought, but his throat felt too dry to speak. He tossed the shovelful of dirt aside.

"Grave robbing," Gunter said.

The coyotes cried. An owl *hooted*.

"Owl. That's a bad sign."

"Shut up," Daniel snapped.

He prayed, in Comanche and in English the way they had taught him at the Industrial School, that he remembered this right. Naséca had dropped some of her son's most prized possessions into the grave, for the journey to The Land Beyond The Sun. One of those had been a *chimal*. Right? It had to be. Closing his eyes, he could picture that scene. Daniel hadn't made any notes in the Old Glory tablet about Jimmy's burial, hadn't thought anything of it, not until now. Just a few days ago, Naséca had told Daniel that Jimmy had learned, or was trying to learn, the ways of making weapons, lances and shields, from Isa Nanaka. Maybe Isa Nanaka had been trying to tell Daniel something, giving him the shield. Not that his father's friend had any part in the crimes. No, nothing like that. Isa Nanaka was an old *puhakut*, wanting to show Daniel the path to the answers he sought.

The spade bit something, and Daniel handed it to Gunter, the Cherokee just standing like a tree, weaving in the wind, eyes wide, scared. Daniel dropped to his knees, and worked like a badger, digging with his hands, probing with his fingers.

"I don't like this," Gunter said for about the twentieth time. "Stealing a body."

"I'm not after the bones," Daniel said. "I'm after. . . ." His fingers struck something. "This."

It took him almost five more minutes to pull out the shield. He couldn't tell much about it, not in the darkness, not with it covered with dirt and mud. He held it out to Gunter, had to force it into the Cherokee's hand, then began covering the grave, thanking Jimmy Comes Last in Comanche for not taking the *chimal* with him on his journey to The Land Beyond The Sun.

Dawn was breaking by the time they reached Ben Buffalo Bone's home, and Daniel carried the shield into the building, brushing off the globs of mud as he ran, leaving the Cherokee to tend to the horses.

A fine *chimal*, Daniel thought. Yellow buckskin, most of it painted white. A design in the center looked blue, but Daniel couldn't make anything out about it, surrounded by blue dots. Sinew had attached feathers to the center design, but those had not survived the journey out of the grave. Red and blue lines had been drawn from the upper part of the shield, where the white met the unpainted buckskin, and Daniel knew these would represent rifles. Yes, a fine shield, one a Comanche warrior would have been proud to carry into battle. Jimmy Comes Last would have learned the ways of The People, the true ways, would have carried on the tradition.

Had he lived. Had whiskey not consumed him.

"What's all of that mean?" Hugh Gunter had walked inside, the Winchester Centennial in his arms.

"His medicine," Daniel said with a shrug before turning the shield around. "But that's not what interests me." He unsheathed his knife, and ripped the back of the shield, reached inside, and pulled out pages and pages of paper.

Paper from books. From ledgers. Letters. He remembered walking around Jimmy's lodge, the one Naséca, in the tradition of The People, had burned after her son's death. He had picked up a burned piece of paper, had wondered what an illiterate Comanche boy would have been doing with paper, letters, books, things he couldn't read. Isa Nanaka had shown him that, too. He was stuffing the paper inside the shields he made.

Daniel grabbed a fistful of letters and pages, thrust them toward the Cherokee. "You can read, can't you?"

Leaning the big rifle against the wall, Gunter took the papers and sat, back against the wall, crossing his legs. He stuck the batch between his legs, brought up one paper, and stared at Daniel.

"What are we looking for?" he asked.

"I wish I knew," Daniel answered, and began to read.

He wished he knew what he needed to find. Wished he knew how much time he had to prove the agent guilty ... of something, likely murder. Sergeant Sitting Still was in the Fort Sill stockade. Ephraim Rueben didn't know that, yet ... maybe. Daniel had asked the sergeant and the lieutenant not to inform the agent, but how long would those Long Knives keep such a secret? For all Daniel knew, the lieutenant had sent a courier off to the agency as soon as Daniel had ridden off.

Had the soldiers sent that wire to Fort Smith? Maybe, but that wouldn't do him any good. Not with Harvey P. Noble down in Wichita Falls. Rain Shower had galloped off to fetch the federal lawman last night, but it was fifty miles, more than fifty, to Wichita Falls—and a lot could happen to a horse and rider over fifty miles. Especially a Comanche woman, without a pass from the agent. Especially in Texas. She'd have to take the ferry across the Red River, or swim her horse across. Then she'd have to find the marshal. Probably her brother, too. Would Noble believe her? Daniel had to think he would, and, even if he were skeptical, the chance that Hugh Gunter had killed Murt Jones would be too intriguing. He'd proceed to the reservation with all due haste, but how long would it take him to get here? And what if he had already left Texas and was riding back to Fort Smith before Rain Shower reached Wichita Falls?

Daniel knew he'd have to do this alone.

Gunter grunted, wadded up a letter, and threw it.

The ball of paper bounced off Murt Jones's nose. "What the U.S. government pays for flour," he said, "is criminal."

"Especially the flour they feed us." Daniel smiled.

No, he told himself. *Not quite alone. I'll have this Cherokee to help me.*

Chapter Twenty-one

"Killstraight!" Ephraim Rueben called from the front of the agency. "Got a chore for you."

Swinging from the saddle, Daniel glanced over his shoulder before addressing the agent. "Yes, sir?"

"Sergeant Sitting Still is missing," Rueben said. "I sent Twice Bent Nose to scout the pastures north of here after his wife came in, worried sick. Nobody's seen him since yesterday, and it ain't like him not to show up. I need him. McBride's bringing in a herd for ration day, be here late today or tomorrow, and we're shorthanded something fierce. When's the last time you laid eyes on the sergeant? It's not like him to just up and disappear."

Hoofs beat behind him, and Daniel nodded. "I saw him yesterday," he said, but the agent was no longer listening. He stepped around Daniel to watch the newcomers. Likewise, Daniel also turned as Hugh Gunter and two officers from Fort Sill reined in their mounts.

"What's going on?" Rueben asked. He studied the Cherokee. "You're Gunter, right?"

The policeman nodded.

"You're a long way from home. And what brings the Army here, Lieutenant?"

When no one answered, Rueben licked his lips. "Is it about my sergeant? Sitting Still? He's missing."

"He's in our stockade," one of the officers said.

"Stockade!" Instantly Rueben turned to Daniel. "What's the meaning of this? What's going on?"

Daniel reached into his parfleche and withdrew a paper, crumpled and dirty, but legible.

"I cannot arrest you," Daniel said, his voice even. "Indians are not allowed to arrest white men, not alone. But the soldiers will hold you until Marshal Noble arrives from Texas." He held the paper closer to the agent, who had started sweating.

"McBride didn't want me burning your trash," Daniel said. "Because I can read. I think he was mad at you for not realizing this. Jimmy Comes Last could not read. You let him burn trash. I remember Ben Buffalo Bone telling me this. But Jimmy didn't burn everything you threw away. He used it to put inside the shields he was learning to make."

The agent straightened, still refusing to look at the paper, so Daniel went on. "McBride has an agreement with The People to lease pastures, but. . . ."

"That's absolutely right." Rueben had found his voice. "And he pays you Comanches for that right. There is no. . . ."

"He pays to graze five thousand head of cattle on pastures just across the Red River."

"And he feeds you beef. He. . . ."

"Shut up!" Daniel had lost all patience with this thief. "McBride has cattle grazing in the northern pastures, too. Hundreds of them. That is why Sergeant Sitting Still always patrolled those pastures. Ben Buffalo Bone and me always rode south. McBride paid you, paid you handsomely, for this robbery."

"That is an infernal lie." Rueben turned back toward the soldiers. "I will not tolerate this, not from a. . . . By God, I'm a white man. Do I look rich? You want to telegraph my bank in Dallas? They'll show you just how poor I am!"

Daniel waved the paper. "How about your bank in Wichita, Kansas?"

"I don't. . . ." Rueben wet his lips again.

"McBride paid you well. So did the Creek whiskey-runners."

"I. . . ."

"Your sergeant told us about the whiskey-runners, Rueben," one of the officers said. "Nice little deal you had there."

"Especially," Hugh Gunter weighed in, "after Tom Benton was out of the picture."

"Benton? Now. . . ." Color drained from the agent's face. "Now, wait, I had nothing to do with Benton. Jimmy Comes Last killed him. You all know. . . ."

"Murt Jones is dead," Daniel said.

"I killed him," Gunter added with pride.

"J-Jones . . . listen . . . there's . . . this is just some misunderstanding."

"Murt Jones ambushed us in the Choctaw Nation." Daniel pressed his hand against his bandaged stomach. It still hurt a little. "He knew exactly where we would be. And we'd be dead if Hugh Gunter hadn't shown up when he did." Daniel nodded in the Cherokee's direction. "That ambush happened shortly after I told you and McBride that I didn't believe Jimmy was guilty. Later, when you sent me down to patrol along the river, I was bushwhacked again . . . right after I asked about that Circle Nine brand, after I asked you and McBride and his hired hands some other questions. And then, Murt Jones showed up trying to kill me last night. Maybe he would have killed me if not for Hugh, again."

"I don't know Murt Jones. Or the Circle Nine
brand."

"Maybe you don't know Jones," Daniel said, "bu
you do know the Circle Nine." He pulled out an
other paper. "I'm not too smart in all ways of white
men. McBride said he didn't know the brand. I be
lieved him. But McBride also said something else a
while back. He had mentioned riders for his brands
Brands. More than one. It didn't occur to me that a
rancher would have more than one brand, not unti
Quanah told me differently. I only thought of Mc
Bride as the Bar TA Slash, but the registry here
shows that McBride has about a dozen brands. Tha
includes the Circle Nine. I guess you both figured
was too dumb to figure that out." He shrugged
"You were almost right."

"I'm not going to stand here and be accused by
some damned savage who's wet behind his ears,'
the agent said, staring at the officers from Fort Sil
but yelling at Daniel. "You're not a detective! You're
just a dumb Metal Shirt. I don't know all of Mc
Bride's brands, and I've never been to Wichita, Kan
sas. This is a mistake. That paper's a forgery."

Daniel was shaking his head. "Senator Dawes
says he met you once in Wichita. By happenstance,
he says. I guess the senator's word carries a lot more
weight than your denial. Along with this deposit
note."

Rueben forced his way toward the two officers.
"You believe that pack of lies?"

"Captain Dittmer said to bring you in," one of the
officers said. "Let's just say the captain and colonel
want to talk to you about it. It'd be more pleasant if
you come along peacefully."

More hoofs beat up dust, and a squad of black

soldiers, led by a gray-bearded sergeant, rode up toward the corrals. Eyes filled with rage, Rueben shot a long glare back at Daniel, then swallowed and looked back at the first officer.

"I'll be happy to clear up all of this," he said tightly, his Texas twang becoming more pronounced as his jaw unclenched, "but then, you two bluebellies, your damned Prussian captain and that bootlicking colonel, will all rue the day. I'm an agent of the United States government, and I won't stand here and be slandered by a damned Comanche! Hell, he's not even Comanche. He doesn't know what he is!"

Daniel handed the lieutenant the two papers he had dug out of Jimmy Comes Last's shield, and watched as the soldiers escorted the agent, riding rigid, back toward Fort Sill, leaving Daniel alone at the agency with Hugh Gunter.

"Now what?" Gunter asked. "You think them papers will be enough to make the soldier boys believe us?"

"The sergeant confessed," Daniel said.

"Injun's word against a white man's."

Daniel shrugged. "I want you," he said, "to ride out. See if you can catch up with Marshal Noble and Ben Buffalo Bone." He was also worried about Ben's sister, Rain Shower. Funny he should start thinking of her suddenly. He had scarcely noticed her during the previous few months. After all, she was full-blood Comanche, and he . . . well, it was like Rueben had said. He didn't know what he was.

"I can do that." Hugh Gunter's dark eyes stared through Daniel. "What are you going to do?"

"Wait," he said. "Think."

"You ain't going after McBride by yourself, are you?"

"He's driving a herd up from Texas," Daniel said. "For ration day. I'll wait. Can't arrest a white man."

"You do that," Gunter said. "And remember that."

"I will."

Both men recognized the lie.

Twenty minutes after Gunter had ridden away, Skunk was carrying Daniel southward in a full gallop. Daniel had left the parfleche with the Old Glory tablet, its pages almost full, in the agent's office. Not that anyone would be able to make sense of his notes, but he didn't want J. C. C. McBride to destroy that—just in case things didn't go the way he hoped.

Oh, he could wait on Deputy U.S. Marshal Harvey P. Noble, could wait for a posse of federal lawmen, could sit back and watch, and pray, that justice prevailed. Probably should wait. But he was Kwahadi. At least, he kept trying to tell himself that's who he was, no matter what blood had flowed through his mother's veins, no matter how many years the pale eyes had taught him to act civilized. Waiting was not in the nature of The People, and he wanted to face McBride himself. Alone. Like two warriors. The way his father would have fought a *taibo* like McBride.

Besides, right now the only evidence he had against the Texas rancher was defrauding the Comanche people and agency out of money. McBride was a free grazer. Daniel wanted to prove the man guilty of murder. He had slain the Bentons, after Tom Benton discovered the scheme between McBride and Rueben, then had made it look as though Jimmy Comes Last had killed the couple. Or maybe McBride had hired Murt Jones to do his killings.

Jones had grown up in Missouri, the stories went, but had gotten his first taste of outlawry in Texas. The Texas Rangers, including McBride and Rueben, had chased Jones into Indian Territory, but maybe, just maybe, McBride and Rueben had caught up with Jones, only, instead of arresting him, they had let him free. Jones would have owed those two a big debt. He might pay it off with murder. Murders.

Skunk screamed, stopped, and buckled, long before the gunshot ever registered, snorting, coughing, taking Daniel down with him, pinning his left leg underneath the paint horse's body, twisting his knee.

As the report of the rifle echoed across the blackjacks and swells, Daniel moaned, biting back the pain that shot up and down his leg. He tasted blood. Reached up, felt his nose, blood oozing from both nostrils. Sand and dead grass covered his face. He must have hit his head hard when Skunk went down.

The horse snorted, and, once he saw the blood, tears flowed freely from Daniel's eyes. He tried to pull his leg from underneath, couldn't, called out to Skunk, reaching for his mane, whispering for him to lie down, be still.

"Rest," he said. "Close your eyes."

His heart felt as if it might explode, and he knew he should have waited. Waited, like the Cherokee had told him to do. He wasn't some warrior of The People, just a confused boy not yet twenty-one. He hadn't caught J. C. C. McBride, defeated him. All he had done was get his horse killed.

The man came along whistling. Daniel looked up, saw the rider on horseback. He reached for his Remington, drew it, started to thumb back the hammer, when suddenly a boot kicked it from his hand. Daniel turned, just as the same boot connected under his jaw, snapping his teeth.

Two men. The nearest one laughed. The rider kept whistling.

By now, Skunk was dead.

"You're a peck of trouble," the man on the horse said, shoving a Winchester into the saddle scabbard. J. C. C. McBride smoothed his ancient mustache. "Anybody else with him?" he asked the man behind Daniel.

"He's alone." Shad Carter stepped into Daniel's line of vision.

"You were in a big hurry," McBride said, slowly dismounting, handing the reins to a big bay gelding to his *segundo*. "Shad and me was riding out ahead of the herd, scouting. Lucky for us." He hooked his thumbs in his shell belt.

"Murt Jones is dead," Daniel said.

McBride spit. He started to speak, shot a glance at Shad Carter, then shook his head, and pushed back the brim of his hat. "I don't think you was riding so hard to pay a visit to that schoolmarm. Coming to pay us a visit, I warrant. Coming for me."

Daniel dammed the tears. The knife wound across his stomach was bleeding again. "You're on a Circle Nine horse," he said.

McBride laughed. "Yeah. I got a rule. Don't allow nobody who draws wages from me ride nothing but one of my brands. Guess you learned that already. Smart, for a Comanch'."

"You used the pastures up north to graze. Paid Rueben to overlook it, and Rueben paid Sergeant Sitting Still. On top of the money they got from the Creeks."

"Sure. We'd leave a few head, mingle them with Jeddah Tompkins's Herefords. Fatten them up before trailing them to Dodge City. Had us a little deal with your good sergeant and my stupid pard, Rueben. Didn't hurt nobody."

Daniel spit. "The Bentons. Jimmy. Tach! You hurt. . . ."

"Shut up," Shad Carter barked.

"First time I mentioned Tom Benton's name," Daniel said, "you pretended you didn't know him. Later, you called him a troublemaker. I didn't think about it, didn't notice it, till I was rereading my notes."

The rancher shook his head. "My pa always warned me that lies'll trip a fella up."

Another rider came up, and Shad Carter started cursing Cotton Henry.

"What's going on?" the young cowhand asked.

"You damned idiot!" Shad Carter snapped. "Get back to. . . ."

The old rancher cut him off. "Be careful who you're calling an idiot, Shad. Remember, it was you who gave that drunken Comanche one of our horses."

"You said to pay him off! Said it'd keep him quiet."

"Not with a horse from our damned string! Not something that could lead the law back to me! I don't know who's dumber, you or Ephraim!"

"What's goin' on?" Cotton Henry repeated.

Smiling, J. C. C. McBride looked across the rolling plain toward a deepening arroyo that stretched southward. Then he answered Cotton Henry's question. "Cotton, we're fixing a problem, is all. You've been a top hand, the way you done me at that hanging and all. Top hand. You ride for the brand. Lots of riders these days tend to forget that. But you ain't. You ride for the brand, and I'm reminding you that's what you're gonna be doing now. You savvy?"

"Yes, sir."

Daniel could barely hear him.

"This Injun's caused us some trouble, like most Injuns do. That trouble ends here."

Shad Carter started to draw a big Colt pistol from his holster.

"No, damn it!" McBride roared. "I'm doing this my way." McBride's eyes kept shining as he pointed at the arroyo. "Carter, you and Cotton get back to the herd. I want y'all to start feeding those dogies into that arroyo. When you hear my pistol shot, stampede them."

"Stampede?" Cotton Henry asked, still staring at his horse's withers.

"That's right. Mister Killstraight here's going to get hisself caught in a stampede." He nodded at his plan. "I'll drag this boy over there. Stay with him. Maybe tie his legs to that dead bit of scrub, though I don't think he'll be going far with his leg busted up and his gut bleeding a mite."

Shad Carter scratched his chin. "Leave him there . . . alive?"

"He'll be alive. When you hear my pistol shot, you start the herd running. Don't fret none, boys. I'll be out of that arroyo when I pull the trigger. Have me a good seat to watch the show."

"We'll lose some head," Carter said.

"I don't give a damn."

"You mean to kill him?" Henry looked up, maybe understanding at last what was about to happen.

"He's Comanche!" McBride fired back. "No matter how good he speaks. No matter nothing. He's Comanch'. Don't you forget that. And he's a burr under my saddle that I ain't tolerating no more. And you work for me, Henry. You ride for the brand."

"Good God," Carter said. "Kill him now, Mister McBride. Kill. . . ."

"I want him to suffer! I want him to know those longhorns are gonna be running over him. I want him to feel that first hoof or horn. I want him to die. And die hard. I want him to know it was me that done it. I want him to suffer. Like my ma did. Like my sisters. When his kind got a-hold of them. I want him to look like they did . . . my mother, damn it, my two sisters . . . when those murdering, savage pack of Comanch' raiders killed them." His face had reddened under his white whiskers. "You two ain't that young that you can't remember what it was like ten, fifteen years back when these pieces of filth could raid and ravage and murder and steal. Hell's fire, I ain't! I ain't never forgetting what it was like to see my own ma, my. . . ." Choking on his words, he turned away.

"I've been feeding you bastards on that reservation," he said after a moment, quieter now. "Feeding you my own beef, making pretty fair money. Hating every damned minute of it. Hating you." He spit again. "Comanches. It galls me, eats at my craw. Well, Daniel Killstraight, you know why!"

Chapter Twenty-two

Once Cotton Henry had been sent trotting back to the herd, McBride and Shad Carter roughly pulled Daniel, gasping from the inferno burning up and down his leg from ankle to hip, from underneath Skunk's body, then dragged him across the rough ground. When they reached the edge of the arroyo, Carter booted him down the embankment, laughing as he pitched, face-first, in the dirt. Daniel screamed.

"I thought you Comanches didn't show no pain," McBride said mockingly.

Rolling over on his back, biting his lower lip, trying to tell himself not to yell out again, trying to keep the tears from rushing down his cheeks, Daniel looked up through blurred vision as the rancher fished out a cigar, bit off an end, and fired it up with a Lucifer he struck on his thumbnail. "Get back yonder," he told Carter. "Make sure Henry don't botch things up."

"I think I should stay," the *segundo* suggested.

"Appreciate the offer, but I'm doing this myself. Besides, I don't trust Henry. Not on this job. He's soft."

McBride's horse had been ground-reined at the top of the arroyo. The rancher shot a quick glance at the mount, then started down the arroyo, slipping, kicking up a small avalanche. When he hit bottom, he brushed off his chaps, and looked up at Carter to repeat his instructions. "Feed the herd in here. I'll give you twenty minutes. When I pull the trigger, you start them running. I'll be up where you are now, watching."

"I still say you should just kill the bastard," Carter tried again.

"And you ain't bossing this outfit. Now, git!"

Daniel choked back the pain. His leg wasn't broken. At least, he didn't think so, but it hurt like a son of a bitch, already swelling so that it pressed tightly against his trousers, and his stomach was not bleeding too badly. McBride hadn't noticed the knife sheathed on Daniel's belt, or maybe the rancher just didn't care. He wasn't sure he could reach it. He glanced around. Small brush atop the other end of the arroyo. Narrow defile that grew pretty wide across here, maybe sixty yards. Banks eight feet high. With luck, he could crawl out, but McBride wasn't going to give him that chance. He tucked a pigging string inside his belt, pitched the cigar, and leaned over, grabbing Daniel's collar, dragging him to the center of the arroyo.

"They know your scheme," Daniel managed, desperate. "The soldiers arrested Agent Rueben. They know all about you free grazing. We found a Circle Nine steer. . . ."

"I don't give a damn." McBride stopped to catch his breath and get a better grip. "Let them fine me. Be glad to pay it."

"That's why you killed Tom Benton. He found out about it."

Again the rancher laughed. "You idiot. You think Benton was a sky pilot. He ran whiskey all through the territory. He was going to blackmail me. That's what he planned on doing. Greedy, Creek-loving bastard."

They covered barely five yards before the rancher had to stop again.

"That's why you killed him," Daniel said.

"You think you're so smart. I didn't kill Benton or his squaw."

They went another few yards. Sweat dampened the rancher's shirt, rolled down his face. The old man was heaving.

"Then you had Murt Jones do it," Daniel said. "You're still just as guilty."

"You damned . . . fool." His voice turned hoarse, out of breath. "They hanged the . . . right person, boy. You went . . . around stirring up . . . all this trouble . . . for nothing." He loosened his bandanna to mop his face, tried to spit, but his throat was parched. "Your pal . . . Jimmy . . . he killed the Bentons. Both of them."

Now, McBride had to use both hands to drag Daniel.

"I don't. . . ." Pain stopped him. Pain from his leg and stomach, his aching head, but mostly from the knowledge that the Texian told the truth. He didn't want to accept it, believe it, but why should McBride lie? Daniel's heart burst. He couldn't dam the tears any more. Some Kwahadi warrior. Some detective. Trying to prove Jimmy Comes Last innocent, when, in fact, he had committed those awful murders.

They covered another couple of yards before McBride had to sit down, panting, sweating.

"He would . . . do anything . . . boy." Somehow McBride smiled as he added: "For a . . . drink!"

"You made Jimmy do it."

"Didn't stop him. . . . Riled him up . . . I reckon. But. . . ." The rancher's joints popped as he rose. "Keep forgettin' that . . . I'll be sixty . . . years old . . . next spring."

Drops of sweat rolled from the rancher's face and onto Daniel's forehead as the rancher heaved him just a few feet, then stopped, straightening, groaning, pulling the pigging string from inside the gun belt. Just like that, though, he dropped the rope to the ground. After a quick glance down the arroyo, McBride reached for his own sheathed knife.

Daniel did the same.

"But Shad's right." McBride's bowie knife came up. "Best to just . . . kill you now. I ain't no . . . spring chicken . . . no more."

Just as McBride started to stab, a hawk swooped from the clouds, talons flashing, silently, startling the rancher as it came close to taking off his hat. "What the hell . . . ?" McBride began, looking up, watching the marsh hawk fly away, turn, dive again.

McBride ducked as the bird shot over his head again, then the rancher turned, cursing, remembering Daniel. He shifted his grip on the bowie, crouching, moving closer, not seeing Daniel's knife until the blade had been buried to the hilt in the rancher's groin.

Moaning, grabbing the deer antler handle with both hands after dropping the big bowie, J. C. C. McBride collapsed in the sand, dark blood pooling quickly between his legs as the marsh hawk swept down again, the wind from the swooping bird of prey causing a loud *whoosh.*

"Damned . . . Co-manch'. . . ." McBride fell on his back.

Daniel rolled over, dragged himself, jerked the Smith & Wesson from the rancher's holster. The old man didn't resist.

"Damned . . . hawk." McBride let go of the knife, crying out in torment when Daniel, with his left hand, jerked the weapon free, wiping the iron blade on his trousers, sliding it back into the sheath. Sitting up, biting back the pain, Daniel glanced upward at the circling marsh hawk.

He remembered the story Isa Nanaka had told, how Daniel's father had turned himself into a hawk to escape the Long Knives along the railroad tracks in Florida, how the marsh hawk was always there to watch over Daniel, to protect him. Later, he would recall the other times he had heard a hawk's cry. Right before he had tried to kill Hugh Gunter, a hawk had stopped him, prevented him from killing an innocent man, maybe from being killed himself. Later, he had heard a hawk right before that ambush along the Red River. And now . . . here. . . . Coincidence? Imagination? A pale eyes might argue that this raptor was merely protecting its nesting grounds, marsh hawks being notorious for such behavior.

Daniel would think of this later. At that moment, he heard bawling cattle, and thought only of his predicament, and of his boiling hatred for J. C. C. McBride.

Awkwardly he thumbed back the Smith & Wesson's big hammer, and aimed the big revolver at the rancher's head.

"Do it," the man said tightly. "Finish it."

The gun shook, even when Daniel gripped it with both hands.

"You ain't got . . . the guts," McBride hissed. "I . . .

t your friend killed," he taunted. "Killed your
rse. Cheated all . . . you people. I. . . ."

Tears and sweat burned Daniel's eyes. He tried to
hten his finger on the trigger.

'You're weak. Not Comanch'. What you gonna do,
y? Arrest me?" McBride tried to lift his head. "Go
ead. Watch me when I walk . . . out the court-
use. Free. Then watch me when . . . I come back to
s . . . reservation. . . . and kill ever' one of. . . ."
s head dropped, and he groaned, mouthing now,
ading: "Kill me . . . you . . . yellow bastard."

Lowering the revolver, Daniel struggled to his
t, and limped away, crouching in case the hawk
ooped down on him. He tripped once, crawled,
mehow pushed himself back to his feet, finally
ched the embankment.

"Yellow . . . !" McBride called out weakly. "Cow-
."

Three times Daniel slipped, trying to climb out of
arroyo. At last, he made it, drenched in sweat,
od, dirt, and grime. He could hear the longhorns,
ser now, even caught the yipping and cursing of
whands, pushing the cattle. He gathered the reins
McBride's horse and the horn, pulled himself into
saddle, keeping his left foot out of the stirrup.
ing his good knee and the Smith & Wesson barrel
a gentle prod, he edged the horse closer to the ar-
yo.

McBride glared at him.

"You're worthless," the rancher said. "I got
re . . . respect for . . . them red niggers . . . who
led my family. You're. . . ." He shook his head, fell
ck. "I will kill you, boy."

Daniel lifted his head skyward, found the marsh
wk still circling, watchful. Briefly he turned toward

Skunk's lifeless body. He thought of Tach, and
Jimmy Comes Last, and blood rushed to his hea
He was Kwahadi, and this *taibo* son of a bitch, if
didn't bleed to death, would live up to his word, I
threats.

He still held the rancher's revolver in his rig
hand. Daniel waited, until McBride looked up, b
fore aiming the .44 at the old man. McBride's ey
hardened. "Do it," he mouthed. Daniel let out
heavy breath, wet his lips, took one more glar
down the arroyo. He could make out the rising du
from the herd. McBride coughed out a laugh, a
Daniel looked down at the man, raised his ar
pointing the barrel skyward, satisfied when the c
rancher's paling face at last showed fear.

"No," the rancher said. "Don't you . . . !"

The pistol's heavy report cut off the old ma
cries. Seconds later, scattered shots down the arro
answered the signal, almost immediately drown
out by the thunder of *crashing* hoofs.

He didn't watch. Quickly he tossed the Smith
Wesson to the ground, turned the big horse, alrea
beginning to panic from the gunshots and sta
peding herd, and galloped away.

Chapter Twenty-three

out a mile from the agency, he gingerly dis-
unted, and turned the horse loose. Daniel walked,
re like staggered, using McBride's Winchester as
rutch. He didn't know how he managed to cover
last dusty trail, twice falling hard, but he didn't
nt to be charged with horse theft, even if it might
ve pleased Quanah Parker. Pale eyes frowned on
ch things. And, of course, the law might say he
d murdered J. C. C. McBride.

He could live with that.

To his surprise, the agency was abandoned, and
dropped the rifle into the well. No evidence, he
d himself, something else he had learned from
vmen like Noble and Gunter, although he won-
red how Shad Carter and Cotton Henry would
plain the death of their boss. Old-timers, the Texians,
ybe even some of The People would mourn the
ssing of J. C. C. McBride, calling it fitting that a big
ncher went under the hoofs. Sad, the newspapers
uld lament—the way that reporter had written
ingly, dramatically about the passing of Randi
dan's father—a good man like J. C. C. McBride
led delivering food on the hoof for those poor In-
ans on the reservations. They'd make the bastard
t to be a saint.

Daniel collapsed inside the lean-to, massaging his
, closing his eyes.

A horse in the corral whinnied, and he looked at

it. Lame. Still carrying the saddle and war bag, a
he forced himself up. That had to be Murt Jone
horse. He limped to the corral, held out his har
and gently called the horse.

After untying the war bag, he rubbed the ge
ing's neck and gingerly hobbled back to the shade
the lean-to. He wasn't sure what he'd find, but
emptied the contents into the dirt. Hugh Gunter sa
there had been some money, but the Cherokee mi
have confiscated that. Daniel couldn't blame hi
Deck of cards. Razor. Tintype. What else had Gun
said he'd found in the sack? A token from son
brothel in Wichita. Well, Gunter must have kept th
for himself, too. He picked up the tintype, brush
off the dust, and stared at the fading picture, th
reached inside his pocket and drew the map Gun
had found on Murt Jones's body, the map that led
Ben Buffalo Bone's place and the house that serv
as a stable, and Daniel's home.

"Shit," Daniel said. His head fell back, striking t
rotting wood, and, gritting his teeth, he stood a
staggered across the yard to the agent's cabin, a
found his parfleche, from which he retrieved his C
Glory writing tablet. He made his way to Ephra
Rueben's chair, and sat down to reread his notes.

He slept that night in the agent's chair, slept late, c
spite the throbbing leg, until horses woke hi
Horses, and voices. Leaving the tintype, map, a
writing tablet on the desk, he hopped to the doc
way, peered into the morning light, and stepped o
side, gingerly moving on to the hitching rail, whi
he leaned on for support, suddenly wishing
hadn't dropped that Winchester into the well.

"You red bastard," Shad Carter said. He had dis-
ounted, and made a beeline for Daniel. Behind the
rk cowhand sat Cotton Henry on his Circle 9
estnut, and two other riders, one in the bowler hat
d pince-nez glasses, the other a cowboy Daniel
d never seen.

Carter's right hand gripped the Colt's butt as he
lked.

"Leave it go!" Cotton Henry called out, his voice
usually high-pitched.

"He killed Mister McBride," Carter said. The Colt
rted up and out of the holster.

"I don't know how you got out of that arroyo,"
rter began.

"Shad!" Cotton Henry raised his voice.

"But," Carter went on, "I'm gonna kill you."

"It's over!" Henry reached behind him.

Shad Carter kept walking. Daniel just watched.
wouldn't show fear. Not to the likes of Shad
rter.

Carter stopped, about ten feet from Daniel, eared
ck the Colt's hammer.

"Don't make me do it!" Henry said, and Shad
rter whirled, hearing Henry jack a round into his
inchester.

Carter snapped a shot at the mounted cowhand.
e Bar TA Slash rider with the spectacles blurted
t a surprised oath. The other horse started buck-
g. Carter cocked the Colt again, and Cotton Henry
led him with one shot from the .44-40.

They were standing over the body, three Texas
wboys and a gimpy Comanche, when Deputy
S. Marshal Harvey P. Noble rode up with Ben Buf-
lo Bone, Hugh Gunter, and Rain Shower.

* * *

Apache, Kiowa, and Comanche children sang
they played outside the mission school. Usin
makeshift crutch, Daniel hobbled up the stairs i
the church, and looked at the newspaper clippir
pinned to the wall. The longer article, the one fr
the St. Louis *Globe-Democrat*, interested him. Ac
ally he was more intrigued by the name the repor
had signed. At first he read hopefully, but so
frowned, shaking his head, and leaned against
rear pew.

Looking equally uncomfortable, Harvey No
and Hugh Gunter studied the articles, only reme
bering to take off their hats when Randi Jord
raced up the steps.

"Daniel!" she called out, stopping, staring, cc
fused at the sight of the two other men. "What . .
I. . . . Who . . . ?"

Daniel didn't want to look into her beautiful ey
didn't want to believe what he was about to say, l
he steeled himself. Told himself that he was Kv
hadi, that she was a pale eyes. That she really did
care for him at all.

"Your brother is dead," he said.

She didn't give anything away. Stepped back, sl
another glance at Gunter and Noble, then look
hard at Daniel. "I don't know what you mean."

Daniel pointed at the *Globe-Democrat* story.

"Mister McBride's dead. Cattle stampeded ov
him. Shad Carter's dead, too. Cotton Henry kill
him. Killed him to save me." Daniel shook his hea
He couldn't quite figure out why Cotton Henry h
intervened, even after Harvey P. Noble had qui
tioned the cowhand and the witnesses, but Dan
wasn't sure he would ever understand the pale ey

Cotton Henry had said there had been too much
ling, had said that McBride wanted Daniel dead,
nned on murdering him, that he hadn't found
courage to stop his boss and Shad Carter, not at
t, that his boss had sent him to watch Jimmy
mes Last hang. "Need you to do me a favor," the
cher had said. "I'm just curious if that drunken
manch' says anything before his neck breaks."
ving never seen a hanging before, Henry had
ped at that chance, but since the execution,
ll . . . he had been sickened by it all. Henry had
e on to tell Noble that he hadn't figured out all
whys and what fors, just knew he had to prevent
ad Carter from killing Daniel.

Daniel had figured out the rest of it. At least, he
ught he had.

"Your brother's dead," he told Randi. "Murt Jones."
pointed at the newspaper clippings. "Those sto-
s don't mention him."

Randi took another step back. "I have no . . .
other."

"Yeah, you and Shad Carter pretended you didn't
ow him. I guess that was for my benefit. Maybe
rter was protecting you, and you protecting your-
f. And when I read that story when I was here a
ile back, I didn't think anything of it." Daniel
hed heavily. "Nice story, I guess. But then I saw
t name at the end. P. F. Palazzo. Italian, I think.
en Cotton Henry and I went to the execution,
en we saw Jimmy Comes Last hang in Fort Smith,
got two passes from reporters. One was from a
wspaper in Arkansas City. I can't remember the
me. But I was pretending to be Palazzo with the
be-Democrat in Saint Louis. You told Shad Carter,
maybe you told McBride, to look up P. F. Palazzo,

told one of them they could buy a pass from t
newspaperman. The story on the wall there says
writer knew your father well. Knew the family w
I guess you knew Mister Palazzo well, knew he'c
willing to sell Cotton Henry a pass to the execut
knew he was a drunk, like Jimmy Comes Last."

She shook her head, forced a laugh. "Why wou
do that? Daniel, you. . . ."

"Cotton told us why he was at the hanging.
said McBride told him what to do. Told him to s
out Palazzo in the hotel saloon. Cotton though
would be quite the adventure." Daniel choked b
the memories from that day. "I guess it was . . .
both of us. McBride, and you, needed some
there. Wanted to make sure Jimmy didn't conf
before he died."

Her head shook, more forceful now, and
blurted out in anger, "Jimmy Comes Last killed. .

The sigh silenced her. It came out more as a ga
a cry. "Yeah." Daniel nodded. "McBride told me t
before he died. I didn't want to believe him. Dic
want it to be true. I kept telling myself that Jim
Comes Last was Comanche. That he wouldn't
that to . . . to. . . . But Jimmy was a drunk. He'd
anything for whiskey. Forget all we are taught. I
get everything."

He stopped, looked at her, saw she wasn't go
to speak, and continued.

"So Jimmy killed the Bentons. But how did he
there? And why? Marshal Noble here figured t
Jimmy came hunting whiskey, must have be
crazy, crazy drunk, probably both, and all that tur
out to be true. But there was something else M
Bride told me. He said Benton was planning
blackmailing him. Not *was* doing it. He *planned*

doing it. Tom Benton found what he was looking for up north. Found the pastures McBride was using illegally. He told you about this, and you told McBride. You told McBride to take Jimmy Comes Last. Or maybe it was Ephraim Rueben. Maybe it was Sergeant Sitting Still. But it would be easy to kill the Bentons, and, well, you wanted Tom Benton dead. And Jimmy would get blamed for it. Rightfully so, I guess. Jimmy was too ashamed of what he had done to speak of it. Maybe . . . maybe he wanted to die. Maybe Tom Benton deserved to die. But Karen Benton. . . ."

"Tom Benton was. . . ." She couldn't finish.

"Yeah. I know. I wanted him to be this champion. I think that's what you called him. Champion or crusader, something like that. Helping The People. That's what you wanted to believe, too. Only, he wasn't. He was a rotten man. Liar, thief, cheat, whiskey-runner. And he was using you."

Her head fell against her chest.

"When you found that out, when you found out he was married, well . . . maybe I can't blame you for wanting him dead."

She started crying.

He fingered the tintype, held it toward her. "Hugh Gunter thought this was a picture of Murt Jones and his sweetheart. But Hugh had never seen you. Your hair's so light, and his was so dark. But the eyes . . . you can see the resemblance in your eyes. He was your brother."

She looked up, knocked the tintype to the floor, and wailed: "He was my father!"

Sobbing, she slid down the wall, pulling her knees up tightly against her chest. Daniel's mouth fell open. Father?

"He was my father," she said over the tears. "When my mother, my real mother died, Papa brought me to Saint Louis. Left me with my uncle and aunt to raise. Then he rode back to Texas."

It hit Daniel then. "That's why you called them Father Wayne and Mother Henryetta."

She nodded. "You. . . ." She looked up. "You killed Papa?"

"I did," Hugh Gunter said. "After you told your bro . . . after you told your daddy where to find Daniel."

Her head dropped. "Papa always told me not to cry over his death, that it was bound to happen." She went through another crying spell while the three men waited patiently. She shook her head. "Did he . . . suffer?"

"It was quick," Gunter said.

Daniel helped her to her feet. "I didn't want . . . ," she began. "I didn't want . . . I didn't want him to kill . . . Missus Benton. I just. . . ." Her head shook savagely. "I . . . I must have. . . . Oh, God." She reached for him. "And, I swear, Daniel, I swear . . . I didn't want you hurt. I. . . ."

"You sent me north," Daniel said, and he showed her the map. "You told me that Benton found his answers north. I guess that was to get me up there. Maybe I'd get killed by whiskey-runners. If not, your father would kill me when I got back. That's why you came up to the agency, I think. Came to Agent Rueben, to find out exactly where I lived. And, with Rueben's help, you drew your father this map."

She stopped crying, and her lips mouthed: "I'm so sorry."

"Why didn't you get your pa to kill Benton?" Noble asked. "If that's what you wanted."

"I wanted to leave Papa out of it." Her body trembled. "I never wanted Papa. . . . Rueben saw me in Wichita. I'd gone up there to see Papa. We'd meet up there sometimes. That's where we had that tintype made."

"I know," Daniel said. He had found the name of the photographer on the picture.

"Rueben recognized Papa. He'd been a Ranger in Texas, him and McBride."

"Yeah," Noble said, and stared at his boots.

"I just wanted Tom Benton to pay . . . pay for. . . . I really thought he was . . . I . . . just. . . . He. . . ."

"I know." Daniel looked at his moccasins.

"Then . . . when . . . after you started . . . digging into things . . . Rueben, McBride, and Shad paid me a visit. They arranged that ambush near McAlester. Said for me to get in touch with my father or. . . ." Again her head shook. Her fists clenched.

"And again along the Red River?" Daniel still looked down.

Her head shook hard. "That wasn't Papa. I swear to it. I think it was Shad Carter and Ted Peavy. I swear that wasn't Papa."

Daniel decided she was telling the truth, recalling Rueben's bewilderment when Daniel had lied, saying he had heard the outlaw's name during the bushwhacking. Her father would have been back in the Choctaw Nation at the time of the ambush along the Red River, but after Daniel had mentioned his suspicions, she had sent for her father.

"I never wanted you dead, Daniel," she was saying. "I. . . ."

He looked at the map in his fingers, remembering the questioning look McBride had shot Carter after Daniel told them Murt Jones was dead. No, the final attempt on Daniel's life had been all Randi's doing. Perhaps she had sent him north, telling her father to kill him there—where Creek whiskey-runners could get the blame—but Jones's horse went lame, so he had waited at the lodge. The map she had drawn was a backup.

Daniel couldn't say he had figured everything out. Just enough. Gently he waved the map at her.

"But that was later," she said. "By then . . . I . . . I don't know . . . I felt trapped. I felt if you kept prying. God believe me. I didn't want anyone hurt. I must have been out of my head when I. . . ."

Outside, the children still sang.

"And Cotton Henry?" Noble asked. "McBride just used him, right?"

"Cotton's a nice young man. I'm sorry McBride and. . . ."

Noble started making scratches in his notebook. Randi walked to the doorway. "I never had much luck with men," she said, staring at the children, her quivering lips trying to form a smile. "Look at them. I really wanted to help them." She looked back inside. "I really wanted to help you, Daniel. I really wanted to like you. I. . . ."

Harvey Noble cleared his throat, and tucked the notepad and pencil in his pocket. "I brung along a horse for you, ma'am," he said. "Sidesaddle and all. Brung along some irons, but I don't want to use 'em."

"You won't need them, Marshal."

"There's a stage we can catch at Hill's Ferry for Fort Smith," the lawman continued. "Not many folks there, usually. Good place to wait. You want to gather up some belongin's?"

"Thank you, Marshal," she said. "You're very kind." She looked back at Daniel, then at the children, and walked outside. Daniel never looked up, not until she had gone.

He didn't know how long he waited. He just stood there, leaning against the pew, heart hurting worse than his wounds, waiting, until he heard the horses beating a drum down the path toward the main road, waiting until a handful of children rushed inside the church and asked where Miss Randi was going, what was going on, firing off other questions that Daniel didn't want to answer.

"School is dismissed," Hugh Gunter told them. "Y'all run along back to your lodges. Everything's all right. Everything's fine."

A moment later, Daniel felt the Cherokee's arm on his shoulder. He made himself lift his head. "Everything's fine," Gunter said. "Everything's all right. You done good, Killstraight. You done what had to be done."

Chapter Twenty-four

When his leg felt strong enough, and the knife wound healing, after about a week of pampering and doctoring (but never any questioning about Randi) from Rain Shower, he mounted the skewbald mare Ben Buffalo Bone had presented him, and rode to the Wichita Mountains. Ben Buffalo Bone had named the paint horse Talking Beaver—his friend hadn't explained why. Feeling the wind in his hair, the smooth gait, Daniel had to admit she was a fine horse. Maybe, someday, he'd think as highly of her as he had of Skunk.

On a tall zebra dun, Rain Shower rode beside him. He had told her he wanted to go alone, that he needed to go alone, but she had replied that she must come with him. She didn't know why. Just knew she needed to be with him on this journey. So he relented.

Jimmy Comes Last still haunted his dreams, and his heart ached for Randi Jordan. Maybe he had spent too many years with the pale eyes. Maybe he'd never be true Kwahadi. Yet he hoped old Isa Nanaka would help him again. Despite himself, despite wanting solitude, deep down, having a strong woman like Rain Shower accompany him pleased him.

He slowed Talking Beaver to a walk over the last few rods to the *puhakut's* lodge, saw the man sitting there, on one of those canvas chairs Long Knives officers liked so, pipe in his hands, as if making an offering, lips turned upward in a smile, gray braids blowing in the wind.

Talking Beaver snorted, afraid, and Daniel swung to the ground, dropping the hackamore to the dirt, frowning as he walked toward his father's friend. "Come," he told Rain Shower, and she dropped from the dun. Even before they had dismounted, he knew that the lung sickness had finally claimed Isa Nanaka, that the old man must now travel to The Land Beyond The Sun.

"You knew I was coming," he spoke in Comanche, sinking to his knees, pulling the beautifully adorned pipe from the dead man's hands. "I had hoped to ask you questions, hoped you would show me the way to find my vision." He looked behind the lodge. Isa Nanaka had built a sweat lodge. *For me*, Daniel knew.

He buried Isa Nanaka, the man known as Wolf's Howl, in the way of The People, burying him with his pipe and prized possessions. It was good this way. A man should attend to the body of another man. Burial should be done quickly, and Isa Nanaka had not been dead long. After Daniel had bathed the body and dressed the great *puhakut* in his finest clothes, he painted the man's face with vermillion, and covered his eyes with red clay. Then, as Rain Shower stood silently, crying, he bent Isa Nanaka's knees toward his chest, brought the head down to the knees, using a rope the old man had left behind to secure the position, and laid the body on a colorful Navajo blanket that Isa Nanaka had traded for years ago. Or had stolen on a raid.

Standing, crying without shame, Daniel looked down at Isa Nanaka. Silent. No singing. No praying.

Next, he drew the iron blade of his deer-horn handle knife over his forearms, letting the blood flow freely. Over the months since he had arrived back in his own country, he had let his hair grow, but now he cut off the locks, cropping his hair close, for he knew he had loved this man so much, and owed him more than he could ever repay.

"Your suffering is over," he said. He started to sheath the knife, but Rain Shower held out her hand, and he understood, handing her the blade, letting her cut her own arms, cut her own hair. "You are in a land of many buffalo," he told Isa Nanaka as Rain Shower dropped the bloody knife. "I hope you will go hunting with my father. I hope. . . ."

He folded the blanket, its colors still bright after all those years, over the corpse, securing it with rawhide thongs, and, struggling, got the body on one horse, an old bay, the only horse Isa Nanaka had. He was glad Rain Shower had come with him. Now he knew why she was here.

She mounted the bay behind Isa Nanaka's body, holding it in place, and Daniel led the horse and its riders to the base of the mountains. *A good place,* he thought, remembering Isa Nanaka's story of how these mountains came to be, a fitting place to bury this great man.

Along the highest peak—what the pale eyes called Mount Pinchot—they found a deep wash, and there they placed Isa Nanaka, west of his lodge, on the southern side of the hill. They set him down, facing east, where the sun would break the next morning and Isa Nanaka would begin the long journey taken by his ancestors. Then, the wounds on their arms starting to clot, Daniel and Rain Shower began covering the grave with rocks and blackjack bles. When they had finished, Daniel killed Isa anaka's horse for the journey, and walked back to the lodge with Rain Shower. He burned the teepee, and they slept that night on the ground.

The next morning, Rain Shower helped Daniel prepare for his sweat bath.

Two days he stayed there, fasting, sweating, singing, waiting to see the truth. The first to visit him was Jimmy Comes Last, who still cried out: "Brother, have you forgotten your promise? Tell her I am sorry." Later, late on the second day, he followed the marsh hawk, watched it fly across the Wichita Mountains, fly east and north, fly to the lodge of Naséca, circle there, cry out, and disappear.

When Daniel stepped out of the sweat lodge at dusk, he knew what he must do, knew why Jimmy Comes Last still tormented his sleep. He ate pemmican, and smiled as Rain Shower brought him a gourd of water to drink. Again, they slept underneath the shadows of the Wichita Mountains, and the next morning mounted their horses.

"I must go alone," he told Rain Shower.

"I know," she said. "I will wait for you."

Naséca greeted him warmly, ushering him inside her lodge, lamenting the fact that she had not much beef to offer him, shaking her head, telling him that the spirits had not left anything recently, but ration day would soon be here.

He smiled politely, said he wasn't hungry, although he felt famished, and wondered about the quarter of beef he had found in her brush arbor so long ago. Maybe there had been some good in Sergeant Sitting Still. Yes, he worked with the Creeks, but Daniel didn't believe, not now anyway, that the sergeant had used the beef to buy the woman's silence. No, he had merely brought food to an old woman. To help her. Yet he had sold the butchered beef to others, as well as the pistol the Lazy B cowhand had dropped.

No, Daniel could never forgive Sergeant Sitting Still for everything. In many ways, the sergeant must be blamed for Jimmy Comes Last's death. Aged Ephraim Rueben shared some of that responsibility, too. And, of course, J. C. C. McBride and Shad Carter, Randi Jordan. To some degree, they were all guilty. Of sending Jimmy to Gibson Station. Of getting him drunk. Of enraging him. Of pushing him to the cabin where he would kill Thomas Benton . . . and Benton's wife. Maybe, Daniel thought, it was good that the cabin had burned. What was it the doctor had said? Bad blood there, bad memories.

But . . . now . . . well, now Daniel knew that no matter their parts, no matter the hand they had had in the Benton murders, Jimmy Comes Last's soul remained stained with that blood. He had killed them, and he had paid for the crime.

Naséca squatted, saying something, but Daniel heard her words to him during their journey from Fort Smith: *You make things right. Make things right with my son. Make things right with the pale eyes. And tell me, when you make things right. Tell me, so I can rest. So he can rest.*

Maybe a pale eyes would see no need for what he was about to do. Inflict pain on a sad woman. But it had to be done. This was why Jimmy still troubled him. This was why the hawk had led Daniel to her lodge in his vision. A white man would not understand, but Daniel did. He was Nermernuh. Not white. Not Apache. He was of The People. He would

ot forget his promise to Naséca. It's what her son
anted. So he could rest.

"Mother," he said softly, and called her again. She
oked up, saw the truth in his eyes, and sat back
iffly. "A long time ago," he said, "you asked me to
elp you, to help the son of yours who breathes no
ore." He swallowed. "Mother, forgive me for caus-
g you this pain. I mean no disrespect, but this is
hat your son wants you to know." Her lips began
tremble. "You asked me to make things right with
our son, and with the pale eyes. You wanted to be-
eve that your son was not to blame for those . . .
ose bad things . . . that happened." He shook his
ead. "I wanted to believe the same. But . . . it was
ot to be."

So he told her, as quickly as he could, that Jimmy
omes Last had murdered the Bentons. Yes, he had
een pushed into it. Yes, others were responsible,
nd those others—from Sergeant Sitting Still to
C. C. McBride and Shad Carter and Ephraim Rue-
en to Miss Randall Jordan—they were now paying
or their parts in that miserable affair. But it was
ver. At last, her son, and Daniel, and Naséca could
nd peace.

"He came to me in a vision. He told me to tell you
hat he is sorry. I am sorry, too. Sorry to tell you
vhat I have learned." Slowly he rose, and headed for
he teepee opening.

When she called out his name, he turned. Naséca
miled.

"I am glad you have come home," she told him. "I
hank you for your words, but you must know this.
he man . . . the boy . . . of whom you speak, he did
ot do this awful thing. My son died a long time
go. That was not the boy of whom you speak. That

was someone else, someone stolen by pale eye
whiskey. I thank you for your words. I thank you fo
coming. The People need you." She called out h
name again, then lowered her head and went bac
to whatever she was fiddling with.

Daniel stepped through the flap, closed it, heade
for his horse. He thought of her words, and straigh
ened, walking taller, knowing he had found h
place, and found out who he really was. Isa Nanak
and Rain Shower had helped him, but so, probabl
more importantly, had Naséca. Just now, she hadr
called him Daniel, hadn't called him Killstraigh
but she had spoken his true name, in the languag
of Nermernuh, The People, the name his father ha
given him years ago, the name his father had ca
ried as a warrior long before that: His Arrows F
Straight Into The Hearts Of His Enemies.

  High above him, a marsh hawk soared.

Author's Note

No Comanches took part in the original class at the Carlisle Industrial School, although Richard Pratt had wanted to recruit Comanches, Kiowas, and Cheyennes, since he had worked with them in Indian Territory and later at Fort Marion in Florida. However, I wanted a Comanche as my detective-in-progress, so I took the liberty of changing history slightly for the purpose of this novel.

Comanches often get a bad reputation in Western fiction: the nameless savage, brutal, racist, pure embodiment of evil. The Comanches I know, however, are wonderful people, loyal, good-natured with a great sense of humor, although, as my friend artist, Pocona Burgess, once told me with a smile: "We can be aggressive to a fault."

Spellings vary for Comanche words, so much in fact that it's hard to find any consistency among scholars, so I have had to pick and choose. That said, for Comanche language and grammar, I primarily turned to *Comanche Vocabulary: Trilingual Edition*, compiled by Manuel García Rejón and translated and edited by Daniel J. Gelo (University of Texas Press, 1995).

In addition, I relied heavily on two books by William T. Hagan for research: *Indian Police and Judges* (Yale University Press, 1966) and *United States-Comanche Relations: The Reservation Years* (University of Oklahoma Press, 1990).

For Comanche culture, sources included: *The C manches: Lords of the South Plains* by Ernest Walla and E. Adamson Hoebel (University of Oklahor Press, 1952, 1986); *The Comanches* by Joseph H. Ca and Gerald W. Wolff (Indian Tribal Series, 1974); *C manches: The Destruction of a People* by T. R. Fehre bach (Alfred A. Knopf, 1974); *Los Comanches: T Horse People, 1751–1845* (University of New Mexi Press, 1993); and *The Comanches: A History, 1706–18* by Thomas W. Kavanagh (University of Nebras Press, 1996).

Information on the Indian boarding schools car from Richard Henry Pratt's autobiography, *Batt field & Classroom*, edited by Robert M. Utley (Univ sity of Oklahoma Press, 2003); *The Indian Industr School: Carlisle, Pennsylvania 1879–1918* by Linda Witmer (Cumberland County Historical Socie 1993); and *They Called It Prairie Light: The Story of C locco Indian School* by K. Tsianina Lomawaima (U versity of Nebraska Press, 1994).

Other sources include *Law West of Fort Smith* Glenn Shirley (University of Nebraska Press, 195 *Quanah Parker, Comanche Chief* by William T. Hag (University of Oklahoma Press, 1993); *The Last C manche Chief: The Life and Times of Quanah Parker* Bill Neeley (John Wiley & Sons, 1995); *War Dance Fort Marion* by Brad D. Lookingbill (University Oklahoma Press, 2006); and two seminal volum from W. S. Nye, *Carbine & Lance: The Story of C Fort Sill* (University of Oklahoma Press, 1937, 194 1969) and *Plains Indian Raiders* (University of Okl homa Press, 1968).

Thanks also go to the staffs of the Vista Gran Public Library and the Fort Smith Historical Socie Thanks also to Mike Blakely of Marble Falls, Texa r his help on Comanche culture (and for bunking ith me on all those road trips); and Robert J. Con-y of Norman, Oklahoma, and Don Birchfield of klahoma City, for help understanding tribal police erations.

Most thanks, however, go to my Comanche friends, e Burgess Boys: Nocona, his brother, Quanah, an complished artist in Oklahoma, and their father, nald L. "Chief Tachaco" Burgess, also an artist as ll as former chairman of the Comanche Nation. l of them are pretty good storytellers, not to men-n thankful, and proud, of being Comanche.

Johnny D. Boggs
Santa Fé, New Mexico

About The Author

Johnny D. Boggs has worked cattle, shot rapids in a canoe, hiked across mountains and deserts, traipsed around ghost towns, and spent hours poring over microfilm in library archives—all in the name of finding a good story. He's also one of the few Western writers to have won two Spur Awards from Western Writers of America (for his novel, Camp Ford, in 2006, and his short story, "A Piano at Dead Man's Crossing," in 2002) and the Western Heritage Wrangler Award from the National Cowboy and Western Heritage Museum (for his novel, *Spark on the Prairie: The Trial of the Kiowa Chiefs*, in 2004). A native of South Carolina, Boggs spent almost fifteen years in Texas as a journalist at the Dallas *Times Herald* and Fort Worth *Star-Telegram* before moving to New Mexico in 1998 to concentrate full time on his novels. Author of twenty-seven published short stories, he has also written for more than fifty newspapers and magazines, and is a frequent contributor to *Boys' Life, New Mexico Magazine, Persimmon Hill,* and *True West*. His Western novels cover a wide range. *The Lonesome Chisholm Trail* is an authentic cattle-drive story, while *Lonely Trumpet* is a historical novel about the first black graduate of West Point. *The Despoilers* and *Ghost Legion* are set in the Carolina backcountry during the Revolutionary War. *The Big Fifty* chronicles the slaughter of buffalo on the southern plains in the 1870s, while *East of the Border* is a comedy about the theatrical offerings of Buffalo Bill Cody, Wild Bill Hickok, and Texas Jack Omohundro, and *Camp Ford* tells about a Civil War baseball game between Union prisoners of war and Confederate guards. "Boggs's narrative voice captures the old-fashioned style of the past," *Publishers Weekly* said, and *Booklist* called him "among the best Western writers at work today." Boggs lives with his wife Lisa and son Jack in Santa Fé. His website is www.johnnydboggs.com.

Five-time Winner of the Spur Award

Will Henry

There is perhaps no outlaw of the Old West more notorious or legendary than Billy the Kid. And no author is better suited than Will Henry to tell the tale of the young gunman . . . and the mysterious stranger who changed his life.

Also included in this volume are two exciting novellas: "Santa Fe Passage" is the basis for the classic 1955 film of the same name. And "The Fourth Horseman" sets a rancher on the trail of a kidnapped young woman . . . while trying to survive a bloody range war.

A BULLET FOR BILLY THE KID

ISBN 13: 978-0-8439-6340-3

The Classic Film Collection

The Searchers by Alan LeMay

Hailed as one of the greatest American films, *The Searchers*, directed by John Ford and starring John Wayne, has had a direct influence on the works of Martin Scorsese, Steven Spielberg, and many others. Its gorgeous cinematic scope and deeply nuanced characters have proven timeless. And now available for the first time in decades is the powerful novel that inspired this iconic movie.

Destry Rides Again by Max Brand

Made in 1939, the Golden Year of Hollywood, *Destry Rides Again* helped launch Jimmy Stewart's career and made Marlene Dietrich an American icon. Now available for the first time in decades is the novel that inspired this much-loved movie.

The Man from Laramie by T. T. Flynn

In its original publication, *The Man from Laramie* had more than half a million copies in print. Shortly thereafter, it became one of the most recognized of the Anthony Mann/Jimmy Stewart collaborations, known for darker films with morally complex characters. Now the novel upon which this classic movie was based is once again available—for the first time in more than fifty years.

The Unforgiven by Alan LeMay

In this epic American novel, which served as the basis for the classic film directed by John Huston and starring Burt Lancaster and Audrey Hepburn, a family is torn apart when an old enemy starts a vicious rumor that sets the range aflame. Don't miss the powerful novel that inspired the film the *Motion Picture Herald* calls "an absorbing and compelling drama of epic proportions."

COVERING THE OLD WEST
FROM COVER TO COVER.

Since 1953 we have been helping preserve the American West
with great original photos, true stories, new facts,
old facts and current events.

True West Magazine
We Make the Old West Addictive.

INTERACT WITH DORCHESTER ONLINE!

Want to learn more about your favorite
books and authors?
Want to talk with other readers that like
to read the same books as you?
Want to see up-to-the-minute Dorchester
news?

VISIT DORCHESTER AT:
DorchesterPub.com
Twitter.com/DorchesterPub
Facebook.com (Search Pages)

DISCUSS DORCHESTER'S NOVELS AT:
Dorchester Forums at DorchesterPub.com
GoodReads.com
LibraryThing.com
Myspace.com/books
Shelfari.com
WeRead.com

☐ **YES!**

Sign me up for the Leisure Western Book Club and send my FREE BOOKS! If I choose to stay in the club, I will pay only $14.00* each month, a savings of $9.96!

NAME: _____

ADDRESS: _____

TELEPHONE: _____

EMAIL: _____

☐ I want to pay by credit card.

☐ **VISA**   ☐ **MasterCard.**   ☐ **DISCOVER**

ACCOUNT #: _____

EXPIRATION DATE: _____

SIGNATURE: _____

Mail this page along with $2.00 shipping and handling to:
Leisure Western Book Club
PO Box 6640
Wayne, PA 19087
Or fax (must include credit card information) to:
610-995-9274

You can also sign up online at **www.dorchesterpub.com**.
*Plus $2.00 for shipping. Offer open to residents of the U.S. and Canada only.
Canadian residents please call 1-800-481-9191 for pricing information.
If under 18, a parent or guardian must sign. Terms, prices and conditions subject to change. Subscription subject to acceptance. Dorchester Publishing reserves the right to reject any order or cancel any subscription.